ADVANCE PRAISE FOR *THAT'S NOT MY NAME*

"Secrets. Lies. Betrayal. Get ready for a roller coaster ride where nothing is what it seems. *That's Not My Name* begs to be read in a single adrenaline-fueled sitting."

—April Henry, *New York Times* bestselling
author of *Girl, Stolen* and *Two Truths and a Lie*

"Tense, heart-wrenching, and addictive, Lally's pulse-pounding debut is an exciting first entry for an author we should all be watching."

—Courtney Gould, author of *The Dead and the Dark*

"With her masterful use of carefully-placed details to build suspense, Lally asks: just because something is obvious, does that make it true?"

—Jessie Weaver, author of *Live Your Best Lie*

"A gripping, emotional page-turner with an undeniable tenderness at its center. Megan Lally's writing is sharp and wholly immersive, with a keen eye for detail and a sly sense of humor. This book will leave you breathless."

—Rachel Lynn Solomon, bestselling
author of *Today Tonight Tomorrow*

T0245861

MEGAN LALLY

sourcebooks
fire

Copyright © 2024 by Megan Lally
Cover and internal design © 2024 by Sourcebooks
Cover design by Erin Fitzsimmons/Sourcebooks
Cover photo © Magdalena Russocka/Trevillion Images
Internal design by Laura Boren/Sourcebooks

Sourcebooks and the colophon are registered trademarks of Sourcebooks.

Published by Sourcebooks Fire, an imprint of Sourcebooks
P.O. Box 4410, Naperville, Illinois 60567-4410
(630) 961-3900
sourcebooks.com

Cataloging-in-Publication Data is on file with the Library of Congress.

Printed and bound in the United States of America.
KP 10 9 8 7 6 5 4 3 2 1

For my dad.
You would have been the most excited
about this. I miss you always.

ONE
GIRL

DAY 1

I think I might be dead.

I try to gather my bearings, but I can't see. I feel *nothing*. Not even my own body. The lack of sensation, the way the silence wraps me in a hug and squeezes—it's unnerving. I want it to stop—

Until the pain comes.

It hits like a full-body punch. My mind scrambles to catalog what hurts, but it *all* hurts.

My hand twitches against something scratchy beneath me. I'm lying on my stomach, and something pointy presses into my ribs. I move my chin, and my cheekbone drags against damp earth. It smells like decay and old leaves.

Fear kicks up my pulse.

I'm outside? How the hell did I get here? I try to look around, but my eyelids scrape like my lashes are made of glass and nails. They slam shut before I can see anything.

An engine roars and I tense, pain shooting down my arms. My

hair blows across my face as a vehicle whips past, then it's quiet again.

I'm beside a road. Did the driver see me? Why didn't they stop? I make another desperate attempt to see. My eyes flood with tears this time. I blink to clear my vision and shake the hair from my face.

Holy shit. It's *so* dark.

No streetlights, no houses. There aren't even stars in the sky.

My eyes slowly adjust. No wonder the car didn't stop. I'm lying in a long ditch, sunken into leaves and bracken. Twigs twist up into the air like claws. The ditch clings to the side of a narrow dirt road that runs straight out ahead of me, then disappears in a wobbly blur of trees.

Panic nests in my throat, and my mind fills with more questions I can't answer.

Where the hell am I?

How did I get here?

Am I in danger?

Why does everything hurt so bad?

I need to get up. I don't know where I'm going, but moving seems safer than lying here. My fingers dig into the dirt as I try to drag my knees beneath me. And for the first time, I notice how cold I am. I can barely feel the tips of my fingers.

My arms threaten to buckle, but I push myself to my feet.

Bruises stretch around my bones, and an involuntary wail escapes my mouth. For a moment, I forget how to breathe. The pain is everywhere. My heartbeat pounds in my ears, and it's at least eleven *ba-dubs* before I can draw in another breath.

Tears spill down my face, stinging my cheeks. I lift my icicle fingers to my nose. It feels hot. Swollen. My fingers come away dark and wet. I taste blood.

Fuck. My nose might be broken.

I have to get out of here.

The road looks the same in the other direction, only dirt and trees. I slowly make my way out of the ditch. Briars scrape at my bare arms. I duck to pass under a tree limb, and its branches pull at me like hands.

An image soars through my mind without warning. Tiny square doors with keyholes in a box by the road. A cluster mailbox, maybe? A burned-out streetlight. Big hands reaching for me.

I recoil and stumble into the middle of the road.

My heart rattles against my rib cage until my chest muscles hurt.

What the actual fuck was that?

Did someone grab me?

They're simple questions, but my mind supplies zero details. It just throbs. Like there's a wall between me and understanding what's happening. I clench my teeth and force another step. I need help. Maybe another car will pass or I can find a house. I have to keep moving.

I don't know how long I stumble along, but it feels like hours. My mind zones out and snaps back so many times that I wonder if I'm losing consciousness.

Maybe I already have. Maybe this progress is all in my head, and I'm still in that ditch. Or worse, maybe I *am* dead and this is hell. An endless purgatory of pain and solitude I'm doomed to wander until the end of time, looking for help that will never come.

Red and blue lights flicker on behind me, filling the road with color. A *whoop whoop* from a police car almost startles me to the ground, but sheer relief keeps me standing. Someone's going to help me. Tires crunch as they come to a stop and the lights create a me-shaped silhouette in the dirt. I start to turn—

"Do *not* move. Hands where I can see them!" a man shouts.

My hands go up automatically and a moment later a door slams.

What is this? Did I do something wrong? Is that how I ended up here? Am I running from the cops?

Should I run *now*?

"Turn around!"

I do, squinting into the bright headlights of the patrol car. An officer stands beside his vehicle, face in shadow, hand on the gun in his holster. I feel whatever blood's still in my face drain away, because when I glance down at myself in the light, all I see is dirt and blood.

There's *so* much blood.

"Jesus, you're just a kid," the officer says, taking his hand off his weapon. He creeps forward. "What happened to you? Did someone do this?"

I open my mouth to answer, but my knees give out and I drop. The cop tries to catch me, but we both hit the dirt hard.

He grabs at the radio receiver on his shoulder, but I can't hear what he says over the roaring in my ears and the caged animal thrashing around in my chest. I stare at my hands, my jean leggings, the front of my light gray T-shirt—covered in blotches of dried mud and dark rivers of blood.

Hands grip my shoulders. I look up at the officer. His words defog in my mind.

"Can you hear me? Paramedics are on their way, but I need to know who you are," he pleads. "What's your name?"

My name?

I blink at him and reach for the answer, but no matter how hard I try, I hit that wall in my mind every time. What's my name? How is that a hard question? I try to breathe but it's too much. I start hyperventilating. Fresh tears pool in my eyes.

What's your name?

I grab my throbbing head. "I don't know!"

TWO
GIRL

The gray walls of the police station look as lifeless as I feel.

The patrolman who found me, Officer Bowman, sits across the table from me. We're in a conference room—or maybe it's an interrogation room. There's only one window, but it faces the interior of the station and it's blacked out. He left the door open though, so I must not be someone they want to keep locked in. That's good at least.

He hasn't stopped worrying at his lip since I refused medical treatment.

I may not know who I am, but I sure as hell know that nobody can make me go to the hospital if I don't want to. Bright lights and loud sounds, more faces I don't recognize, no way of telling who is a threat and who isn't... No thank you.

A few hours ago, the paramedics cleaned the blood from my skin, which apparently all came from my nose. It's bruised, not broken, but hurts like a bitch all the same. And I have a lump on the side of my head. I've been told to look for concussion symptoms for the next few days. They declared the rest of my injuries superficial and bandaged what they could.

"You look pretty bad," Officer Bowman said after the paramedics failed one final time to get me to go to the hospital. "There's a process here, procedure we need to follow. You should get checked out by a doctor. Get a rape kit—"

I blocked out the rest. There are some things I can't even begin to think about. Not today. Maybe not ever. That's one of them.

When they realized I wouldn't budge about going to the ER, both paramedics and Officer Bowman exchanged a look and left me alone on a stretcher inside the ambulance to talk outside. If they didn't want me to eavesdrop, they should have whispered. That creepy road was silent as the grave and did nothing to keep their voices from drifting back to me.

"All her bruises look new. I'd guess within the last couple hours. Fresh swelling," the tall, wiry paramedic said. "That, plus the injuries to her face, could point to some kind of an impact. Maybe a car accident. She doesn't have bruising from a seatbelt, but the injury to her nose could be from an airbag or a steering wheel. With a head contusion on the left, it's possible she might have hit the driver's side window. But it's only a guess. Regardless, her vitals are fine. She's not in any immediate medical danger."

I clung to that version of events, my hands fisting in the papery stretcher sheets. A car accident was better than the other, darker, possibilities. And it didn't require a rape kit.

Bowman took notes while Tall-and-Wiry climbed back into the ambulance and handed me a fresh icepack. "Good luck," he said as he helped me down.

That icepack sits on the table between me and Officer Bowman, though it's warm now. I've been here for hours. He squints at me, like he's waiting for me to start screaming or for my head to spin around. And who knows, maybe it will. I mean, I'm basically a character from a teen horror movie.

Covered in blood? Check.

Bruised to hell? Check.

Wandering, terrified, in the middle of the night? Check.

A steaming cup of hot chocolate sits next to the room-temp ice-pack, but I don't reach for it. I don't move. I don't say a word. Wrapped in the scratchy blanket the officer draped around my shoulders, I try not to think. Because the alternative means navigating the holes in my memory, and I can't bear to do any more of that than I already have.

Officer Bowman's chair creaks as he leans forward. He's young… ish. Maybe twenty-six or twenty-seven. With a baby face and eager blue eyes, he looks like a lemur with a badge. "You should drink that," he says, nodding at the mug. "You may be in shock."

I shrug.

When the paramedics left, Bowman switched gears, apparently determined to make me feel better however he could. He brought me to the precinct, though I don't remember much of the drive. When he noticed my wrecked shoes—I don't know what color they were before, but they'd become a tie-dye of dried blood and forest sludge—he gave me a clean pair of black socks from his work bag and a sweatshirt. It's navy blue and says "Alton Police Department" on the upper-right side. It fits like a shower curtain, but the fabric is soft and warm.

Once I was dry, he smiled. "Feel better?"

I did. Right up until I caught sight of my reflection in the dark interior window and didn't know the person staring back at me. Now I don't want to talk. Ever. I don't have anything to share with him anyway. I'm a nobody, with no name, and a stranger's face.

"Miss?" he says. "Can you hear me?"

I nod.

"Miss, you need to drink something. I really wish you'd let me take you to the hospital. You're very pale."

The thought of the emergency room sends another barb of anxiety through my body. Being pale is the least of my worries. I shake my head.

Officer Bowman sighs. "Miss—"

I glare at him. "Stop calling me Miss."

He sits back in his chair, and it creaks again. "Okay. What should I call you?"

Good freaking question. "I don't know. But don't call me that."

My voice sounds a thousand miles away. Was that one of the concussion signs the paramedic warned me about? I should have paid attention.

Officer Bowman pushes the mug closer to me. "I'll make you a deal. You drink some of this and try to help me figure out where you came from, and I'll stop calling you Miss *and* I'll cool it about going to the hospital. For now."

I eye him.

"You have a nasty goose egg, but you're alert and responsive. You can walk unassisted, and the lights in here don't seem to be bothering you. If you start to slur your speech, lose your balance, throw up, black out, or show any other warning signs of a concussion, we're going to the ER. Until then, I can get you a fresh icepack and we can talk. Deal?"

Whatever. I nod and take a sip.

I won't admit it, but the warmth feels good on my throat, and it settles in my stomach like a rock thunking into a puddle, which makes me think I haven't eaten in a while.

He leaves the room, and I readjust the blanket around my

shoulders. The wool prickles against my neck but I can't muster enough energy to care. Between the blanket and the sweatshirt, I've created a cocoon of heat around me, but I still can't stop shivering.

Bowman returns with a fresh icepack. I carefully press it against my hairline. It stings but dulls the throbbing.

He pulls his notepad from his pocket and sits. "Okay, so let's talk. I want to go on the record and say you're not in any kind of trouble. I only want to figure out what happened to you out there."

How could he know if I'm in trouble or not if neither of us have any clue where I came from? I could have stabbed someone in the face, and he'd have no idea. "You and me both."

His brow furrows. "You don't have any memory at all? Nothing before waking up in the ditch?"

I shake my head. "I thought I saw hands reaching for me, but I might have been spooked by the dark."

He writes on his pad. "Do you know how old you are?"

"Nope."

"What about family? Can you tell me who your parents are?"

I stare at the clock on the wall, watching the second hand tick around. "No."

"Okay. You look young enough to still be in school. Do you remember its name? Maybe the mascot? A phone number we can call? Anything?"

I shrug again. "I don't know."

"Did you run away?"

"I don't know that either."

"*Could* you have been in a car accident?"

I let out the most epic sigh. How many times do I have to say it before "I can't remember" clicks in his brain?

When I don't respond, he frowns and taps his pen on his chin. "Okay. New plan. I'll be right back." He disappears into the main office and reappears a minute later with a laptop. "To be honest, this is way above my pay grade. I basically write speeding tickets. I put in a call to my boss, but he probably won't answer until morning when the precinct reopens, and I don't want to wait that long to start getting you some answers."

That makes two of us.

"So let's do what we can in the meantime. Since you have no ID, we'll search missing person reports, first here in town and then expand our reach. Someone must be missing you, and your face could be here in the database attached to a name and contact info for your family. It might take us a while but finding out who you are is the first step to finding out what happened. So let's see what we can dig up, hmm?"

I nod, and he starts typing.

We spend the next hour sifting through files. We weed out the locals almost immediately. There's only one missing person in town, and it's some old Santa-looking man who "disappeared" while barhopping. Bowman makes some comment about having to track down that guy every other month, then moves on to the county's missing list. Turns out Alton is about halfway up the Oregon coast.

I wait for any of this to feel familiar, but it doesn't. I can't even tell him if I live in this state. How messed up is that?

I mostly sit and drink my hot chocolate. He convinces me to drink another cup and eventually the sandwich he packed for his night shift.

"Well, you're definitely not eleven, so this isn't you," Bowman mumbles at about one thirty in the morning. He clicks to another listing and squints at the screen.

I wonder how long we're going to keep this up. At some point, I have to leave this place, right? The thought fills me with dread. Where would I even go?

"What happens if you can't figure out who I am?" I ask.

He looks up with his kind lemur eyes. "You have nice clothes—if you look past the blood. Name-brand shoes. You're in good health. You don't appear to have been living on the streets. You must belong to someone. We'll either find your people, or they'll find you. We may have to kick this up to a more-equipped precinct in the morning though. This is a small office for a small town. We don't have the same resources as the larger stations. I have to sift through these reports one at a time, and I've barely worked through half the missing persons in this county, much less the state or beyond."

I nod. That makes sense. This whole office is basically an open space with two desks, this conference room, a short hallway with bathrooms, a break room with a copy machine, and a holding cell.

A loud bang comes from the front of the precinct. I jump out of my chair and into the corner of the room.

Officer Bowman peers though the doorway and turns back with his hands out, palms facing me. A gesture clearly meant to calm the spooked animal in front of him. Someone's knocking on the front door. "You're safe. Nobody's going to hurt you here."

I nod. My head throbs from standing so fast, and my heartbeat thumps like a Lizzo chorus.

Oh, hey. I guess I remember Lizzo. If all else fails, at least I like good music.

"Stay here. I'll be right back," Officer Bowman says. He walks out, and I hear the metal-on-metal creak of the front door opening. "Can I help you?"

I can't see him anymore, not from this angle. I pull my blanket tighter around me and creep toward the door, curious who would show up at a closed precinct this late.

"God, I hope so," a man says. His voice is much deeper than Bowman's but also a lot quieter. I have to lean toward the doorway to hear the rest. "My teenage daughter is missing. I can't reach her on the phone; I've been driving around for hours trying to find her. I think I have to file a missing person's report."

Holy shit. Missing daughter? Was Bowman right? Did my people find me?

I inch closer until I can see out into the precinct. Bowman stands with the front door cracked open, his entire body blocking the open space. I can't see the man in front of him.

"What's your name?" Officer Bowman asks.

"Wayne Boone."

"Okay, Mr. Boone. How old is your daughter and what does she look like?"

"She's seventeen, with short brown hair, freckles, and green eyes. Around five foot five."

Bowman looks over his shoulder and locks eyes with me. His gaze flickers toward the conference room, and I reluctantly slip back out of view, fighting the urge to check my swollen nose for freckles in the reflection in the glass.

"Step inside for me. I'm going to need some identification."

The door creaks and I hear it click shut a second later. "Of course," the deep voice says, closer now. "I also have photos of her if you need them for the report?"

"Actually, I have someone here matching that description, and I—"

"She's here?" the man shouts. "Mary's here?"

Mary? My Lizzo heartbeat speeds up. Is that me?

I peek around the corner again. The men are in the entryway, standing by a long wooden bench. Mr. Boone is kind of wiry. His arms are slightly shorter than they should be for his height. His hair looks like it's thinking of going gray but hasn't committed to the change. The silvery strands stand out around his ears, but he's slicked most of it back. Not with product though, like he's been running his hands through it for so long it's been forced to obey. He's wearing a black sweater and dark jeans.

I don't think I've ever seen him before.

But what would I know?

"We have *someone*," Officer Bowman says, carefully.

Mr. Boone folds his arms, looking impatient, and as his eyes sweep the station, he catches me staring at him. His arms drop and his face glows with relief. "Mary?"

I freeze.

He tries to step toward me, but Bowman stops him with a hand to his chest. "Oh my god. I've been looking for you for hours. Are you okay? What happened to your face?" He says all this in one breath. Each word more panicked than the last, and I flinch because I know exactly what he means.

It was a shock to see myself too. I look like I lost a fight with a two-by-four.

I stare back at him and wait for...a rush of knowing? A giant lightbulb to shine through this numbness and tell me who I am? For his face to unlock a memory? Nothing happens. He's still a stranger.

"She's okay, a little bruised. She might have a concussion," Officer Bowman says, blocking his advances. "Now I need you to give her some space while I run your ID and verify who you are."

The man looks at Bowman and finally takes a step back. "What do you mean? She's right there. She can tell you who I am." He looks at me like he can't understand why I'm not running to him.

"She can't remember anything, Mr. Boone. Now please sit down while we sort this out."

Mr. Boone looks at me again, his confusion morphing into unease. "You don't remember me?"

I don't know what to say. How can my supposed father be standing right in front of me and I still can't remember him?

"I'll prove it," he says. "I can prove who I am. I have pictures on my phone."

Pictures? I inch sideways until I'm out of the conference room. The promise of clues draws me forward. Mr. Boone pulls his phone from his pocket and swipes a few times. I creep up behind Officer Bowman as he turns the phone to show us his screen.

Sure enough, it's me. Same stranger from my reflection, same girl he described at the door. Dark brown chin-length hair, green eyes, freckled nose—though my face looks different when it's not so bruised and swollen. In the photo, I'm sitting on brick steps, smiling at the camera and sticking out my tongue. He swipes again and I'm with a group of kids my age on the dock of a lake or pond. He swipes again and I'm younger, sitting in a restaurant, surrounded by gift bags stuffed with pink tissue paper. There's a rainbow-sprinkle-covered birthday cake in front of me with a giant 15 candle dripping pink wax. I smirk at the camera, sitting beside the man standing in front of me now. In the picture, Wayne grins for all he's worth.

Nothing about these photos feels familiar...except maybe the candles? I can't figure out if it's *actually* familiar or if I'm so desperate for a connection that my brain is fabricating one.

But it's me in these pictures. That's hard to argue with.

"You really don't remember anything?" the man asks.

He looks so upset I almost want to pretend I do, but that wouldn't help anyone. When I don't say anything, he shakes his head. His sadness slipping away, replaced with something like...determination?

He holds out his hand. "I'm Wayne Boone," he says. "And you're my daughter, Mary Boone. You're seventeen. You're loved very much, and...I'm so happy I finally found you."

I look at Officer Bowman. He nods, so I tentatively reach out and shake Wayne's hand. His skin is soft, and his hand is warm while mine is made of ice.

"How about we sit down and sort this out," Bowman suggests, subtly maneuvering himself between us again. "In the conference room?"

I nod and shuffle back to my chair. Wayne sits across the table from me, and Bowman sits to my left. I stare openly at Wayne. He has a weathered look about him. The skin on his cheeks is rough, like it's been permanently chapped from the wind, but he's clean shaven. His features are all sharp: cheekbones, the line of his nose, the angle of his jaw. It looks like someone chiseled him out of granite and someone forgot to smooth the edges.

He smiles at me and some of the hardness lifts.

"Let's start at the beginning," Officer Bowman says, tapping his notebook with his pen. "How did you get separated from your daughter?"

Wayne leans forward, his forearms pressed to the table. "Our house is undergoing some renovations. All the floors are being replaced. So rather than tiptoe around subfloor, tools, stacked furniture, and dust the whole time, me and Mary decided to stay at my fishing cabin for a few weeks while the work is being done. I packed up my van, she

THAT'S NOT MY NAME | 17

packed up her car, and we were supposed to meet there. She never showed up."

I stare at him. Nothing sounds right, but it doesn't sound wrong either.

"When was this?" Officer Bowman asks.

"We left our house at around four this afternoon. It's an hour's drive. We live in McMinnville. I got to the cabin first, obviously, and by five thirty it was getting dark and I started to worry. I called her phone but she didn't pick up. So I started looking for her."

"Where's the cabin?" Bowman asks.

"On Ridge Road. Up the mountain from here."

Bowman nods like he knows where that is. "That's close to where I found her, walking down the mountain."

The forest flashes in my mind. The darkness, the clawing branches reaching for me... I glance down at my scratched hands. I want all of this to be over.

"You found her *walking* down the mountain like this?" The alarm in Wayne's voice is palpable. He gestures at my fucked-up face. "Did anyone see what happened to her? Where is her car?"

"Nobody's called in about a vehicle. She was on foot and already injured when I found her." Wayne looks like he's about to ask more questions, but Bowman holds up a finger. "Now hold on. Let's get through your statement, before we get off track. What happened after you left the cabin to look for your daughter?"

Wayne fidgets in his seat, clearly unhappy he can't ask more questions. "I retraced the route we took, first around the mountain and then all the way back to McMinnville. I checked the turnoffs and convenience stores and gas stations. I called the hospitals, but nobody had admitted her. I even called you guys. Twice. Nobody answered the phone. I'm only here now because I noticed the light on. I've driven through town a million times tonight."

Officer Bowman frowns. "I'm sorry about that. We're a small station, and too rural to be manned around the clock. Normally the building is closed by six, and night shift is all patrol. I'm only here because of her," he says, smiling at me. "You should have called 911. They would have dispatched someone to help you or called me into the office."

Wayne sighs. "I should have." He shakes his head. "I wasn't thinking straight."

He looks…wrecked.

"It probably wouldn't have made a difference," I say quietly, and both of them look at me. "No matter who you called, I was unconscious in the woods. If you drove up and down the mountain and didn't see me, what would the police have done differently? I still would have wandered into the road when I did. Nobody could have prevented this from happening." I gently touch the swollen skin under my eyes.

Wayne looks at me. "Yeah. Yeah, maybe you're right."

Bowman clears his throat. "Can you explain your daughter's condition, Mr. Boone? She has a lot of injuries."

Wayne's concerned gaze never leaves me. "She was fine when I last saw her. If you found her walking, my best guess is she crashed her car. It's the only way she wouldn't have shown up at the cabin. The power steering has been giving her some trouble lately, but I didn't think it was bad enough to cause an accident. Maybe it went out and she lost control. Those mountain roads are full of twists and turns."

As he talks, I imagine winding roads, and the steering wheel locking. Crashing into a tree. My face hitting an airbag. My body knocking around inside the car. Slamming my head into the window.

Relief prickles through me. Maybe it *was* an accident.

"What kind of car does she drive?" Bowman asks.

"A '96 Oldsmobile station wagon. A gray-blue beast of a thing, with pink seat covers. Someone must have found it by now. Filed a crash report?"

Bowman shakes his head, writing everything down. "Not to my knowledge, but I can look into it."

"I'd appreciate that." Wayne catches me staring and winks at me.

A jolt of familiarity hits like a blast of warm air, and I sit back in my chair.

I might remember him.

Wayne looks up at the clock. "I'm sorry, but do you know how much longer this is going to take?"

Bowman arcs an eyebrow. "I'm going to need quite a bit more information from you. Are you in a hurry?"

Wayne rubs a hand down his face. "No, of course not. But it's incredibly late, and…" He waves a hand at me like my face should finish his sentence for him. "She's been through a lot tonight, and I'd like to get her home so she can rest."

"I understand, Mr. Boone. I really do. But I can't release a minor, especially one who has been through a trauma, into the custody of a stranger."

Wayne closes his eyes. His jaw sets and his shoulders tense. "I'm not a stranger. I'm her father."

"Can you prove that?" Officer Bowman looks over at me, then turns back to my maybe-dad. "Do you have a copy of her driver's license or any documentation to prove her identity? I need to establish not only who *you* are but who *she* is as well. For everyone's safety."

Wayne deflates. "Her license would have been with her in the car, probably in her wallet. I don't have that if you don't. And she's been homeschooled since freshman year, so she doesn't have a current school ID." He fishes his wallet out of his pocket. "I think I have her ninth-grade one though? She was always losing the damn thing, so I held onto it for her."

He slides an unassuming piece of lamination toward us. A face stares back at me from a McMinnville High School ID. Brown hair, cut to the chin. Green eyes. Happy smile. Pink shirt—pink seems to be a recurring theme here. The same stranger from the pictures on his phone, though slightly younger. Rounder, softer. A lot less bruised.

And there, printed in big block letters next to my face: Mary Boone.

I mouth the name, letting the shape of the syllables find history on my lips.

Mary Boone.

I may have no memory of what happened tonight, and I may hurt like hell, but I have a name. And a parent who remembers everything I don't. That's so much more than I had an hour ago.

Wayne continues, "I have her birth certificate and Social Security card up at the cabin. I can bring everything in, or you're welcome to follow us out there. You can take a look at the house and all her documentation to make sure everything is on the up-and-up. I'll sign whatever you need me to sign. Tell me what I have to do to prove she's mine."

Officer Bowman looks uncertain. "Well…I suppose that would work," he says. "If you can provide the documentation to verify who she is, I can release her into your custody. I'll be taking you up on the offer to visit the cabin though. And I'd like an update on her condition in the morning. You're also going to have to give a full report about the accident and the missing vehicle before you leave. We'll need your contact information, your address, and *your* vehicle information as well."

Wayne nods vigorously. "Of course. Whatever you need."

They both look at me. Suddenly it's on me to decide?

"Can I see those pictures again?" I ask Wayne.

He slides the phone to me. "Sure."

They wait in silence as I swipe, lingering on each picture. There are hundreds, some from more than eight years ago. The girl is so young in some of these, she almost looks like a different person. As I swipe, she slowly ages and turns back into me. It's the weirdest thing, not recognizing your own face. But the proof is right here. Her face is my face. In many of his photos, Wayne smiles at me, or his arm is wrapped around my shoulders, or he's laughing in the background.

A sense of finality sinks in. This is me.

This is my father. I belong with him, and this life is mine.

I am Mary Boone.

THREE

DREW

Life really goes to shit when everyone thinks you killed your girlfriend.

The screen flashes another error message, and I kick the base of the photocopy machine. The clang of shoe-to-metal echoes through the library, and one of the elderly community volunteers shoots me an annoyed glance from the travel section. But really, how many errors can this thing have in ten minutes?

I point at the machine, in a *Hey, this thing is junk, and you know it* way. The old guy shakes his head and goes back to organizing travel guides, pretending I don't exist.

Just like everybody else.

I jam my pointer finger against the unresponsive touch screen until the "copy" button lights up and asks me how many copies I need.

Finally.

I pull a folded piece of paper from my back pocket and smooth it across the edge of the machine. Her face stares up at me, and it suddenly feels way too hot in this stupid library. I slide my finger over the crease that cuts across her eyes, and I frown. I shouldn't have folded the flier, but I didn't want to lose it at school, and if I tried to run this errand before class, I would have been late. Again.

With the sheriff pulling me out of school every other day to ask me the same damn questions, I can't afford to miss any more classes. My lawyer seems to have put a stop to it, but the damage is done. I'm barely clinging to graduation, and only my parents give a shit.

Because when your girlfriend vanishes into thin air, you instantly become the person who had something to do with it. At least in the court of public opinion. And maybe in the actual courts if Sheriff Roane has anything to say about it.

Rage rolls up my neck and pounds in my ears, but losing my temper won't do me any good. It certainly won't convince her parents, the town, or Podunk PD that I'm not the reason Lola hasn't come home.

I slide the flier across the glass of the copier and punch buttons until the display says two hundred copies. I hesitate and check my wallet to see how much cash I have on me. I change it to seventy-five instead and feed the bills into the machine, cursing my printer at home for running out of ink.

And the random locals who stop to point at me every time I leave my house.

And the cops for not doing their job.

And, most of all, the world at large for going on with their lives like it doesn't matter she's gone.

The machine whirs to life, and Lola's beautiful face multiplies over and over in the tray at the side of the machine. The giant MISSING headline printed at the top. Those fat letters are probably what killed my ink cartridge.

Someone taps me on the shoulder, and I jump straight into the side of the copier. I whirl around, expecting the library volunteer, but it's my cousin.

Max holds up both hands and takes a step back. "Whoa, Drew, chill out."

I cover my face with my hands and scrub them down to my chin. "Holy shit. Don't sneak up on me like that."

"I didn't sneak anywhere. I called your name twice." He tosses his curly black hair from his forehead. It sticks up in every direction, some parts longer than others, and I wonder if my aunt tried to cut it for him again. She's never been as good with scissors as she thinks, but Max doesn't seem to mind. He puts a hand on my shoulder. "You okay?"

I shrug him off. "Yeah, sure. Fine."

Max hooks his thumbs in the pockets of his jeans and gives me his *you're full of shit* look. I ignore him and grab my fliers. Lola's picture— one my dad took of her smiling on her front porch before her family's annual Fourth of July BBQ—takes up most of the space. I listed her information at the bottom as simply as possible.

Name: Lola Elizabeth Scott

Age: 17

Hair color: Dark brown

Eye color: Green

Last seen: 10:55pm on September 29th at the Willamette River boat launch in Washington City

And in bold at the bottom, "If you see this girl or have any information regarding her whereabouts, please call…" and my phone number. Because Washington City PD don't seem to be following up on any leads these days. Not anymore. Not when they have their prime suspect.

Me.

Max leans over my shoulder. "More fliers?"

I tap the papers on the top of the machine to straighten the stack, and head for the door. The volunteer at the front counter doesn't look up as I pass, much like I don't answer Max's almost-but-not-quite-a-question.

Not that being ignored will stop him. Max is many things, but a quitter is not one of them, tenacious string bean that he is.

I shove the door open and hear it swing again about two seconds later. I pull the cords on my sweatshirt to keep the chilled November air from crawling down my neck and brace for his guilt trip.

"Hold on," Max calls, jogging to catch up with me. "I'm trying to touch base. See how you're doing."

I keep walking. My SUV is parked around the corner. This side of town is all trees sunk into circles in the sidewalk and murals painted by middle schoolers. Even in the dead of fall, it's sickeningly alive and colorful. I focus instead on my feet and the aged asphalt.

"Your dads are super worried about you, man."

Ah, there it is. The guilt. I stop and let my head fall back until my chin points up at the darkening sky. I blow out a breath that feels like concrete in my lungs. "I know they are."

"So stop for a second and talk about it, dude. We're trying to help."

I lower my chin. "All anyone wants to do is talk. I'm tired of it, Max. Talking won't bring her back." I turn and brandish the fliers. "The cops are barely looking for her anymore. This is the only thing I can think of to help bring her home. No one will let me do anything else."

He bites his lip and I deflate a little.

Okay, fine. The fliers haven't exactly proven helpful. I've been posting them for weeks and received exactly ten calls. Nine of them were pranks, and one was an old lady telling me I should be ashamed of myself. But I don't know what else to do.

Max's kind brown eyes fill with sadness, and his whole face droops. "She's been gone a long time…"

"I'm sorry, what does that mean? You think I should give up?"

"What? No, of course not. But you might have to accept—"

"Please stop. I love you, and I know you're trying to help, but I can't. I can't stop looking. Because that means she might not come home, and it's—"

…all my fault.

"It's what?" Max asks, stepping closer.

Some wild mix of guilt, anguish, and fury presses down on my chest, suffocating me. "It's unbearable," I choke out.

He hugs me. I want to pull away, to be alone, but this hug is for his benefit, not mine.

He steps back with a clap to my shoulder and smiles. "Let's go to your place. Everyone's heading over there for family dinner. Your dads are making hilachas. What do you think?"

I think it sounds like another thing that used to make me happy and now sounds like a nightmare. But I'm not about to say so.

My family is…a lot. White on Dad's side, Guatemalan on Papá's, and they love to get together. My dads adopted me three weeks before my third birthday—I don't really remember anything before them—and my whole life has been these big gatherings. Everyone talking, happy, in each other's business—just like Max. Which was fine when they were pestering me about asking Lola to homecoming freshman year or crowding around to show her my gap-toothed tee-ball photos from kindergarten after she'd become a regular at family dinner. But now it means forced smiles and not talking about the one thing that consumes me. Everyone wants to help, but there's nothing they can do.

When I don't say anything, Max smiles wider, like he thinks I'm about to agree.

"I'm sorry, Max. I'll make it to the next one, okay? Today's not good for me. I have to do something."

His face falls, but he nods. "Yeah. Okay."

"Tell my dads I'll be home when I'm done?" I say, turning away with my fliers.

His sigh fills the sidewalk behind me. "You're going to the river, aren't you?"

I stop and turn back. "Why would I be going to the *river*?"

His eyes look like they're about to burst from his face. "I meant Dairy Queen. And their…river of milkshakes."

He knows I haven't been back to the river since the night Lola disappeared, so why would I go there today? Unless there's a reason to.

"What's happening at the river today, Max?" I say through my teeth. "Or should I drive out there and see for myself?"

Panic explodes across his face. He must have been given instructions to keep me from doing exactly that. Was it my dads? His mom? Both?

"If I tell you, do you promise not to go?"

I glare at him.

"Fine, *fine*. Okay, so… There might have been another search today, and your parents wanted me to make sure you didn't interfere with it. But they're probably done by now, so there's no point in going down there. Also, you didn't hear any of this from me."

My brain spins trying to understand. "But that doesn't make sense. Why would they search by the river when they've been through those woods ten times already? *Weeks* ago."

"I have no idea." He throws up his hands. "I don't have any details. So let's pretend we never talked about this and get some food at your place instead. I'm starving."

Dozens of thoughts tumble through my mind all at once. Lola's been gone for five weeks, almost to the day, and in that time I've watched the investigation shift from worry that she ran away to a full-blown Amber Alert–style missing person investigation. The police pulled out all the stops. They set up roadblocks throughout the county, shoved her photo into the hands of every local news station, and posted all over social media. They've searched everywhere, starting at the boat launch where she was last seen, growing their radius based on tips and possible sightings until, eventually, their leads dried up.

Why would they double back to ground zero with a search party? It didn't make any sense. I mean, do they think Lola's been foraging by the water's edge, waiting to be found? *Oh hey guys, thanks for coming, I was getting really sick of tree bark and algae water.*

The only way she'd still be at the river is if—

I take a step back.

They're not looking for *Lola.*

They're looking for her remains.

It feels like the fliers in my hands are about to burst into flames.

"...and it's a great day for hilachas, amiright?"

I blink; Max has been talking this whole time. "What?"

He groans. "Surprise, surprise, you're not paying attention. Just... come back to your house with me, okay? You're not allowed to be down there anyway, and the alternative is food. Let's *go.*"

"I'm not hungry."

Max's hands flap around. "This is a monumentally bad idea."

I make a beeline for my car and pretend I can't hear him. I climb into my dented white Isuzu Trooper and chuck the fliers onto the passenger seat. They don't matter as much as they did ten minutes ago. I have a new mission.

I put the Trooper into gear as my passenger door flings open. Max's tall, lanky self jumps in, rocking the entire SUV as he slams the door.

"Are you insane? I was about to hit the gas!" I yell at him.

"Good. I'm just in time then." He buckles in and flips his curls from his forehead. "I'm not letting you do this alone. Somebody has to keep your ass from getting arrested."

I wonder how hard it would be to kick him out of the vehicle, but the determined look on his face and the grip he has on the oh-shit handle tells me he's prepared for a sneak attack.

"You're stuck with me," he says. "If you want to creep, I'm creeping too. Let's do this."

"You're annoying. You know that?" I turn back to the road and take off before I punch him. My aunt will have my ass if I harm one hair on his precious little head, and he knows it.

It only takes a few minutes to get to the edge of town, where the boat launch is, but the drive feels like it drags. I haven't been within a mile of the river since Lola went missing, and it feels like sinking into a black hole of awful memories and pain the closer I get.

I follow a curve in the road and when it straightens, the boat launch comes into view.

The river borders Washington City like an arm slung around an old friend, but the only part of the bank that's low enough to reach the water is here. The boat launch is a narrow parking lot set into the trees with a concrete slab slanting down into the ice-cold Willamette River.

This time of year the launch is normally deserted, but today it looks like peak boating season. Every one of the ten parking spaces is full, except one, and cars line the road on both sides.

The steadfast townspeople coming together to find closure for poor Lola and her family. They should be out in the world looking for *her*, not here looking for bones. The thought makes me sick to my stomach. This whole place makes me sick. The lot, the water, the November sunset filtering through the pine trees. I hate it all. I hate everything that happened here and what it's done to me. What it did to Lola.

I park along the side of the road behind another car and cut the engine. I fold my arms across the top of the steering wheel and lean forward. It looks like the search is wrapping up. People emerge from the overgrowth on the far side of the parking lot to join the small crowd waiting by the tree line. A couple deputies stand among them, chatting away. There's no sign of the sheriff.

I parked too close. Dozens of eyes flicker toward the Trooper, shooting daggers through my windshield. Sometimes I think this car is as notorious as I am. If I gave it more than a second's thought, I would have asked Max to drive. His car's the same color as the trees and might have blended in.

I fucked up again.

A little old lady with a clipboard narrows her eyes at me, and I wonder if she's the one who left the voicemail.

You should be ashamed of yourself.

Joke's on her, I already am.

"So what's the plan, Drew?" Max presses his insanely long legs against the floorboards, yanks the stack of fliers out from under his ass, and chucks them in the backseat. "Is there a purpose to crashing this shindig?"

I hold the old woman's stare a minute longer, and she flips me off.

When I don't respond, he says, "I mean, you can't exactly walk over and join them. You'd get arrested for harassment or teenage fuckery in ten minutes flat."

I make a disgusted sound in my throat and lean back in my seat. He's right. Roane or his officers wouldn't hesitate to put me in handcuffs if I got anywhere near the do-gooders. Especially the way the sheriff's been leaning on me the last few days, desperate to not have the case of a missing girl bungled on his watch. Hell, the only reason Roane hasn't put me behind bars already is because I'm a high-achieving *white* kid from a family that's financially stable enough to pool funds and get me a lawyer. If I happened to look more like Papá and the Diaz side, that might not have been the case.

It also helps that Roane doesn't have any actual evidence against me, and his entire investigation seems to hinge on me eventually confessing. Still, I know I'm pushing my luck by being here.

"I don't want to join them. There's no point. Lola's not in there."

I feel his stare bore into the side of my face. "And you know that because...?"

"Don't start. I don't know *where* she is, but I know she's not in those woods. She's not dead."

"How do you know? For sure?"

"Because she can't be. That's...impossible." I drag my fingers through my hair. "She ran away, or she was kidnapped, or...I don't know. But she can't be dead. They're wrong, and I'm going to prove it."

Max shifts in his seat, leaning forward with a wince. "Okaaay, so if you're not planning to cause drama, what are we doing here?"

"That's a good question." I look across the parking lot and my gaze lingers on the only empty parking spot. Home to Lola's shrine. It looks run down even from all the way over here.

Old flowers and half-burnt candles, framed pictures of Lola pulled from her Insta, now waterlogged and forgotten. A blue and gold uniform lays across the pavement, partially covered in leaves. There used to be an identical one by her locker until someone on the staff put it away last week.

Monuments, care of the classmates who lost their minds with worry when she went missing, but quickly lost interest once the shock of her being gone and the attention from pretending to miss her wore off. Like the participants in this search party, who would rather stumble upon a body in the woods and be done with it.

"I just wanted to see who came," I say. "I think I would have felt better if there weren't so many cars. It would mean everyone thinks this is as pointless as I do."

"I don't see Mr. or Mrs. Scott. That's a good sign, right?"

Maybe.

I scan the cars again, and glare at an old, dented Volkswagen across the road. Autumn's here somewhere. What would a search party be without the sobbing best friend? I guess that explains why she wasn't at school today.

Max is right though. I don't see Mr. Scott's Wrangler or Mrs. Scott's sedan. A spike of hope shoots through me. Maybe they haven't given up either?

Or maybe they rode with the deputies and haven't made their way out of the woods yet...

"We should get out of here before someone calls Roane," Max says.

I know he's right, but I can't tear my eyes from the tree line. The crowd keeps growing. Almost fifty now, as more and more people emerge from the forest.

Please don't be here with them.

My fingers tap an anxiety rhythm on the steering wheel.

"Drew? Come on. We don't have to go to family dinner, we can go wherever you want. I'll buy us some ice cream. Whatever it takes to get you out of here. Please?"

I sigh and reach for the ignition as the crowd parts and a tall figure steps from the trees. The sight of him chills like a bucket of ice water straight down my spine.

And now I'm nauseous.

"Oh *shit*," Max whispers. "Her mom's here too."

I watch them join the others. Mr. Scott looks like half his hair has gone gray since September, and his wife has lost so much weight the breeze coming off the river might be enough to carry her away. She clutches her black coat at the base of her throat and pushes her long dark hair out of her face. Someone says something to him, and Mr. Scott turns and glowers at me. Like a living skeleton, promising to haunt me until the day I die.

My face burns with shame. This man, who knew me almost as well as my own parents, and still turned on me like everyone else.

I slam the Trooper into gear, make a U-turn, and take off.

He wasn't supposed to be here. Neither of them were supposed to be here.

Who's still looking for Lola?

"Are you okay?" Max asks, carefully. Like he spent a long time choosing his words.

I shake my head, taking the corner too fast. "You were right. I shouldn't have come here."

FOUR

DREW

I take Max back to the library. He doesn't speak the whole drive—must have killed him—but he also doesn't move when I double-park by his Liberty, so I know it's coming.

I wave a hand at him. "Go on, say what you want before I get a ticket."

He fumbles with his seatbelt, twisting it in his hands like a piece of licorice. When he lets go, it rolls up into the holder with a clatter. "You know I love you, and I don't want to sound like I'm not on your side here, because I am. But showing up to the boat launch like that makes you look guilty. You get that, right?"

I want to argue with him, but I can't. So I say nothing at all.

"The bad guys always return to the scene of the crime, and that's all anyone saw when you pulled up. Guilty Drew. Not to mention your dads are going to flip when they find out you were there, and my days will be numbered when my mom finds out I spilled the beans. All in all, this wasn't a great move."

I trace the emblem on the steering wheel with my thumb. I hate that he's right. "I know. I'll keep quiet if you do?"

He blows out a big breath and shakes his head. "As far as I'm concerned we got a Blizzard. And that's what I'll say if they ask me, but dude, get your shit together."

I nod, my stomach filling with acid and regret. "I need someone to find her."

"We all do. But this isn't how to do it. Use that big brain of yours and find another way. Today's search doesn't mean anything. She's been gone a long time. Everyone's grasping for answers in whatever way they can."

"But they're wasting time, Max. Every hour spent in those woods is an hour they're not getting any closer to her."

"So give Roane fewer reasons to worry about you, and more reasons to look elsewhere." He points his thumb toward the mess in the backseat. "Are those fliers really helping Lola? You're not the only one who needs her to come home safe. We're all struggling, and we can't lose you too."

He gets out and slams the car door. In the sudden silence, I almost wish he'd come back.

Almost.

Max pulls out ahead of me, and I watch him disappear down Main Street. I should be right behind him. I should go home to family dinner because it's the right thing to do, and it'll make everyone happy. But I'd rather eat my fliers than face my family right now.

I circle around the outside of town, careful to stay far from the river. I park in a neighborhood in the opposite direction from home and gather the fliers from the backseat.

Time to piss off some homeowners' associations.

Because Max is only half-right: The fliers probably won't lead me to Lola. But they *are* something. They're proof that I kept looking. And when she comes home, everywhere she goes, there'll be a picture of her face and my phone number, and she'll know that I never gave up. Which is the only thing I can give to her now.

I grab my backpack and the stapler from the backseat and get to work, tacking her face on every telephone pole and stop sign I pass until a streetlight flickers on above me. I look up in surprise. It got dark fast.

I look up and down the road. I've zombie walked straight into Lola's neighborhood. In fact, her cul-de-sac is a block ahead of me.

The dwindling pile of paper in my hands feels like lead.

I shouldn't get any closer. I know that. Her family is suffering enough. They don't need to see me lurking twice in one day. I zip my supplies into my bag, but my feet take me to Lola's corner on their own. I'll only stay a minute.

The Scotts' big gray Craftsman sits one house down. The downstairs lights blaze warmth across their wide porch and perfect lawn. Nothing moves beyond the glass and the driveway is empty, so I take a few steps into the road.

I remember the first time I saw this house. When Lola introduced me to her parents. The place seemed so imposing with its big windows, glossy white porch swing, and manicured hedges. It doesn't look imposing anymore. It looks sad. Like the walls themselves feel the absence of the girl in the corner bedroom the same way I do.

The light in her room tugs at a familiar hole in my chest. Lola left it on the night she disappeared, and her parents haven't touched it since. It's like they can't bear to cast what's left of her in darkness. I understand and hate it at the same time. I wouldn't be able to turn it off either, but seeing that window illuminated on the second floor messes with my head every time. It tricks me into thinking she might have come back, that she's in there, talking to Autumn about what a jerk I'm being or the history midterm.

But Lola's not in there, my minute is up, and I don't belong here. This town is full of places I don't belong anymore.

I turn and find a red Wrangler idling in the road behind me. Every bone in my body turns to stone as Mr. Scott locks eyes with me over the steering wheel.

For one wild heartbeat I wonder if he's going to run me over and put us both out of our misery. But instead, the Jeep pulls past me into the driveway. Mr. Scott parks and crosses the lawn in long strides.

I brace for his anger, but he stops on the sidewalk and practically whispers, "Come here."

The fact that he doesn't yell is somehow twice as terrifying as if he'd screamed in my face. Getting closer is the last thing I want to do. I can't even meet his eyes; how am I supposed to talk to him?

I take slow steps, dread hanging from every part of my body, until I'm standing in front of him.

"What are you doing here?" He doesn't sound as furious as I expected. He sounds...hollow. His eyes are bloodshot, and his cheeks are gaunt. He's wearing a button-down shirt, but the skeleton man beneath it looks like he's trying to disappear, same as his daughter. The passenger door of the Jeep slams, and his wife stops at the back of the vehicle. She looks straight through me.

Guilt wraps around my throat and squeezes. "Fliers," I croak.

"Why won't you leave us alone? Haven't you done enough?"

Yes.

The strangest urge to defend myself bubbles over me. I respect the hell out of this man. Always have. I don't want him to look at me the way everyone else does. "I'm trying to find her. Same as you. Mr. Scott, I've eaten a million meals at your house. Our families went camping together last summer. You went to every one of my swim meets. You *know* me. And you know I'd never hurt Lola. Not ever."

His glare sears into me, and I think he might regret not running me over when he had the chance. "The kid I knew would never have left her alone at night. He wouldn't have waited until the next day to call and see if she got home okay. He wouldn't stop cooperating with the police. I don't know you at all."

The truth of his words slams into me and tightens the grip this guilt has on my throat. I couldn't speak if I tried.

He takes a long measured breath, but before he can say more Mrs. Scott appears behind him, her fingers wrapping tightly around her husband's arm like she needs the support to stand. Wide green eyes bore into me. "Just tell us what you did, okay? Tell us where she is and let this all be over. I...we can't...I need you to tell me what happened," she pleads. "The sheriff is saying there's little hope after all this time. They're looking for a body, and we don't know if that's the right call. Everything in us is screaming to keep looking for *her*. And *you* are the only one with the answers."

Jesus. They should have hit me with the car. It would have been less painful.

I can't make a single word form on my lips. I don't have any answers. I don't know what to tell her. I don't know how to breathe.

Mrs. Scott chokes out a sob. "For god's sake, Drew. She's my fucking child! Just tell me where she is!"

"I swear I didn't hurt her. I swear on my life!" Bile rages up my throat. "I'm sorry I came here. I'm not trying to hurt anyone, least of all you or your family."

A tear slips from the corner of her eye, and she wipes it with the back of her hand.

Mr. Scott puts his arm around her shoulder and shakes his head at me. "Get out of here, Drew. And don't come back."

He guides his wife up the porch and vanishes inside, slamming the front door behind him.

I have no idea how long I stand there, but at some point, it starts raining. I drag myself across the intersection. Having the whole town hate me is awful, but his words are a red hot poker to the guts. I keep finding myself in places I don't belong today.

"Hey, asshole."

I jump and spin toward the voice.

Autumn's sitting on the curb across the street, just beyond the streetlight. Watching me.

Irritation bubbles up inside me, but I'm so exhausted that it dies there. She's been like an extra shadow these last few weeks. Everywhere I go, she's always in the background, glaring at me like she's hoping I'll burst into flames and she'll get to watch me burn.

"What are you doing here? Following me again?" I mean to sound harsh, but it comes out a strangled whisper.

Autumn stands and pushes back the hood of her silver glittery sweatshirt. She looks like a furious disco ball as she walks into the light. Waves of long red hair fall from where she'd tucked it back. "How dare you come to her house? You have balls even coming to this neighborhood after what you did."

"For fuck's sake. I didn't do anything."

"You and I both know that's not true," she says, stuffing her hands into her sweatshirt pockets. "Lola was my best friend, and I'll be damned if I let you get away with this."

"Is."

"What?"

"*Is*. She *is* your best friend. Present fucking tense," I yell, stepping toward her.

She recoils, fear blossoming across her face. She backs up and glances toward her house up the road—mapping an escape from Big Bad Me.

I shake my head. I can't get used to people who've known me all my life treating me like I'm a monster. Hell, I knew Autumn long before Lola and I started dating, not that it stopped her from turning on me too.

I don't want her to be scared of me though, no matter how angry I am with her. I keep my distance. "I didn't hurt Lola. I never would, and I'd *never* hurt you either. So why don't you stop following me and go tell your father to do his job and find her."

She folds her arms, regaining some of her bravado. "He's the sheriff. He's supposed to question suspects. He *is* doing his job. The only way he could do it better is by locking your ass up."

"Whatever, Autumn. If you put half as much energy into looking for Lola as you do harassing me, she'd be home by now and we'd all be in a lot less misery."

I stalk off in the direction of my car.

"I'm not falling for the steadfast boyfriend act," she yells behind me. "You did something to her and everyone will know the truth eventually."

Her words hit like a slap. I turn, barely recognizing the hostile person staring back at me. "You know what's funny? If the tables were turned, there isn't a person on this Earth who could convince me you were capable of hurting anyone. I'd defend you until the end, Autumn. When she comes home, I don't want to hear how sorry you are for stabbing me in the back. I'm fucking done with you."

Regret fissures down her face before she wipes it away. "You think I *wanted* to find out my friend is a monster? I wanted to defend you, but history only goes so far. I know you're to blame. I've known it for weeks."

"What the hell does that mean?"

"It means I may not know what you did, but I know all this is your fault." She stomps toward her house around the corner, leaving me alone with a knot in my stomach.

Because she's absolutely right. This *is* all my fault.

I am to blame.

The rain slowly picks up, growing to a full downpour by the time I reach the Trooper. Water soaks through every layer of my clothes, down to my bones. I shiver all the way home, but I don't bother with the heater.

Call it penance.

I park in front of my house, surprised to see only two cars in the driveway. My parents' matching silver Volvos. The rest of the family must have gone home already.

Thank god.

The front door's unlocked, and I don't bother calling out. I don't want to talk. I want a hot shower and some sleep. I hang my keys on the hook by the door, so they'll know I'm home, and trudge upstairs. I stop in the hallway to throw my dripping sweatshirt in the dryer and close my bedroom door behind me. I smack the light switch by the door and my desk lamp flickers on.

I sigh. Even my room doesn't feel like it's mine anymore.

A collection of swim team trophies and grunge band posters decorate my walls. Video games and scattered textbooks litter the carpet. But *she's* had her hands on everything in here. She went to every swim meet, every concert—even though she would have rather seen Taylor Swift. She studied here with me every day after school. Complained about the video games but still watched me play. She even picked out my comforter. Said the blue in the plaid matched my eyes.

Now they're all artifacts of my old life. I've been asked to sit out this swim season, step down as captain—and nobody on the team will speak to me. I haven't listened to music or picked up a controller in weeks. It's all waiting on her. I need Lola home, so I can go back to a life that's more than missing person posters and guilt.

I kick off my shoes, tug on a pair of sweats, and collapse into my desk chair. Maybe I don't have it in me to take a shower after all.

Despite the exhaustion, I pull my whiteboard from the wall above my desk and flip it over, revealing the only thing I care about these days. The back of the board hides my entire pathetic investigation. Post-it notes, a printed map of Washington City marked with everywhere Lola went the day she disappeared, and photos of her. So many photos. I brush my thumb against one of us parked at the boat launch. The dark river in the background barely illuminated by the flash. We both smile like idiots, no idea what's about to happen.

It's the last picture I have of us.

Taken the night she disappeared.

This simple four-by-three-foot collection is everything I know about that last twenty-four hours—which isn't much. I scan the time-line, scribbled on the back of some old homework, detailing every-thing that happened from the moment I picked her up for school in the morning. Her classes, after-school practice with the team, the fight with her parents, me picking her up at her house at just after 10 p.m., the boat launch, the stop she made at the convenience store right before midnight, and finally the cops finding her phone by the side of the road the next morning.

I have no information to add. Same as yesterday and the day before. I flip the whiteboard over and hang it back on the wall, frustration rising. Max was right. The fliers aren't helping, but I don't know what else I can do. I need new information, a clue, a starting place. The silent phone on my desk mocks me. I *need* someone to tell me something I don't already know.

No, that's a lie. I need Lola to call. All these weeks later, I still expect to see her name on my screen every time it rings. With every ping of a text message, I think it's her. And every time it's not, I feel it all over again—the suffocating loop of hope turned to dread.

My elbow brushes my laptop keyboard as I sit back down, and the screen lights up. The background is another picture of me and Lola. The last time we went to the beach with Autumn and Max—though neither of them were dumb enough to get in the water. My arm is stretched out to take the photo while we hug and laugh. We're calf-deep in the unbearably cold ocean, jeans rolled to our knees, her huddled against the wind in her flowery jean jacket. The photo feels like karma punching me in the face.

She's everywhere and nowhere at the same time.

I slam the laptop shut and brace my elbows on my knees, eyeing the trash can next to the desk in case what little I've eaten today makes a reappearance.

How could I do this? How did I let this happen?

There's a knock on my door, and I look up as it creaks open. My dads stand shoulder to shoulder in the doorway. Something is wrong. They're smiling, but not really. Tiny smiles. Don't-panic-Drew smiles.

Dad scratches a patch of graying blond hair near his ear and drops the façade. He grimaces. "Hey, kiddo. Do you have a minute?"

Papá pulls off his glasses and squints at him. "What your dad means to say is how was your day?"

"Fine," I say, mechanically. "What's wrong?"

Papá comes in and sits on the edge of the bed. Dad follows him. The springs creak under their weight, and they both look like they're dreading everything about this conversation.

Did something happen?

Did the sheriff call? Did someone tell them I was at the river?

"We missed you at family dinner," Dad says. "Everyone was looking forward to seeing you."

I nod. "I know. I'm sorry, I should have texted. I had to take care of something."

"More fliers?"

I nod again, surprised they haven't mentioned me crashing the search yet. Maybe they don't know? "But I don't think you guys came in here to talk about fliers. What's going on?"

They lock eyes for a moment, like they're comforting each other before ripping off a Band-Aid. The nausea returns. Maybe I'm not in trouble. Maybe it's worse than that.

The whites of Papá's eyes are pink behind his glasses, like he's been crying.

Maybe this isn't about the sheriff after all.

Dad leans forward and takes a deep breath. "Kiddo, the lawyer called. He… He thought we should know…thought that we should tell you…"

Papá gives Dad's pale knee a squeeze and my whole body tenses.

Lola called from…California, Florida, Vegas, somewhere. She ran away and she's never coming home.

Lola's in the hospital.

Lola's kidnappers came forward with a ransom.

Papá's red-rimmed eyes meet mine. "Hijito, they found a body."

I turn and hurl into the trash can.

FIVE

MARY

An hour later, Wayne holds the precinct door open, and I step into the fresh air for the first time in what feels like days. It rained sometime since Officer Bowman brought me in. The parking lot shimmers with it. Cold moisture-heavy air prickles the skin on my bare arms, and I regret giving Bowman back his sweatshirt.

The town looks dead to the world. The short little strip mall across the street is dark. Several streetlights are burned out. I look up and down the road, but the only things I see illuminated are a gas station with a flashing twenty-four-hour sign and a deserted motel.

Wayne walks around me and heads for the only car in the lot that's not a police cruiser: a gray work van, covered in rust spots and peeling paint. He opens the passenger door and smiles. "Do you need anything before we drive up to the cabin?"

I shake my head and step beside him to look in the van. Considering how dented and messed up it is outside, the interior looks almost new. But climbing into a van with a stranger still feels like a red flag, even if he is my dad.

He stands with one hand on the door. "Are you sure? We should get you some ibuprofen, or icepacks—I'm not sure what's at the cabin. Maybe some bandages, in case any of your cuts need more cleaning—"

"Okay, okay," I say. "Whatever you think we need."

"Sorry." He frowns at his feet. "Don't get me wrong. I know a Band-Aid and a shower won't fix things, but I'll be here for you while you piece it all back together. We can get through anything. Even this."

A mix of feelings knots my stomach. I'm grateful, but terrified. I'm relieved, yet unsettled. I'm happy and lost…I can't pick a side. I know he's trying to be comforting, but I don't even know what to *call* him. Wayne? Dad?

Split the difference, call him Dwayne?

"Do you mind if I call you Wayne?"

"I'm not going to lie, that'll be strange. But if it makes you feel better, you can call me whatever you want." He smiles, though it's a tiny fragile thing.

Dwayne it is.

He gestures toward the open door. "Ready?"

Officer Bowman steps out of the precinct behind me, locks up, and pockets his keys. "Hold on. Until everything checks out, she's riding with me." He catches my eye and smiles. "We'll follow Mr. Boone up to the house."

I look between the van and the cruiser. Part of me wishes I could be at ease with Dwayne and be done with it, but I'm glad that Bowman is coming along. It gives me a little longer to adjust.

"Of course," Wayne says, jarring me back to the conversation. "Like I said, whatever you need me to do. You should at least have a jacket though. It's freezing out here." He reaches into the space between the front seats and holds something out to me.

It's a jean jacket, with rose gold buttons and pastel, floral sleeves. Periwinkle, orchid, and lilac on white fabric, with vintage leaves. I fight the urge to frown. Apparently I'm a floral person?

I slide it on like I'm not unsettled by the look of it. I can't even put on a jacket without mixed feelings. "Thank you."

"Not a problem."

"We'll be right behind you, Mr. Boone," Bowman says, leading me away with a hand on my shoulder.

I give Wayne a small wave.

"I'll see you in a minute, kiddo."

It sounds like a promise.

We climb into the front seat of the police cruiser, and the first thing Bowman does is crank up the heat. The warmth feels good on my face.

"Don't worry about all this," he says, gesturing to the precinct and the van. "We're just covering our bases. He had to fill out a preliminary report. I ran his license and registration. He has no warrants or arrests. I'll check out the paperwork at the house, but it's not easy to fake a birth certificate. I won't leave if anything seems off. I promise."

Of all the people who could have found me, I'm glad it was someone as nice as him. "Thank you for helping me."

He gives me a deep nod. "Are you ready to go?"

I click my seatbelt and grip the shoulder strap. They keep asking me if I'm ready. Can anybody be ready for this kind of day? I feel like I'm test driving my own father.

I nod, and Bowman pulls out of the parking space.

We turn onto the deserted main street, the headlights of the cruiser illuminating the back of Wayne's van ahead of us. We take a right near the little motel by the edge of town and follow Wayne up the mountain, winding along half a dozen roads that all look like the one I woke up on. Wayne drives carefully, signaling for all his turns, never driving faster than the speed limit, and I don't know if that's because he's being followed by a cop or if he's always this cautious.

About fifteen minutes of bumpy roads later, Wayne turns down a short driveway and parks in front of a log cabin. We pull in behind him, and I lean forward.

A set of stairs leads up to a porch on the front of the house. Two big windows with drawn curtains sit on either side of the door, but I can't see much else. The van blocks half the cruiser's headlights, and when it's dark on this mountain, it's *dark*. I can't even see the edge of the driveway.

It's creepy.

Bowman reaches for his door. "Wait here while I check out the house, okay? I'll lock the doors. Just in case."

I send a panicked glance at the darkness waiting outside the window and wring the seatbelt strap in my hands. "In case of what?"

Wayne had my school ID and all those pictures in his phone. He had enough proof to get us this far. What does Bowman think is going to happen in there?

"It's procedure," he says, and I wonder if he saw the panic on my face. "Your safety is my concern."

In reality I'm sitting in a police cruiser, but in my mind, tree branches reach out for me with menacing fingers. The grip on my seatbelt tightens, and I look him straight in the eye. "Please don't leave me in the dark. I don't want to be alone."

He holds my gaze for a beat, glances up at the house, and sighs. "Fine, but you stay right beside me."

I nod and we climb out, but I'm more on edge than I was a minute ago. Wayne rounds the front of the van as we come up beside it. A motion light over the door flickers on, illuminating us and the driveway. The darkness pushes back to the tree line and hovers there like a living thing.

"Welcome home," he says with a smile.

I try to smile back, but "home" looks pretty ominous at three in the morning.

He heads up the steps, unlocks the front door, and disappears inside. I wait for Officer Bowman to go in first, but I'm right on his heels. Wayne circles the living room turning on lights, and the place is ablaze in a few seconds. I relax a bit.

He catches my eye from the kitchen. "Figured you wouldn't be in the mood for shadows tonight."

I give him a grateful smile and hang by the door while Officer Bowman pokes around. The main room is open and small, with a living room near the door and a kitchen in the back. Everything is yellow, from the plaid couches to the afghan flung over the back of it, but it smells nice. Like caramel or something sweet. It's way less creepy inside than out.

A woodstove fills the corner to my left, sitting on a little raised brick platform that also supports a firewood holder and one of those racks with a fire poker and little shovel.

Four doors sit in the wall to my right. Three are open. The first looks like a bedroom, with a sheetless queen-size mattress on a log frame. The second is a bathroom. I can't see well enough into the third, and the last one is closed with a latch on the outside.

"What's that?" Bowman asks, knocking against the locked door.

"Basement," Wayne says. "The key is downstairs, but we can get in through the door out back if you want to take a look."

"I'll check it out before I leave," Bowman says, continuing his sweep.

Wayne sets his keys on the wood island, holding his arms wide. "It's not much, but we can make do while the floors are being fixed, huh?"

Again I'm struck with a sense of familiarity. I don't know if it's him or this cabin, but something feels…normal about this, and my nerves settle a bit more.

"Yeah, it'll work," I say.

"That's my room," he says, nodding toward the one with the bare mattress. "This one is yours." He walks to the third door and turns on the light.

I look to Bowman and he nods, so I cross the space. I lean on the doorframe and peek inside. The room is small, but not exactly a closet. A twin bed fills one corner. Wayne stands beside a wooden desk that's covered in old books. Mostly weathered Christian fiction and Chicken Soup for the Soul books. I don't think those are mine.

A nightstand sits by the bed with a lone lamp on it. An inspirational poster hangs on the wall above the headboard, with a beach and bold pink letters that say "Don't Worry, Be Happy…"

Well, that's coming down immediately.

"What do you think?" Wayne asks, brushing dust off the books. "We won't be here forever."

I shrug. It's a room with a bed when a couple hours ago I thought I'd be sleeping in a police station. I have no complaints. "Looks fine to me."

Wayne waves us out toward the kitchen. We shuffle back to the main room, and he turns to Bowman. "What do you say I grab that birth certificate and we wrap this up? She looks like she's about to drop."

Bowman eyes me. "Sure. Where's the paperwork?"

"I've got it right here." He slips into the first bedroom and emerges with an accordion file folder. He sets it on the island and pulls out a paper, setting it on the counter.

There it is. Mary Ellen Boone. Born 10:56am, on October 11th in Newberg, Oregon. It's stamped with the Oregon seal. He slides my Social Security card toward Bowman too.

Bowman examines the documents, and all the muscles in his shoulders loosen. I can practically see the transition from potential perp to cooperative father. He looks at me.

"We good?"

He nods. "As soon as I run all this information through the system from the car. Do you want to wait here or with me?"

I plop down on the sofa and every bone in my body sags. God, I'm so tired. "Here, please."

"Okay. We'll be right back. Mr. Boone?"

Wayne gives me a wink and leads the way. They disappear out the front door.

I'm only sitting a minute before my chin droops toward my chest. I zone in and out, so much I don't know how long they're out there, but at some point, the front door opens and Wayne comes back in wearing a giant smile. "We're in the clear, kiddo."

Bowman steps in behind him. "Everything checks out, Mary. These documents are genuine, and I'm confident we've figured out who you are. I'm comfortable leaving you in your father's care if you are?"

I look around the cozy cabin. Wayne may feel like a stranger, but the logical part of my brain tells me he's not. The evidence is overwhelming. I'm fairly certain the alternative is the hospital or state custody, so really, it's no choice at all.

I smile. "Yeah, I'm good. I don't want to go anywhere else tonight."

"Me either," Wayne says. "You need some sleep and maybe some food. If you're up to it?"

The bathroom door calls to me. "Actually, all I want is a shower and sleep."

"Of course. Towels are on the shelf above the toilet. I'm sorry we don't have any of your clothes." He nods toward the dirty, disheveled stuff I'm wearing. "They were all in your car, so I'll have to find something for you to wear."

"Yeah, sure. Sounds great."

Bowman reaches out and puts a business card on the arm of the couch. "On that note, I'll let you both settle in. Mr. Boone, I'll be in touch when we find the car, and Mary, call me if you need anything, okay? I'll check in again soon."

I smile and take the card. "Sounds good."

He shakes Wayne's hand and leaves.

A moment later I hear the sound of his cruiser crunching out of the driveway. For some reason, my stomach sinks. Bowman wouldn't have left if there were any doubt. He promised. But I clutch the business card tight in my hand.

Wayne strides into the kitchen. He pulls open the fridge and shakes his head. "Why don't you jump in the shower and get warm? I'll run back into town and grab us some food and whatever I can find first-aid-wise from the convenience store."

That sounds amazing. I doubt I'll make it to the food though. It takes most of my energy to stand up. "Good plan."

He smiles and grabs his keys from the counter. "Do you want me to lock the door?"

"Yes, please," I say, a shudder rolling down my back.

"You got it. Oh, and Mary?"

I pause halfway to the bathroom and turn to him.

"I'm so glad to have you back, kiddo."

The sincerity in his voice tugs a genuine smile across my face. "Me too."

I lay my jacket over the back of the couch and kick off my disgusting shoes before I step into the bathroom, which looks a lot like the rest of the house. Bright artificial colors and wood tones everywhere. There's a pedestal sink, toilet, and tub/shower combo with a small window. I set Bowman's business card on the windowsill.

I shed the rest of my dirty clothes and take what's probably the best shower of my life. The hot water rushes over my skin and for the first time today, I feel alive again. Like I'm experiencing rather than drifting. I crank up the heat and the water washes away blood, dirt, and the worst parts of this unbearable day.

I imagine all the chaos swirling down the drain.

Well, maybe not all of it.

I try not to look at the bruises birthing their way across my knees and arms. Ghosts of blue and purple draw an ache through my muscles that even the hot water can't quite touch.

Car accidents suck.

I run out of hot water long before I run out of chaos. I'm mostly dried off before I remember I don't have any clean clothes. But when I poke my head out of the bathroom, I find a pair of too-big sweatpants and a black T-shirt hanging on the other side of the doorknob. A pair of clean socks too. And my jacket has been moved to the hook by the door. The bloodstained shoes are gone.

Wayne must have done this before he left; I'm so grateful I could cry. I tug everything on, not caring that none of it fits. It's clean; that's all I want tonight.

I absently wipe the steam on the mirror with my towel before I hang it up—an old habit, maybe?—and again, my reflection makes me stop.

This is my face. It's the same as the precinct reflection, though this version is cleaner. My cheeks are pinker. The garish sight of two black eyes is a lot to deal with, but it's not the jarring part. The *face* is. I still don't know her.

How can I not know my own face?

My stomach churns.

I turn away from the mirror and gather my dirty clothes and the business card. Wayne hasn't made it back yet. I pad to my room, where I discover he's made my bed too. Incredibly soft jersey sheets stretch across the mattress with a massive white fluffy down comforter that weighs a ton and smells like a good night's sleep. The kindness of these simple gestures nearly breaks what's left of me. I drop my dirty clothes by the door, lean Bowman's business card against the floral lamp base, and use my last shreds of energy to sink into bed.

My bed.

Mary's bed.

I close my eyes and burst into tears. They flow like a torrent. No matter how tightly I curl into my blankets, or how long I shower, or how many locks are on the front door, I feel exposed without my memories. I can't own my name or my face.

"I'm Mary Ellen Boone," I whisper to the darkness. "*Mary*. My name is Mary."

And I cry myself to sleep.

SIX

MARY

DAY 2

I wake up half a second before my eyes open to flashes of a long, darkened ditch. Panic shoots through my body and my scratchy eyes rip open...but I'm not in the dark. I blink up at smooth half-circle logs lining the ceiling. Sunlight streams in through a window highlighting that goddamned beach poster.

Don't worry, be happy.

I gingerly sit up, and the events of last night roll through my mind like a creepy television recap I really could have done without. Fresh tears sting my eyes, but I take a deep breath to make them stop. The last thing I need is misery-fest round two.

No. I have to stop crying. I have a life to piece back together.

I swing my legs over the side of the bed and stretch. My joints move like rusty hinges, but the stretching helps. I stand and it's not outwardly painful. More like a dull ache that happens to cover nearly every inch of me.

I guess that's not much better.

The unmistakable smell of breakfast wafts through the crack beneath the door, and my stomach growls in response. I tug my door open and grin. The cabin smells like things I want to eat as fast as humanly possible—scrambled eggs, maple sausage, butter, toast.

The woodstove in the corner is bursting with flames, clearly reloaded recently, and pumps out heat that instantly relaxes me.

Wayne looks up at me from the kitchen island and smiles. He's halfway through slicing a carton of strawberries. "Dang it. I wanted to get this all ready before you woke up."

I look at the counter. A platter of scrambled eggs sits beside a mess of bowls and eggshells. A cast-iron skillet sizzles on the stove with medallion sausages full of fennel and grease.

My mouth waters. I sit on the barstool across from him. "Nice fire."

He nods and goes back to chopping. "I know how much you hate being cold. Plus this place can be drafty."

He places the bowl of fresh strawberries beside the eggs.

The normalcy of this is comforting. Like I didn't wake up in a ditch ten-ish hours ago.

"Hungry?" Wayne asks.

"Starving, actually." My stomach makes a sound like a whimpering dog.

He laughs and turns back to the stove, stirring what looks like pancake batter in a big measuring cup beside the stove. "Grab what you want. Your pancakes will be ready in a second."

I don't need to be asked twice. I pile eggs and sausages on my plate. I stab at the sausages first and Oh. My. God. It's like I forgot what food tasted like. I scarf them down in less than a minute.

"You weren't kidding," he says, looking back at me before pouring the pancakes onto a fresh pan. "Your appetite's coming back. That's a good sign."

"Thank you for making all this."

He waves at the spread with a spatula. "Breakfast is our thing. I couldn't miss the chance to give you a little slice of normal, even if this kitchen isn't as up-to-date as the one at home."

Breakfast is our thing? I should ask him about this, because it might shed more light on this life of mine, but I'm too busy forking mouthfuls of eggs into my face. I scoop some strawberries onto my plate too. They're a little watery, but I'm not about to complain.

Wayne drops a plate of pancakes onto the island and piles some food onto his own plate. "Are you feeling better?"

I nod because nothing can make me stop stuffing my face at this point. I snag a couple pancakes and scratch at an itch on my neck.

"Good. I'm thinking we'll hang out here today. You can watch TV and rest. We don't have anywhere to be, and it's important you have time to recover. What do you think?"

I start to respond, but there's something stuck in my throat.

No. Nothing's in there.

I try to clear my throat, to dislodge this feeling, but it lingers. A crawling itch works its way through my mouth and down my neck. My nails rake across my skin.

What is happening?

I clear my throat again and the itch spreads down my arms. I look down and freeze. My forearms are covered in newly forming hives.

Wayne does a double take and reaches for my arm. He examines the hives, his face as white as a sheet, then looks at the counter. "Did you eat the eggs?"

I nod.

He doesn't walk, he *runs* to a brown paper bag sitting by the front door and spills the contents across the floor—bandages, antacids, Pepto, tampons, ibuprofen, Midol, peroxide, Q-tips, Icy Hot, triple antibiotic ointment, bug bite relief. It looks like he swiped the entire first aid aisle into a cart. He snatches a box off the floor and runs back to me, wielding extra-strength liquid Benadryl like it's the holy grail.

I take whatever dose he gives me. The itching is like little pinpricks all over the inside of my mouth and the hives make me want to claw my skin from my body.

Wayne brings me water and rubs the spot between my shoulder blades. I blink over and over, taking in shallow breaths until his words make sense again.

"—so, so sorry. I should have been paying better attention," he says. He looks miserable. "I made breakfast on autopilot. The eggs were for me—it never even crossed my mind that you wouldn't remember you can't eat them. I'm so sorry."

Eggs. I have an egg allergy.

Okay, so…downside, hives suck. Upside, I know one more thing about myself.

Wayne moves me to the couch, and eventually the medicine kicks in. My throat begins to lose the itch, but it's slow going. The hives stop spreading, but they linger. The itching ebbs over the next hour or so until it doesn't consume my mind anymore, but with it comes drowsiness and a self-loathing I didn't expect.

What use am I if I can't even remember what I'm allergic to?

Wayne flutters around me, bringing me water, cold washcloths, asking what I need every other minute until I finally ask him to sit and chill because he's making me feel worse. This isn't his fault, it's mine. He didn't force-feed me an allergic reaction.

He sits on the coffee table in front of me, and his shoulders sag. "I'll keep a closer eye, I promise."

"Is it always like this? How many allergy attacks have I had?" I croak.

He looks away. "I don't know. Maybe half a dozen before your mom and I got the test done. You were little."

I stare at the hives on my arm. "Do I need an EpiPen?"

He looks surprised. "Um, no. Not that I remember. It's always been itchy and annoying, but nothing life threatening."

I want to ask him more about this, but my eyes flutter closed and the next thing I know, the sun is coming in the windows at a different angle. I look at the clock. I've lost an hour. I find Wayne in the kitchen, making a plate of toast. "Don't worry, this is safe," he says. "Why don't you take this and go back to bed? Sleep it off a bit?"

He helps me stand and I take the plate, though eating is the last thing I want to do right now. "Thanks."

I crash into bed, and he softly closes my door. I pass out before I have a chance to overthink how quickly this morning took a turn for the worse.

Fuck my broken memory. And those eggs.

I wake up several hours later, and surprisingly my mouth feels almost normal. Definitely not full of itchy worms anymore. I'm exhausted though.

It's already three in the afternoon. I don't want to flip my schedule and be up all night, so I force myself out of bed. I half expect to find Wayne camped outside my door, but the cabin is empty. All the shades are drawn. I dump the uneaten toast in the trash and spot a note on the island, held down by a brass ballpoint pen.

Hey kiddo,

If you wake up before I get back, I had to run some errands and check in with the precinct about your car. I'll be back in a bit. Watch some Netflix and stay inside where it's warm—the remote is on the coffee table. I locked the door for you.

Dad

I put the note down and take a deep breath. Maybe Wayne will come back and tell me they found the car and all my stuff. At least then I'd have clothes that fit. If I keep looking on the bright side, I'll be fine.

I pull open the fridge and find a Tupperware full of leftover sausage. I don't bother to heat them up. I'm not particularly hungry, I just want to enjoy something again, and those eggs sucked away all my joy. These sausages are the highlight of my day.

And that's okay.

Tomorrow it'll be something else.

The important thing is I have a tomorrow. I know who I am. The rest will come.

I plop down on the couch while I eat, but I can't find anything to watch. Mainly because all the streaming options stress me out. I can't remember what I've seen before and what I haven't.

When I'm finished with the sausages, I toss the Tupperware into the sink. How do I normally pass time? Do we come to this cabin often, even when our house isn't being renovated? What would I normally do here?

I tug open the blinds on one of the big windows facing the yard and look outside.

The driveway is *much* less creepy in the daylight. In fact, it's not creepy at all.

The gravel is hedged with empty half-barrel planters. Because it's November and everything's dead. Soft sunlight filters through the clouds, illuminating the side yard in patches, and I suddenly want to get out of the cabin and look around.

I look at my jacket hanging by the door in all its floral, rose gold glory, and grab the yellow afghan from the couch and wrap it around my shoulders instead. It smells like dust, but whatever. It'll keep me warm and it's less…flowery. I slip on a pair of rubber rain boots by the door that absolutely do not fit and flip the dead bolts. At first the door won't budge, until I realize I forgot the lock on the knob.

A blast of crisp air shocks some of the tired out of me as I open the door. I step onto the porch with a little more energy than before.

The steps groan beneath me, old wood creaking against old screws. I round the front of the house and stop short. The most beautiful river glistens at me from behind the house. How did I not notice there was a river back here? I guess Wayne did say it was a fishing cabin…

I gravitate toward the slate-colored water.

The side yard is about as wide as the house, but not all at the same level. The ground slopes past the driveway until it's level with the foundation and a gray metal door. That's probably the basement entrance. The left side of the yard is all trees and a massive woodpile covered by a green tarp. The ground dips again past the house, down to the water's edge. The mostly dead grass turns to brush and fallen leaves along the shore.

I come to a stop just shy of getting my borrowed boots wet. If I thought the view of the river was pretty by the house, it's breathtaking down here. The water sparkles as it slides downstream, low-hanging trees trailing branches through the current. A breeze whispers across my face that smells like late fall and wet things. The chains of a wooden bench swing creak, hung from a two-by-four screwed into two trees by the water. It looks old. It might hold my weight but would definitely leave me with a few splinters. I walk over.

I think I like bench swings?

I press on the seat with both hands, testing the strength of the chains. When nothing breaks, I sit down and simply…exist. I pull the afghan close around my shoulders and watch birds swoop down and scoop up tiny fish from the river. I break into a smile and breathe for what feels like a long time.

Long enough to spook Wayne, apparently.

"Mary?" His voice carries across the yard, tinged with worry.

I turn in my seat, but I can't see him. The woodpile stands between me and the house. I cup my hands around my mouth, and shout, "Down here. By the water."

He appears moments later. His shoulders sag in relief. "What are you doing out here? You should be inside."

"Why? It's beautiful out here."

Wayne picks his way over and stops beside one of the trees. He smiles and looks out over the water. "I guess it is. I'll sit with you, but only for a minute. It's cold, and the last thing you need is to get sick on top of everything else."

I'll take it. I shuffle over to make room for him, and he sits quietly beside me. But the serenity isn't quite the same with another person here. The silence feels heavy.

"So," I say. "How were your errands?"

He shrugs. "Fine. Got most of what I was looking for. There's still no sign of your car. Officer Bowman says they're looking."

Well, there goes that dream. I guess I'll have to make do with Wayne's clothes.

"I'm sure they'll find it eventually." I wonder what that'll be like though, rummaging through boxes of my things. Will they feel like mine? Or will everything be like that floral jacket, and throw me off even more?

"Do you have any questions for me?" Wayne asks after a while. "While we're sitting here, I mean. About our life? Anything you want to know?"

I raise an eyebrow. "You're asking the person who can't remember anything, to ask you questions…about the life I can't remember?"

He barks out a laugh. "Fair point. What if I share the basics? Try and jog your memory that way?"

I shrug. "Sure, why not."

"Okay, let's see." He leans back in the swing and takes over the pushing, which lets me fold my legs up on the seat. "You're a senior in high school. You're a great student. Kind of a homebody, definitely not a partier or anything like that. And you spend a lot of time reading. There're a lot of books in your car. All clean books, of course, nothing crude."

Nothing crude? What does that mean?

I guess that explains all the Chicken Soup books in my room.

He pushes off the ground again and we swing a little higher. "I work from the house, mostly. It's been great for homeschooling because I'm usually there to help if you need something, though you rarely do. You're an only child, but not on purpose. Me and your mother wanted more kids, but it didn't work out that way."

"Where is she? My mom?"

Wayne frowns and his gaze drops to his lap. "She's been gone for a while now. It's just the two of us. Both of our parents died before you were born, so we're a smaller family. But we manage."

I look back over the water. Well, that's sad as hell. And fucked up, because now I'm missing dead people I can't remember. "How did she die?"

"Car crash. When you were nine. It's why last night had me so rattled. You scared the hell out of me. I thought I lost you too."

My throat gets thick again, not from an allergy this time. "I'm sorry."

He reaches out and gently squeezes my knee. "Not your fault. *I'm* sorry for what you're going through. I can't imagine how hard it is to forget your life, and I'm kicking myself for letting you drive that piece-of-crap car. When we get back home, we're getting you something better. I promise."

I nod, but I don't really care about a new car. I'm not even sure I remember how to drive.

We stare, the water and this silence a little less awkward. I think about the dead mom I can't conjure an image of.

I guess I get to add it to the list of facts I've collected about myself: Mary Ellen Boone. Seventeen. Good student. Senior. Lizzo. Egg allergy. Floral jacket. Dead mom.

That last one is almost as depressing as needing to compile a list like this in the first place.

"I wonder how long we have," Wayne says.

I squint at him. "What?"

"Before your memory comes back."

"I've been thinking about that too. I wonder if it'll come back in little pieces or all at once. Maybe I'll never—" I can't finish that sentence. I can't imagine living like this forever, never knowing what came before this.

"It'll come back. It's only a matter of time," he says, and stands. "Now come on, let's go back inside. I have to start dinner soon, and I have a surprise for you."

I'm not in the mood for any more surprises, but I'm starting to get cold, so I follow him back to the house.

Inside, he snags a brown paper bag off the couch and hands it to me with a big smile. "I found you some stuff at the little store in town. Some leggings and T-shirts. I thought you might like something that's really yours, until we find the rest?"

I stare down at the bundle of cotton in the bag, and tears prickle my eyes again. I didn't even have to ask him to take me to get my own things. He's already on it. "Thank you, Wayne. This is amazing."

"Anything for you, my Mary girl," he says.

He reaches behind me and locks us in.

SEVEN
DREW

Mr. Moore *drones* on about some dead guys who did something important at some point in history.

I can't stop staring at Lola's empty desk beside me. It feels like a black hole.

Her fingerprints are still there, I bet. Pressed into the underside where she'd grab the armrest and push herself up when the bell rang. She'd stretch her back before lugging her rose gold messenger bag off the floor and throwing it over her shoulder.

I'd try to carry it for her, and she'd refuse, saying she was as strong as me, and I'd make some dumb comment about taking it when she got tired, but she'd drag it behind her before she'd ever hand it over and admit I was right.

Back when things used to be normal.

Before I fucked everything up.

Mr. Moore sits at his desk and opens a textbook. The rest of the class follows suit, but I don't bother. All I can think about is the corpse in the woods.

It turned out to be a hiker who fell down a ravine. It was on the news this morning. Some college student from the University of Oregon who was found by another hiker. Nowhere near the boat launch.

It wasn't Lola. But it could have been.

Where the hell is she?

Someone clears their throat and I look up with a start. Mr. Moore walks over and leans on the edge of the seat in front of me. The rest of the classroom is empty. I must have missed the bell.

"Whatcha doing, Drew?"

Mr. Moore is young. The kind of guy who posts dance videos on social media and shaves his head on purpose. Who wears sweater-vests for the irony, and pairs them with aviator sunglasses. 'Cause he's the cool, relatable teacher. Or whatever.

"Sorry, I wasn't paying attention."

I gather my stuff as fast as I can. I'm over school for today. I won't get any work done, not when I keep imagining Lola's broken body at the bottom of a ravine somewhere.

I shudder and slide past him.

I'm almost at the door when he says, "You might want to reconsider cooperating with the police. We all need a little closure, you know?"

I stop dead.

"*Excuse* me?" I turn to face him. Indignation stings my chest and makes my question come out louder than I intend it to be. "What is that supposed to mean?"

He folds his arms. "It means what it means. We need closure, especially her parents, and you'd be doing the whole town a kindness by telling the truth about what happened."

Yeah, that's what I thought he meant. "I'm sorry, did I miss the day you got deputized by the police department? I thought you were supposed to support your students, not coax them into false confessions." But even as I say it, I know a line has been drawn. Mr. Moore is *trying* to be here for his students—his other students. And Lola. They're all on one side of this tragedy, and I'm on the other.

I shake my head. "You know what? Why don't you make another out of touch dance video and leave me the fuck alone."

Mr. Moore steps back, eyes wide, like that was the last response he expected from me, even though it's the only one he deserves. I leave the classroom before he can give me a lecture on language. Or detention.

If I thought I was done with school earlier, I'm more than done now.

I head for the hallway at the back of the building, passing rows of lockers, alternating gold and electric blue, and glare at the big pelican mural on the wall by the cafeteria. The Washington City pelicans. It's a stupid mascot. Lola always hated that creepy bird.

Hates. She *hates* it.

Present tense.

I pass a wall of windows framing the art studio and instantly feel eyes boring into my body. I almost expect to see the entire class staring me down.

But it's only eagle-eyed Autumn.

This period, the art studio is used for fashion design. She sits at her little sewing machine in the front row with a dozen other people, mutilating some curtains. Well, the rest of the class is mutilating them. Autumn's creation looks great. Floral and bright, with strips of lace around the edges.

She glares at me from her workstation and makes a *V* with her fingers, motioning from her eyes to mine. *I'm watching you.* Or in Autumn's case, *I'm watching you, ya giant piece of shit. Come here so I can sew your hand into this curtain.*

I think about flipping her off, but as much as she pisses me off, she's hurting too.

The side entrance looms ahead of me, and I'm brainstorming what to say to my dads if the school calls to say I ditched, when something catches my eye and I jerk to a stop.

My locker sits in the stretch of wall between the side entrance and the cafeteria, only now, it's plastered with my Lola fliers. They're taped from top to bottom, completely covering the blue metal beneath them. And someone's written "Murderer" down the front in bold letters the size of my face.

Fucking Autumn. Nobody else would have the balls.

I stalk over and rip them off, tearing each flier into little pieces that scatter across the linoleum. I shove the side doors open a little too hard, and they slam against the outside of the building. All the kids pretending to play baseball on the field for PE turn to look at me, but I don't care. I stomp toward the parking lot, cursing Autumn's name under my breath.

What the actual fuck is wrong with her?

Everyone assumes the sheriff's daughter has all the inside information, which means every time she pulls this shit my life explodes with accusations. I have no idea how long that was up on my locker, but it's guaranteed to have the whole school glaring daggers at me again. Explains Mr. Moore's attempt at coaxing the truth out of me too. More spotlight where it doesn't belong, which puts Lola in even more danger.

A lump lodges in my throat. I hope Autumn gets her hair caught in that sewing machine.

I see Lola in my mind. Walking this exact route to my car after school. Arm snaked around my elbow. Smiling at Max's dumb jokes. Making fun of me for getting so stressed about a midterm.

It feels like walking with a ghost.

What if she never comes home?

My stomach rolls, and it makes me want to puke right here on the sidewalk. I yank my phone from my pocket, desperate for any piece of the real, living girl. When she wasn't an empty chair or a shrine or a face on a poster.

I scroll to Lola's name and open the last texts she sent me.

The last texts she sent *anyone.*

9:10pm

Lola: Can you come get me? Parentals are being dicks. Can't
       handle it.

Me: sure. give me a bit. we can grab food if u want.

Lola: Thanks. Where do you want to eat?

Me: don't know. wherever.

And then after I continued playing video games for another thirty-five minutes, because I'm a prick:

9:46pm

Lola: Are you still coming?

Me: yea. be there in fifteen.

Lola: k. Love you.

A flash of what happened next makes my hands shake. That happy vision of her in my mind shifts to tears and absolute rage as she slams the passenger door and storms off. I press the backs of my hands deep into my eyes, until it hurts, so I'll focus on the pain instead of that look on her face.

The screech of car tires grabs my attention. I stopped in the middle of the school driveway. I jump back onto the sidewalk and some lady in a minivan narrowly misses me. She doesn't stop either. She speeds out of the lot like she's going to get arrested for almost hitting a student.

Or maybe she was aiming for me. I'd believe anything today.

I hurry toward my car before anyone else can come for me. Or worse—someone makes me go back inside. But I get to the spot where I parked and whirl around.

My SUV is gone. I look around the lot, hoping maybe I didn't pay attention to where I parked, but no. It's not here.

I unlock my phone to call my dads and find several messages from them in our group chat. In my rush to guilt myself with the past, I didn't notice my new notifications. I scroll through a dozen texts, alternating pieces of the same story, and I get the gist pretty quickly. The sheriff delivered a warrant for my car this morning. And they took it.

They both offer to pick me up, but I'm so disgusted I can barely read their messages.

Why would the sheriff do this? Why now? I don't understand. It's been five weeks of questions and lawyers, but nobody's searched my car before. Or my house. Which means they probably had no cause to get a warrant—so what changed? What do they have now that they didn't have five weeks ago?

Heat crawls up my neck and across my face.

I storm down the school's driveway and fire off a message telling my dads I want to walk and not to worry. They won't be off work for a couple hours anyway.

I pause at the end of the road. Main Street stretches out on either side of me. If I cross and head through that neighborhood, it'll take me home, but something stops me.

If I turn left and keep walking for a few miles, I'll end up at the river.

Another place I shouldn't be. Especially after yesterday. But Autumn's presence in class means there's probably no search party today.

I don't want to be home alone. I don't really want to be in the place responsible for my worst memories either, but I need to walk off this anger and the boat launch was *our* place. The last place I felt any shred of peace, composure, happiness, and stillness. I want that back, but I don't know how to get it.

On impulse, I veer left, whether it's for punishment or absolution.

I only make it a mile from school before a police cruiser pulls up beside me.

EIGHT

DREW

I don't have to look up to know who it is. I groan as the driver's window eases down, but I don't stop walking. The cruiser keeps pace with me.

"Where ya headed, kid?" Sheriff Roane calls across the lane between us.

His gravelly voice makes my shoulders tense. I force a smile. "Out for a walk. They say teenagers don't get nearly enough exercise, so today...I choose health." I shoot him and his beer belly a pointed glance. "You might consider parking that car and following my lead."

He scowls. "You're a smartass."

"Yup. So what brings you to this side of town, Roane? Need to confiscate my shoes too?"

"Maybe."

"You can take my Adidas, but you can't take my liberty."

His mouth twists up into an irritated pretzel. "Shut up, and get in the car. We both know where you're going. I think you've had enough exercise for today."

The cruiser pulls ahead of me, and angles to the left, cutting off my path. He leans over and flings open the passenger door. At least he's not making me sit in the back this time.

I weigh the pros and cons. I mean, I could call my dads and tell them the sheriff is trying to question me without them. Without my lawyer. Even saying that out loud might be enough to get him to leave me the hell alone. It's worked before.

But he took the Trooper. Which means the police must have some new evidence. If I get in the car, maybe I can find out what it is and get ahead of it.

"Any day now, Drew."

I sigh and climb in.

At the very least, I can't make him think I'm *more* guilty. Plus, this is what cooperation looks like, right? That's what everyone wants to see.

The second my door closes, he pulls back into his lane and drives toward the edge of town. He doesn't say anything, and I don't either. He doesn't even have the radio on…and cop cars have some seriously silent interiors. I can hear the air whistling through his nostrils and it's kind of creeping me out.

It only takes about five minutes to get back to the river. Roane barrels straight down the road like it's nothing. Because to him it's a road, not *the road* where everything changed.

There's nobody at the ramp today. My gaze slides across ten empty parking spaces and lingers on the second to last one. Our spot. The one we parked in every time we came out here. A giant tree hangs over it, with branches full of orange leaves.

As if he knows, Roane parks in *our* spot and cuts the engine.

For a second, I feel like I've left my body. This is exactly where she was, only in the passenger seat of *my* car. Smiling. Staring at me with those beautiful, trusting, green eyes. The freckles across her nose peeking out from beneath her makeup.

"Drew?"

I snap back to reality and the image of Lola's face fades from my mind. Roane's paunchy face stares at me and I grimace. "Yeah?"

"You're looking a little green. Anything you want to tell me?"

"For the last time, I didn't hurt Lola. It's just…hard being here."

I look past him at what's left of Lola's shrine in the first parking spot. It's looking sadder by the day, but there's a fresh vase of bright pink lilies that wasn't here yesterday. Probably from her parents.

The rest is a soggy mess after last night's rain.

The sheriff eyes my balled-up hands. "If it's so hard to be here, why'd you crash the search?"

I shrug. "I wanted to see who was dumb enough to give up on her."

"And today? Why'd you leave school?"

"I didn't feel like going home, and my options were limited without my car," I say, pointedly. "I guess I figured I'd have to face this place eventually."

"No time like the present?" Roane shifts in his seat and looks over at me. "Can I ask you a couple questions while we're out here?"

Oh fun, he's playing the supportive sheriff today. Next he'll tell me it's totally understandable if something did happen to Lola, because *we all lose our temper sometimes*, elbow elbow.

"That depends. Can I have my car back?"

He shakes his head. "Not until we're done."

I match his posture, crossing my arms. "Not until you're done doing what? All my car will tell you is that she was in it. Which you already know. I drove Lola to and from school every day for the last two years. Her hair is all over that passenger seat, and she probably has tampons in the center console. So what the hell are you expecting to find?"

"Blood."

I feel all of mine leave my face. "*Blood*? Why?"

He doesn't respond.

"Do you have reason to believe she's hurt?" My volume raises with every word until I'm practically shouting. And I can't stop it because now instead of a ravine, I'm imagining her lying along the banks of this river, slowly decomposing and— "Are you saying she's...?"

He throws up his hands. "Stop. Just stop."

I can't breathe. "No. Are you...are you saying you found—"

He reaches across and flings my door open. The rush of cool air hits me in the face and I gasp it in.

"We don't know anything yet," he yells over my panic. "Listen. We were looking for any sign of her being hurt. And since you were the last person to see her, it's a logical jump to search for signs of injury in your car. If there was blood in the Trooper, that's something we'd need to know."

I take another breath. It rattles in and out. "There's not."

"I know. I got the report twenty minutes ago."

My mind scrambles to catch up. So he knew there wasn't any blood in my car before he even picked me up.

"You take my car, and when that tells you nothing, you try and shock me into admitting I hurt her? Why are you screwing around with me when you should be out there finding Lola?"

"I am trying to find her, and I thought you could help me with that. I need more information. So far, your statements have been vague at best. What really happened that night? Why were you here in the first place?"

I sigh and let my head drop back. My statements haven't been vague—not entirely anyway. Not about the stuff that matters. He's looking for a hole in my story, but I tell him the whole thing again anyway, because I live to disappoint him. "She sent me a message just after nine o'clock. She'd gotten into a fight with her parents and asked me to come get her. They've been fighting a ton the last few months, so this was pretty much a routine. I picked her up a little after ten. We stopped at Dairy Queen and came here with takeout. We talked for a while, then she wanted to walk home, so she got out of my car, and headed toward her house. How many times do we have to go over this?"

"As many as it takes. Why were they fighting so much lately?"

"Her parents are great, but they're in their own world a lot. They wanted her to learn to handle things on her own, be independent, but to Lola, it felt like they didn't care. Like she didn't matter. So she started acting like their rules didn't matter either. Suddenly they were fighting about everything. Her grades, the team, curfew, how loud she played her music, when I was allowed over, how much time she could spend at my house."

He nods, and I wonder if Lola's parents told him this too. "And that night? What was the fight about? Why did she want to leave her house so badly?"

I try not to roll my eyes, because we've been over this multiple times. I can feel him looking for a discrepancy. He won't find one. "Lola wants her own car. She's had her license for, like, a year, but no car to drive, and it made her feel stuck. She tried to make a deal: if she followed all their rules and got her grades back up, would they be willing to match what she's saved so she could get a car by the end of the semester? But they said no. Repeatedly. They said it was important for her to make her own way in the world or some shit, and her mom said she didn't deserve a car yet. Lola flipped out and they started screaming at each other. She said she couldn't be there anymore and waited on the front porch for me."

He nods, like he's digesting new information. He has all this written out somewhere, from interrogation number one, two, five…

"Why are you wasting time with this story *again* instead of going out there," I say, jabbing my finger toward town, "and figuring out where she went when she left here?"

"Because it's become increasingly clear that leaving town wasn't her idea, Drew. We've cleared everyone else connected to Lola. Her family, the clerk at the convenience store, those she had conflicts with at school, even visitors staying at the hotels in the area. We've talked to everyone, and you're the only suspect we have left. Also, and I can't stress this enough, I *don't* believe you. You say she simply got out of the car, but why would she want to walk all the way home from here? It's at least three miles back to her house. Why would you let the girl you love walk home in the middle of the night by herself?"

My mouth goes dry. The kind of dry that seizes up the rest of me. I say nothing.

Roane smiles like he's won and looks out at the shrine. "I have reason to believe you had something to do with this. I've had a feeling since day one, but there was still hope she may have needed a break from all the fighting at home and run away, that we'd find her alive and well. As your lawyer keeps telling me, you're an upstanding kid with 'no motive.' So we looked at all the other options before zeroing in on the honor student swim team captain. But now, I finally have the evidence I need to prove you're involved in Lola's disappearance."

What the hell? What kind of evidence?

"I may not be able to prove you hurt her *yet*, but you and I both know you're to blame."

The *yet* rings in my head. But for once he and I are in agreement.

I am to blame.

I unbuckle my seatbelt. The click is jarring in the silent cruiser cab. "Lola didn't just vanish, and she didn't run away from home. She got out of my car, and…something happened to her. Something that didn't involve me or my car. Lola's story doesn't end at this boat launch, and neither should your investigation."

He slips into a deadpan cop face. "Why'd she walk home, Drew? What made her get out of your car?"

My epic stupidity. But I don't say that. "Do me a favor—don't talk to me again without my dads or my lawyer. If I'm your last real suspect, act like it. Talking to a minor without a guardian or legal representation is illegal, right? Then again, you've never been good at your job before, so why start now?"

He laughs and I slam the door in his stupid face. The sound of his mocking amusement carries across the empty parking lot through his open window.

It's a laugh that says *Just wait, you little smartass, I'll get you for this.*

And he's probably right.

NINE

MARY

It's amazing what a good night's sleep and an eggless meal will do to lift your spirits. I look down at my half-eaten breakfast—cinnamon toast and a sliced banana. I smile, picking up the last piece of toast.

Wayne sits beside me, reading a newspaper and finishing off his third cup of coffee. I like this, sitting together and enjoying our morning.

It feels familiar, and without the catastrophe of yesterday, I love it.

I roll my shoulders back, rocking the sleep from my tired muscles. I ended up going to bed pretty early last night. Wayne made dinner—chicken and potatoes with little crispy bits of garlic on them—and eating expended the last of my energy. I was in bed before he finished the dishes. I fully expected to zombie walk into the kitchen this morning; instead I woke up feeling lighter, more alert, more capable than I had since the purgatory ditch.

I finish my toast, except for the crusts, as Wayne chuckles to himself and folds the paper. "Headlines crack me up," he says.

"Why?"

He lays the paper on the island and points to the big bold letters at the top of the page. MAN EATS OWN SOCKS IN COURT TO VALIDATE INSANITY PLEA.

"Oh gross. Did it work?"

"Nope. Got ten to fifteen for home invasion. At least he was creative though."

"I guess that's one way to put it. Disgusting is another. He's going to regret that decision in a day or two. I'll stick to toast."

I toss my crusts in the trash and put my plate in the sink. Through the window, the river catches my eye. It's super pretty in the morning, with the sun bouncing off it. I watch it for a moment before I turn back to him. "Do you need the bathroom?" I ask. "I'm going to take a shower."

He looks at me over the rim of his coffee cup. "Nope. I'm good."

I snatch the new bag of clothes from my room and slip into the bathroom. I'm so excited to put something on that'll actually fit. In a way, these new things are more mine than anything else because I can remember their whole life with me. I can't say that about any other possession.

The hot water is just as soothing this round, and by the time I climb out of the shower, even my bruises feel better. The blue-black circles under my eyes still need time to heal, and the cuts on my scalp sting like a bitch every time the shampoo slides through my hair, but it feels like all the pores on my body take a collective deep breath.

I towel off and dig through the bag, deciding what to wear. I settle on a pair of leggings and a blue tank top. I pull the shirt over my head, and it rolls into a constrictive bunch under my armpits. Something's not right. I wrestle it off, tugging it up half an inch at a time until I'm free, and hold it out in front of me.

It's *way* too small. Almost comically small. How could he look at this and think it would fit me? I check the tag on the leggings but they're smaller than the shirts. These look like they'd fit a middle schooler. I sit on the floor with the clothing in my hands and blow out a slow breath, holding back unexpected tears.

The loss of the only things in this cabin I thought were fully mine hits hard. But I feel ridiculous for almost-crying about some leggings.

What's wrong with me? It's an honest mistake. We'll find my car soon, or we'll exchange these for a different size. It's not the end of the world. I just have to wait a bit longer.

I take a deep breath, toss it all back in the bag, and maneuver into the clothes I slept in last night: another pair of light gray sweatpants with the drawstrings pulled so tight they dangle to my thighs, and a gray T-shirt with Homer Simpson on the front.

I drop the bag of clothes in my room and return to the kitchen, scrunching my hair with a towel. Wayne crumples the newspaper and chucks it into a basket beside the fireplace with the other cardboard and burning materials. "All right, enough news. What's on the docket for today?"

I press my back to the sink and worry at my lip. If he noticed I haven't changed my clothes, he hasn't said anything. I hesitate, not wanting to upset him when he's trying so hard to help, and his eyebrows come together.

"Everything okay?" he asks.

"Um…yeah, everything is fine. I was wondering if we could run into town today."

He leans forward, folding his arms on the island. "Do you have a fever or something?"

"Huh?"

"You hate going places," he says. "You hate leaving the house. In fact, I have to practically drag you out into civilization whenever we run errands."

Oh right, I'm a homebody. A reader—nothing crude.

But honestly, I'd walk all the way down the mountain on my own if it meant getting out of this outfit. "I guess the need for clothes that fit overrules the urge to stay home?"

"What about the clothes I bought you?"

I grimace, thinking of the wad of fabric in the bag, with a stab of guilt. "They're too small. I'm sorry," I say, before I realize I'm apologizing because the clothes *he* bought won't work for me. Which is ridiculous. I didn't pick them out.

His face falls. "You're kidding. Everything? None of it fits?"

"Well, I could wear the shirts, I'd just have to stop breathing for the rest of the day," I joke, but I immediately regret it when he looks even more upset.

"I'm so sorry. I grabbed whatever looked right."

I wave him off. "It's totally okay. Maybe we can go back and exchange them? I left all the tags on. I can pick everything out this time so you don't have to worry about it."

He looks down at his hands folded in front of him. "I think you need another rest day. Maybe a few, really. You've been through so much."

I throw the towel over my shoulder and gesture to the outfit currently hanging off me. "Please? I want something I can feel like myself in. Something not, *this*. Plus, I feel so much better already. I really don't need a rest day. I won't even look at anything made of eggs."

He stares at me.

"Please?" I cross to the other side of the island. "I'll be in and out, I promise. Ten minutes, tops."

He sighs. "Mary. I'm still worried you'll have a histamine flare-up, not to mention the concussion, and you look like someone punched you in the face. Maybe we can order something online instead. It won't take more than a week to arrive. Besides, there's not much of a selection in town. The store's more of a gas station that also has some clothes in the back. I barely found what I already got for you, unless you're looking for a XXXL men's neon work shirt…"

Ugh. I know it's unreasonable, but the idea of waiting a week for packages to climb the mountain makes my stomach drop. "Can we go to a different store? I really want something that fits."

With a great big sigh, Wayne sits back in his chair. Watching me.

"Please? Please, please, please?"

He rolls his eyes. "Fine. You win. There's a little thrift store down the coast that we can go to. We stop there every time we're in the area. If you're up for a drive, they'll have a much better selection for you, and it'll save you from shopping for another couple months," he says with a laugh. "It won't be busy this time of year either. But you're doing the breakfast dishes first."

I jump up and down. "Deal!"

"Please stop jumping. Your poor brain…" He gets up from his stool, draining the last of his coffee, and brings the cup to the sink. I snatch it and start scrubbing with a soapy sponge. "I'm going to regret this," he mumbles.

I laugh and rinse the cup. Shopping with me couldn't be *that* bad. "I think you'll probably survive."

"We'll see."

Fifteen minutes later, the dishes are washed and I'm back in the rain boots from yesterday. Wayne hands me the floral jacket and a black beanie. "For your wet hair," he explains. "It's cold out there."

I twist up my still-damp ends, and tuck them into the hat. "Thank you."

He unlocks the dead bolts and holds the door open for me. "Of course."

Just like yesterday, the cool air is bracing in the best way. I suck in a deep breath and feel the cold settle into the deepest parts of my lungs. Wayne unlocks the van and I climb in, excitement bubbling under my skin. It's a simple trip to the store, but it feels like an adventure and I'm all for it. I practically bounce in my seat, waiting for him to get in.

I get a closer look at his insanely clean vehicle today. The carpet has those zigzag streaks like it was recently vacuumed, and there are fresh black covers on the seats that smell brand new. A little green air freshener tree hangs from the rearview mirror, though I think it's been there awhile because it doesn't smell like pine in here. It smells like leather and woodsmoke.

It smells like Wayne.

I twist around to look into the back. The carpeted floor hasn't been vacuumed as recently as the cab. It's littered with grass, mud, and pine needles. And two plastic buckets full of tools sit behind my seat, with a shovel stuck between them.

He mentioned working from home while we were by the river yesterday, but I never actually asked what he did for a living.

Wayne's door opens. He pulls off his jacket and throws it over the back of his seat before climbing in. He catches me looking around the van and pauses with his hand on his seatbelt. "Something wrong?"

"Nope, just looking at the tools. Are you a carpenter or something?"

He clicks the seatbelt into place and starts the van. "Sometimes. I'm a man of many talents, and I get bored easily, which means I change jobs every now and then. I finished a house painting job not too long ago, and now I'm taking some time off to deal with anything that pops up during the renovations at the other house."

"Do you own the cabin?"

"Yeah. It was my dad's."

"Must be nice not to have to pay for two houses plus renovations at the same time."

He nods and backs the van toward the road. "Yeah. Those new cabinets are costing me a fortune."

Cabinets? I blink at him, waiting for him to correct himself, but he doesn't. "I thought you said the floors were being replaced."

He hits the brakes, and the van jerks to a stop at the end of the drive-way. For a second I think it's because of what I said, but then a car shoots down the road behind us and he mumbles something about how dumb it is to speed on dirt roads before he starts reversing again. When we're fully backed out, he throws the van in drive again and smiles at me. "They're putting in the floors and the cabinets at the same time. I already paid the flooring bill, and now I start paying on the other half of the project."

"Oh."

Wouldn't all that work take longer than a few weeks?

"You'll have to find another house to paint then," I say to break the silence.

He laughs. "That I will."

Soft jazz plays from the speakers, and he turns up the volume as we make our way down the mountain and onto Highway 101. Soon the road curves and the Pacific Ocean stretches out beyond the stone barrier that lines the highway.

Wayne clears his throat. "You sure about this? It's a bit of a drive— about an hour and a half. Pretty though. Almost all coastal highway, and you love looking at the ocean."

I'll have to take his word for it. Like everything else.

I shrug. "Yeah, I'm up for an oceanside adventure if you are." Ninety minutes does seem like a long drive for a thrift store though. How is there not something closer?

"I'm always up for an adventure with my best girl."

I smile, then stare out the window for the rest of the drive, listening to the music as the ocean flickers in and out of view through the trees. Occasionally Wayne points out a lighthouse or a town and shares a quick memory. I appreciate the effort, but none of his stories spark anything.

After almost exactly an hour and a half, a sign for our exit flies past my window. Waybrooke. One mile. I'm so ready to get the hell out of this van.

I catch him eyeing my face as we take the exit. He glances between me and the road a few times, looking uneasy.

"Everything okay?" I ask.

"Yeah. I was thinking we should probably stop and pick up some makeup or something real quick. We don't need anyone seeing that face of yours."

My face?

I catch sight of myself in the side mirror. The bruises under my eyes look worse somehow in the daylight.

I guess taking me out in public with this face looks pretty bad for him. But he doesn't have to sound so…judgy. I didn't ask to get cuddly with a steering wheel.

He smiles. "Don't worry. Nobody will see you."

I can't explain the stab of unease that sentence brings.

TEN

MARY

Waybrooke looks like every other coastal town we've driven through. Wood shingled buildings, a cute little diner with black and red buoys hanging off the eaves, a few houses that someone turned into real estate or doctors' offices, a hardware store, a beachy hotel, another beachy hotel, a crystal store, a used bookstore, and finally a pharmacy. Wayne insists I wait in the car, so I coach him on what concealer is, and it still takes him three trips inside to get the right thing. When he finally emerges, triumphant, I have to laugh.

I dab it under my eyes, adding a couple coats. It's not perfect by any means, but it's much better than it was. The girl in the visor mirror no longer looks like a human/raccoon hybrid. Though my nose is still a little swollen, it's not as noticeable without the eyes adding to the effect.

The thrift store sits all the way at the end of the main drag of Waybrooke.

Wayne parks in one of a dozen empty spots and cuts the engine.

This place doesn't look at all like what I expected. It too is covered

in ocean-weathered shingles. Old white shutters sit on either side of
the windows, and a bird nest sits atop one. A big pink and white sign
hangs above the front door.

Nana's Favorites

Est 1989

Oh boy.

Wayne jumps out. "Come on, let's find some treasures!"

I muster a smile and follow him inside, but this does not feel like
somewhere I'd want to come back to more than once. If he says this is
a regular stop for us, then maybe the inside is better?

The door jangles as we walk through it, and an old woman with
white hair and thick pink glasses looks up from the counter. She smiles
at us. This must be Nana.

"Welcome!"

I look around the store.

Nope. I was wrong. The inside's just as bad.

The carpet is dark, and not in a good way—it looks like it would
be a much lighter color if someone cleaned it. The walls are all wood
paneled, and it smells vaguely like incense in here. But the clothing
racks stretch all the way to the back of the store, and they look clean and
organized. Possibly because they don't get any customers and this poor
woman has nothing to do but straighten the hangers and de-wrinkle
everything.

Wayne strides over to the woman and unleashes a huge smile. He
says something about this being *our* favorite thrift store, and I wander
away to shop so they don't fold me into the conversation. I don't want
to lie if she asks me about it. I'd rather pretend I can't hear them.

I find the section with clothes that look like they'd fit me and leaf through the hangers. There's actually some good stuff here. I find myself gravitating to all the darker stuff. Blacks and dark jewel tones.

It only takes me a few minutes to fill my arm with things I like. A couple black T-shirts, a long-sleeved eggplant-colored shirt, a loose-fitting gray sweater, a soft black shirt with tiny white horizontal stripes, and a maroon plaid button-down, along with several pairs of black leggings in the *correct* size, and two pairs of dark jeans that might fit. I'm fairly sure of everything else.

At the end of the last rack of shirts in my size, I slide a sequined pink monstrosity out of the way, and a tabby cat stares back at me. Not a real one. It's a plastic decal printed on a white sweater, but the cat looks alarmingly real with its big yellow eyes. I start to slide it aside but I can't stop staring at it.

Suddenly, the cat is moving, except it's not on a shirt anymore. It's on a long red sofa. The cat walks along the arm, then curls around and around before it settles and goes to sleep.

Then I'm right back in the thrift store.

I suck in a breath and practically fling the cat-shirt away from me in surprise.

Okay. O-kay.

That…felt like a memory. I think? We must have a red sofa back at the McMinnville house. He hasn't mentioned any pets though.

Hope flutters through my stomach.

Wayne appears at my elbow. "That's a terrifying cat."

I nod, but I'm too lost in the maybe-memory. "Do we have any pets?"

He scoffs. "No. God, no. I'm crazy allergic. Cats and dogs."

"Oh." Poof, there goes the hope. Not our cat then. Maybe it was a memory from a friend's house?

Wayne leans in to check out my selections, and frowns. "Are you planning to attend a funeral? Where's all the color?"

I look from him to the clothes. "What do you mean?"

"What's with all the black? You're a colorful person, kiddo. You like bright colors and florals and…well, this," he says, plucking another hanger off the rack. It's a peach tank top with a lace overlay.

Peach.

Oh, dear god.

"You don't have to dress like a vampire just because we're staying in the forest. It's not Forks." He laughs at his own joke and holds out the hanger with the hideous peach tank top. "Try this one on."

I try not to make a face. "Um, it's a little cold for tank tops. Maybe in the spring?"

Or never.

He looks down at me and his frown deepens, so I reach forward and grab the tank top. "You know, it's fine. It's hot inside the house anyway, so I'm sure I can still wear it."

Under something.

I add it to my pile. First the floral jacket and now I'm a peach person?

We wander to the shoe section where I avoid the black options in favor of a gently used pair of white sneakers he has no objection with. After a quick trip to the dressing room to try on the jeans, I have everything I need. In and out in twenty minutes. Shopping with me is a breeze.

The old woman beams at me when I load my stack onto the counter. "Did you find everything you needed today?"

"Almost." I snag a couple packages of ankle socks and a generic package of underwear by the checkout that makes Wayne blush furiously. At the last minute I add another beanie. A white one this time.

I hold it out to Wayne, asking silent permission, and he nods with a smile.

"Now I have, yes."

Counter lady looks like she might dance as she rings everything up. Her name tag clings to her knitted pink sweater at an angle. The name's written in a curly font that's almost impossible to read, but my brain pieces it together after a minute. Eloise.

Wayne thumbs through bills in his wallet, counting out exact cash, and I point to the clothes. "Can I change before we leave? It's a long drive back to Alton. I'd rather be in something comfortable."

Eloise smiles even wider. "You're from Alton? My brother used to live up there. Gorgeous trees up that mountain. I've never seen anything like it. But then again, you'd be hard pressed to find any place in Oregon that's not beautiful."

I squint at her. She looks like the kind of woman who's lived her whole life in the same town. I wonder if she's been anywhere else. Alton hasn't impressed me so far.

Wayne smiles down at me. "Of course, you should be comfortable. Change into whatever you want. I'll finish up here."

Though he sends a meaningful look at that peach monstrosity, I snag a black T-shirt, pair of jeans, socks, sneakers, and my first clean pair of underwear in three days and slip into the dressing room. When I'm done changing, I look in the mirror and sigh.

This is more like it. Some well-fitting clothes and shoes are better than an egg-free breakfast experience. I feel like a new me. Or the old me? Whatever.

I tuck my short hair behind my ears, trying to get it out of my face, and wish I'd added mascara to Wayne's pharmacy run, but all in all, I don't look like someone who woke up in a ditch two nights ago, and that excites me more than anything. I pinch my cheeks to bring some color back into them and drag my finger across the freckles on my nose.

I probably stand there looking at myself for too long, but I eventually gather Wayne's clothes and my jacket. I find him waiting for me by the door, holding a big pink bag with the "Nana's" logo on the side.

Eloise looks me over from her perch at the counter. "Much better, dear!"

The heat of a blush crawls across my cheeks and I wish her a nice afternoon.

"You too! You both have a safe drive home, okay? And come back soon!"

"Well, don't you look happy," Wayne says, when we step outside. He holds open the shopping bag so I can dump the clothes I changed out of inside.

"Oh my god, I am." I twirl around in the new clothes. "You were right, this place is great. We'll have to come back."

We cross the parking lot, and a waft of something sweet soars through the air. My stomach grumbles. I suddenly wish I ate something more substantial than cinnamon toast for breakfast.

I spot the diner down the road. "Do you want to grab some food?"

He stops by the front of the van. "We have food at home."

"Yeah, but it's almost two. We haven't had lunch, and it'll be three thirty before we even get back. The diner's right here...waiting to feed us. Please, please, *please*, it smells so good."

He scrubs at his chin stubble and looks down the road like he's trying to predict what traffic we'll hit if we wait. "Fine. But we have to make it quick. I want to get home and so you can rest. If you're going to crash again, I'd rather it be at the cabin."

"Same."

He smiles and hands me the hot-pink shopping bag. "I'm surprised you're not the one dragging *me* home."

Yeah, yeah, homebody whatever. I practically skip to my side of the van. "A new pair of shoes does wonders for the mood."

He rolls his eyes at me, and I laugh. I feel…happy? Or content at the very least. I almost feel normal, even without my memories, and that's a goddamned miracle.

The parking lot of the Waybrooke Diner is mostly empty, which makes no sense because, even from outside, the food smells amazing. Like warm syrup and coffee and baking bread. My stomach growls again as I slip my jacket back on.

The inside is all black, white, and red. Black-and-white checkered floors. Black-and-white photos on the walls, surrounded by red frames. Red curtains. Red salt and pepper shakers. Red ceiling fans.

A round woman with a gorgeous face, and the most amazing eyelashes I've ever seen, shows us to a booth.

Wayne sits facing the door, and I take the opposite bench. I watch a man in a white baking smock pull a whole platter of cinnamon rolls the size of my face out of an oven and sweep them over to a display case by the hostess station. I might die if I don't get one of those immediately. Especially when I see he's stocking them behind a very important sign.

Vegan.

Which means no eggs.

"My name is Sandra," the woman says, forcing me to refocus. She slides napkins and silverware across the fake marble tabletop. "Can I take your drink order or do you need a few minutes?"

"I'll have coffee," Wayne says. "And a water."

She smiles. "You got it. And for this pretty young thing over here?"

I scan the drink section of the menu but all I can think about is that cinnamon roll. "Ummm, I guess water too." I flip the menu over and giant pictures of real fruit smoothies jump out at me. "Actually, can I make that a strawberry smoothie?"

"You got it," Sandra says, scribbling that down. "Small or large?"

"Large, please," Wayne says with a wink, and points at the display case. "Could we also grab a couple of those vegan cinnamon rolls?"

I blink at him in surprise and smile from ear to ear. "How did you—"

He waves me off. "Oh, please. You love cinnamon rolls."

Sandra nods with a bright smile and heads straight for the display case. In moments, one of those glorious cinnamon and icing-covered pastries slides across the table in front of me and I almost clap because up close it's even *bigger* than my face, nearly the size of the salad plate it sits on. I don't know if I've ever been this excited about eating something in my whole life.

I don't notice when she returns with our drinks. Or when Wayne orders real food. I demolish the whole thing.

When it's gone, I sit back and sigh.

I'm not really hungry anymore, but I pick at the other food he ordered for me. The grilled cheese and French fries don't hold a candle to the sugar. I leave most of it uneaten.

Wayne asks for the bill, and silence settles around us as Sandra walks away. Now that we're not stuffing our faces, it's kinda awkward.

I start to ask him a question, but it dies in my throat when I see him staring at my shirt with an almost angry expression. "What's wrong?"

His look intensifies and he glances around the diner. "I guess I wasn't paying close enough attention in the thrift store. I didn't realize your shirt was so low cut."

I look down at my T-shirt. It's a V-neck, but it's not all that low. The bottom of the *V* lands about an inch below my collarbone. "Is that…bad?"

He shakes his head. "It's inappropriate. We can get rid of it when we get home, don't worry. I'll pay more attention the next time we pick out clothes. You can't remember. You don't know the rules."

What. The. Hell.

His attention trails out the window and stays there.

You can't remember. You don't know the rules. There's clothing I'm not allowed to wear? Along with the "clean" books I read? I look down at my shirt again. What's wrong with a V-neck?

The silence stretches on and makes me uncomfortable. I search for a change in subject, and the utter lack of topics that come to mind gives me an idea. "Since we're waiting for the check, how about another round of Mary facts? To pass the time?"

He slides the remains of his BLT away, still looking a little irritated. "What do you want to know?"

I shrug. "Whatever you can think of. Rapid-fire-Mary."

He smiles and it relieves some of my tension. "Okay…your favorite color is purple. Has been since you were about five years old."

I make a face. Really? Purple? I guess I shouldn't be surprised, considering there are about twelve shades of purple on my sleeves right now.

Okay. Time to update the list.

Mary Ellen Boone. Seventeen. Good student. Senior. Lizzo. Egg allergy. Floral jackets. Dead mom. Bit of a homebody. Cinnamon rolls. Purple.

Not too bad for two full days in the life of a stranger.

"Keep going," I say, taking the first sip of the smoothie I'd totally forgotten.

He blows out a breath. "Okay…um… We got really close after your mother's accident. Even closer when we started homeschooling. You're part of some homeschool groups back in McMinnville—they're a great group of kids, really solid friends. No troublemakers."

I forgot I'm homeschooled.

Why does that feel so weird to me? I can practically see the insides of a high school hallway in my mind. The desks. The gym. I can feel myself walking down the hall with too many books in my bag, talking to friends in a cafeteria. Maybe they're remnants of my freshman year? He said I was in regular school until then.

"Why am I homeschooled?" I ask. "I mean, why did I start after freshman year? Was that my choice?"

"In a way. You were having some trouble. Not academically, you've always been on top of your studies, but you…" He trails off and takes a long sip of his coffee. His hands tighten around the mug when he sets it back on the table. "You fell in with the wrong people, and I can't say I'm all that upset that you don't remember *them*. I lost you for a bit, to people who led you down a wayward path. No respect for adults. For the rules. Partying all the time. Inappropriate outfits. Inappropriate music and television shows. No morals. I had to step in before you went too far. Homeschooling has been really good for you though, and in the end, you recognized it was necessary too. We've been closer than ever these last few years."

I have no idea what to make of that story.

Appropriate books. Appropriate clothes. Appropriate friends. Appropriate life.

A pattern is emerging here.

And what does he mean, about going too far? Too far in what way? Is he saying I got into drugs or shoplifting, something illegal? I open my mouth to ask, but the white-knuckled grip he has on his coffee cup makes me think better of it. Whatever happened, whatever I did, it's bad enough that he's still upset about it.

Can you feel remorse for something you don't remember doing? Should I?

I drink some more of my smoothie and stare down at the table, trying to loosen the knot forming in my chest. These life details are giving me anxiety. Or heartburn. Or both. I wish I could remember already. All of it. All at once. A tsunami of all my mistakes and triumphs, so I don't have to rely on someone else's version of it. I want to know what really happened with my friends.

Sandra leaves the bill as she passes by with a tray of food for another table, and I aimlessly reach for my smoothie again, but this swallow goes down weird. Like a whole chunk of strawberry.

I freeze.

My mouth blossoms a familiar itch that once again creeps down the back of my throat and spreads through my body. I rip my sleeves back, but I already know what I'm going to find there.

Baby hives. Fuck. *Fuck*, not again.

We didn't order anything with eggs. Why is this happening?

I look up at Wayne and claw at my itching throat. A wordless plea for help.

He springs from his seat. "Come on. Pharmacy's across the street. Hurry up." He slaps a couple twenties on the bill and shoves me, itching and hacking, out the door and toward the van.

I stop by the passenger door and he sprints toward the pharmacy.

I scratch my neck, my chest. I chew on the insides of my mouth, trying to relieve the itch that won't stop. After what feels like a very long time, he reappears around the back of the van, already pouring a dose of liquid Benadryl into the cap it came with. I take it and he pours another, pressing it to my lips until I drink that one too.

I close my eyes and wait for the first signs of relief, but it takes ages. He helps me into the passenger seat and stands by the open door, shaking his head as we wait, and wait, and wait.

"It must have been the strawberries in the smoothie," he blurts, leaning against the inside of the door. "Not the eggs. It's the only thing you ate both times."

I think of the sliced strawberries sitting on the table at breakfast. It *must have been* the strawberries? Was he guessing the first time?

How can my own father not know what I'm allergic to?

There must be confusion on my face because he adds, "I'm so sorry. So, terribly sorry. Your mother was allergic to eggs. You're allergic to strawberries. I can never keep that straight. You usually remind me, but you can't remember what not to eat." He scrubs his face with his hands. "God, I'm so sorry. I knew it was too soon for an outing. Let's just…go home."

He shuts the door. I try not to frown as I scratch all my skin off for the second time in so many days. I pull the hot-pink Nana's bag from the space beneath my feet and shove it into the back so I can stretch my legs.

Wayne climbs in and starts the van. I reach to the side, still scratching, to grab my seatbelt and catch a woman staring at me from the sidewalk. I don't know her—at least, I don't think I do—but she gapes at me with wide, dark eyes. She's short and slim. Maybe forty? With clearly home-done highlights in her dirty-blonde hair.

She waves, and I instinctively wave back.

The van pulls away and she takes out her phone, almost frantic, and holds it to her ear.

"Don't worry," Wayne says, dragging my attention back to the inside of the car. "Once we get home, we don't have to leave for a long time. I'll throw out every strawberry in the house. I'll do anything to keep you safe. You know that, right?"

Worry curls through my stomach. I click the seatbelt into place. "Yeah...I know."

ELEVEN

DREW

Roane blows past me in the cruiser before I've even left the parking lot, and I'm filled with regret. Sure, it's noble and shit to strut away from the sheriff's accusation-field-trip, but every step makes me more aware that this is where Lola stood five weeks ago. And I'm plunged into the past.

Did she turn left or right when she left the parking lot?

Did someone offer her a ride?

Was she crying?

Did she make it to her street?

Worst of all: Would she still be here now if I didn't do what I did?

By the time I reach the school again, the parking lot is empty, and the past quiets. She wouldn't have made it this far into town without someone seeing her. I've escaped her ghost for now.

About a mile from home, the sky opens and it downpours. Because the universe hasn't crapped on me enough lately. I don't pick up the pace. I all but drag myself home.

I know you're to blame.

The weight of these last five weeks is going to crush me. Roane's new evidence, whatever it is, has him doing searches and taking my car and who knows what else is coming.

I'll never give up on Lola, but how am I supposed to fight for her and for myself at the same time? Roane said I was their last suspect. And knowing him, he won't stop until he's pieced together enough evidence to fit his version of events. Then I'll get arrested, and Lola will still be gone. How do I help her from behind bars?

I scrub at my face in frustration.

I... I don't know what to do.

When I open my front door, Dad shoots up from the stairs and flings himself at me. I grunt at the impact. He wraps his arms around my shoulders and squeezes the life out of me.

"Drew, my god. Where have you been? I called a hundred times," he says. "And why are you so wet?"

I try to answer him, but there's no air left in my lungs. My wheezing response seems to surprise him because he lets go. "Sorry. I'm sorry."

I wave him off. "It's okay. I get it. It's not a good time to not answer my phone." What an understatement. I'm lost for a moment, thinking about him waiting on the stairs, tapping his fingers on his bad knees, wondering if something happened to me too. The guilt sours my stomach. "I'm so sorry. My phone is on silent, and I had a run-in with Roane. I walked home."

"From the school?"

I shake my head. "No. From the boat launch."

His face falls. "Come in. Warm up. Tell me what happened while I make you some food. Your dad is working late tonight, so it's just us."

With a blanket wrapped around my shoulders and a bowl of

leftover hilachas from family dinner, I talk while he sits on a stool across the counter from me. The empty seat in Mr. Moore's class, Autumn, the murder message on my locker, skipping school, the missing car, and what Roane said about Lola. To his credit, Dad doesn't interrupt, not even when I admit to ditching class. His lips thin in that *I don't like this* kind of disapproval, but he doesn't say anything until all my food is gone and my story is over.

He takes a deep breath. "Okay."

I wait for more.

He scratches behind his ear and stares at the black granite countertop between us. Then he takes my bowl, sets it in the sink, and sighs. "You already know how I feel about skipping, but this time I'll give you a pass, because I think what you're going through is justification. I don't want you missing any more school though. You still have to live *your* life, no matter what."

I nod. "I know."

"And I'm glad you told Roane not to talk to you anymore. He shouldn't be following you around. I'll call our lawyer, maybe make a complaint to the police station. You're a minor, he can't just pick you up and question you. I know he has a lot of eyes on him right now, and he's feeling the pressure to figure out what happened to Lola, but that doesn't give him the right to question you without a parent or lawyer present. Your father is going to have a meltdown."

"Do we have to tell him?" I ask, with a wince.

Dad folds his arms. "Drew."

"Okay, okay." I don't want to keep things from Papá, but of the two of them, he worries a lot more. "I don't want him to stress. It's already done anyway. I'm not saying another word to Roane without you guys there."

"I'll tell him what happened, but I'll wait until tomorrow. Deal?"

"Deal."

"Do you need a ride to school in the morning?"

Shit, I hadn't even thought of that. Roane took my transportation for who the fuck knows how long. I have no way to get *anywhere* for the foreseeable future. "No, it's okay. I'll ask Max."

"You sure? I don't mind."

He probably wants to see me walk into school himself, but he shouldn't have to be late to work because the cops took my car. "No, really. It's fine. Max won't mind, and we're already going to the same place."

Tired lines crease the skin around his eyes. "I'm worried about you, Drew. I think this is the first warm meal I've seen you eat in a while. I hear you pacing late at night. Max is the only friend I've seen you with for weeks. You said nothing when the swim team asked you to step down. You always miss family dinner. You're distant…"

Distant is a good way to put it. I would have said completely tired of everyone's shit, but I'm less polite than he is. "I'm fine. You know… processing."

He stares me down.

"Really," I say, twisting my face into what I hope resembles sincerity. "I'm okay. I'm sad, and I want her to come home, and it sucks that everyone turned their backs on me *and* her, but I can't control what anyone else does. I'm trying to get through it, but everything will be okay."

The lies churn the beef and potatoes in my stomach, and I wish I'd eaten less.

The truth is, I can barely sleep because every time I close my eyes, I dream of the river turning into a black hole and swallowing her. I can't sit back and wait for the cops to figure out what happened because I don't trust them.

Dad folds his hands on the counter. "I know this is hard for you. It's been hard for us too. Lola's so important to this family, I mean, she practically lived here over the summer, and it's been an absolute nightmare waiting for news about her, so I get it…"

I can't begin to explain how much I love him for consistently talking about her in the present tense. It makes me feel less alone in this. Like I'm not the only one hoping.

"Me and your father also understand that as devastating as this has been for us, it's even worse for you," he continues. "But that doesn't mean you get to give up on your life either. You can advocate for Lola and still take care of yourself at the same time. *You're* still here."

I nod through the sudden pain at the back of my throat. I know how hard this has been for them, but he got one part wrong.

I don't know that I *am* still here. Not really.

I feel like part of me left when she did.

"I know. I promise I'm okay." I reach out and put my hand over his on the counter. "I'm going to go change into some dry clothes and see if I can sleep. It's been a stupid day."

He looks over at the clock on the stove. "It's only six."

"I know. By the time I change and wind down, it'll be another hour. And you're right, I haven't been sleeping all that well." Also I really need some distance between me and that worry on his face.

I stand and he waves his hands at me.

"Oh, wait. I almost forgot." He walks over to the counter, grabs a bag with an office supply store logo on the side, and tosses it to me. Two ink cartridge boxes clatter together inside. "For your fliers. Max said he found you at the library copier, so I figured your printer was out of ink. I picked some up for you on my way home today."

I stare down into the bag and feel my eyes catch fire. It's such a simple errand, but it feels like a kind hand in the darkness. The fact that he'd buy me what I need to continue this mission of mine, when neither one of us thinks it's doing any good, is the kind of unwavering support that I don't deserve.

"Thank you," I mumble, and hug him.

"You're welcome." He squeezes me extra tight. "We miss her," he says. "We miss Lola too. You're not alone in this."

I hug him a little tighter. A lump has made a home in my throat.

After a long minute, he lets me go. "Goodnight, Drew."

"Night, Dad." I turn and hurry up to my room.

We miss Lola too...

My parents don't deserve a son as careless as me.

If they knew what I did, they'd never forgive me.

I yank the blanket from my shoulders and kick my bedroom door shut behind me with a sigh. I drop the bag of ink on the floor and toss the blanket toward the bed as I switch on the light.

Two things happen at the same time.

The light illuminates a figure sitting on the edge of the mattress.

And the blanket hits them in the face.

I leap back with a half-strangled yelp. The figure rips the blanket off and I sag against the door. "Autumn?"

She stands and throws the blanket on the floor, the sparkles on her sweatshirt catching the light and dancing reflections across my ceiling as she puts her hands on her hips. "Don't throw shit at me!"

I stare at her, heart pounding in my throat. I about peed my pants and she's angry about getting hit with a blanket? After *she* broke in?

"What the fuck are you doing here?" I whisper yell.

"Looking for clues," she says, too loud.

I hold a finger to my mouth. "Unless you want my dad to find you in here, you better lower your voice. I doubt the sheriff would like that call."

She flinches but lowers her voice. "Like you care what happens to me anymore. You're done with me, remember?"

"How did you get in here?" I look around the room. Everything on my desk is messed up, stuff is pulled out from under my bed, the pockets of all my sweatshirts are flipped inside out, and the closet door is open. Clothes and shoes are everywhere. "And who's going to clean this shit up?"

She points a thumb toward the window. "Climbed the tree outside. You left the window unlocked. And the mess is all yours—you're lucky I didn't take a knife to the mattress."

Murderer.

My blood boils. "Get the fuck out."

She casually plucks my whiteboard from the wall and props it up on my desk chair, waving at the evidence of my investigation like a game show host. My sticky notes flap in the airflow from the heating vent like they're waving at me. "Not until you explain what the hell this is."

Shit.

It feels like a violation for her hands to be all over Lola's board. That's mine. It's work I've been doing while Autumn's spent her time making empty accusations.

I clear my throat. "What does it look like?"

"It looks like a creepy wall of a stalker."

She snatches the picture of us at the boat launch from the board and I lunge forward to take it back. She holds it away from me, toward the window. "Is this from that night? Did you take this? Before you…"

I glower at her. "Before I what, Autumn?"

"Before you did what you did."

"I didn't do anything to Lola."

"You're a liar."

"And you're a criminal. Get the fuck out of my house before I call your dad. I mean it."

Her entire face turns red. Not the embarrassed kind, but the Autumn kind. Where she's literally boiling inside. "I have the proof already, so stop lying."

"Then give it to your dad. Don't let the stairs trip you on the way down."

She smirks. "I did give it to him. A few days ago."

She's full of shit. She *has* to be. "Nice try. If you had anything useful, you would have given it to him weeks ago."

"Want me to prove it?" She fishes her phone from her pocket. The screen lights up and I see she was recording our whole conversation. Which doesn't surprise me. Wannabe Nancy Drew over here probably thought she'd get me to confess and then backflip out the window or something.

She scrolls through her voicemail and presses play with the flourish of someone who's about to ruin my day.

A familiar sob comes through the speaker. "Autumn?" Lola cries.

Something vital inside me shatters into a thousand pieces.

"This is the worst time to not answer your phone... You won't believe what he did. I can't...I can't even... He's fucking evil. He's the worst person. I can't believe I spent so much time with him. He never really loved me. I don't think he's capable of love. He's a fucking monster. I can't believe he..." another fit of sobs fills the room. "I can't deal with this anymore. Between him and my parents, it's not...I can't. I can't handle it. Please call me back."

The call cuts off and I crumple to my knees.

Jesus fucking Christ.

I don't think he's capable of love.

I'm going to lose my dinner. I start to retch, and Autumn's eyes pop out of her smug little face. She kicks the desk trash can toward me, and I hold it in front of my face for the second time this week. Slowly my stomach settles, and the food decides to stay down.

Is this their new evidence? Is this what got the sheriff the warrant to search my car? To name me as his last remaining suspect? Is this voicemail the reason he thinks I *killed* her?

I slide back until my shoulders press into the door and I hang my head. "What have you done?"

"What do you mean what have *I* done? What have *you* done!"

The voicemail replays over and over in my mind. I can't stop picturing her walking down the side of the road, sobbing into her phone. All the possible horrors she could have walked into play in my mind. Because of me.

"I didn't hurt her," I repeat.

"The fuck you didn't. You heard the message. She called you a monster. What did you do?"

I look up, catch her blazing blue eyes, and tell her the truth. "I broke up with her."

Autumn's mouth drops open, and I look down at my hands. Shame settles in every nerve of my body.

I broke up with her. I broke up with Lola.

And it may have killed her.

"You did not," she whispers, so quiet I can barely hear her. "You wouldn't."

I glare at her. "Oh, but I'd kill her?"

"Wait. Tell me everything."

That's the last thing I want to do, but she probably won't leave until I do, and I want to be alone when the grief and guilt of that voicemail eat me alive.

Besides, Autumn lost Lola too. And my dad was right, I'm not alone in this. She's my least favorite person right now, but Autumn's had to live with that voicemail for weeks. The stalking and the accusations make a lot more sense. The murder locker was still a dick move though.

"I sigh. She got in a fight—"

"With her parents. I know. She texted me about it while she was waiting for you to pick her up," she says.

I nod. "She was still pissed when I picked her up and wanted to get food and go down to the river. We grabbed some burgers and drove to the boat launch. She vented about her parents, and we brainstormed ways to raise the money without them. She said I was the only person who saw things the way she did."

Autumn's face turns red again, and she sinks to the edge of my bed. "So naturally you dumped her."

I deserve all the sarcasm she can fling at me. "I didn't know I'd do it when I picked her up. She'd been casually dropping little comments about the future. *When* we go to college together. *When* we ditch our parents and move into our own place. *When* we get married. Always *when*, like it was already decided. Like I didn't have a choice in any of it. I felt like I was suffocating.

"Then at the river, she told me she couldn't wait until we have our own kids because we'd help them with *their* first car, and I panicked. I mean, kids? Our kids? We haven't even graduated yet. And…I don't know, I just wanted some breathing space. She looked at me with those big eyes, and I don't know what she said because all the blood was rushing in my ears and all of a sudden I'm telling her I don't want that. It turned into a huge fight. I got so mad, I told her I couldn't be a Band-Aid for her family drama…and I said she was draining the life out of me. That I was done."

Autumn's face goes completely pale. "And she got out of the car."

"And she got out of the car. I asked her to let me drive her home, and she said she wasn't my problem anymore, that she'd walk home. Then she accused me of looking for any excuse to end things and said I probably had some other girl lined up already and stormed off."

"*Do you* have another girl?"

"Of course not!"

She rubs her temple. "But you let her walk off."

I nod. "I was so mad. Not only about the fight, but that she'd think I'd cheat on her. I sat there in the parking lot for a while, crying and squeezing the life out of the steering wheel. I tried to call her three or four times, but she didn't answer her phone, so I drove home. I called again from here and checked her Snapchat location to see if she got home okay. It said she was by that convenience store up the road from the river for a long, long time, and then it disappeared. I didn't sleep, worrying about her. I tossed and turned and thought about everything: how we started, what we've been through. I realized I was being a coward. I wanted to fix it. But by then it was too late. In the morning when I called her house to check on her, her dad told me she wasn't in her bed."

"Oh my god." Autumn sets her phone down on the bed beside her. "That's why she called you a monster. That's why she was crying?"

"Yes."

"She walked off alone in the middle of the night. You didn't hurt her."

I stare at her.

"You know what I mean," she says, rolling her eyes. "You didn't physically hurt her."

"No. Not that your dad will listen, not with that voicemail validating his version of events."

She at least has the decency to look a little ashamed. "I'm sorry. When he told me the case was no longer a missing person's investigation, I couldn't sit on it anymore."

"Why did you sit on it at all? If you thought I hurt her, why not give him the voicemail the day she went missing? Why did you wait?"

She throws up her hands. "Because her voicemail said she couldn't handle it anymore. Everyone was saying she ran away, and I really hoped she did. I hated you for whatever you did to make her so upset, but I didn't want to believe you were actually violent. She was supposed to waltz through the door with some unbelievable story, get grounded again, and that would be that. But then…"

"She didn't come home."

"Exactly. I held out hope, but a week passed. Then two. Then three. The voicemail felt like it would catch my phone on fire. I couldn't stop thinking about it. But I've known you my whole life and contrary to what you might believe, I didn't want to believe you had anything to do with her disappearance. Plus, turning over the voicemail felt like admitting she wasn't coming home, and I…didn't do it. But then you got super combative, and angry, and distant, and my dad thought you were holding something back. I don't know. When he sat me down and said missing teens rarely come home alive after this much time has passed, I couldn't justify keeping it to myself anymore."

I want to hate her for not talking to me about all of this, but I can't. She was in an impossible situation with evidence she didn't know what to do with.

And I hate that she sat alone with it for so long.

"Thank you," I say quietly. "For the benefit of the doubt. I appreciate it, even if it ran out."

She stands and paces from the window to the closet, running frantic fingers through her red tangles. "Shit. I really thought…I really thought you knew more than you were saying. Where the fuck is she, Drew?" She turns toward me, and tears fall down her face. "What happened to Lola?"

My chest tightens. "I have no idea. Everything I know is on the back of that board, but it's really fucking hard when I'm the only one looking for her. Everyone either assumes she ran away or I killed her."

Autumn flinches. "If she ran away, she would have reached out by now. At least to me."

"I know. And if she didn't run away, and I didn't hurt her, then someone took her. Someone who's keeping her from calling home."

Autumn's gaze goes unfocused, and I can tell she's imagining the worst. She swallows hard and shakes away whatever nightmare she conjured. "Okay. How can I help?"

I sit up. "*What?*"

"I mean it. Tell me what to do. How do we find her and get my dad off your back at the same time?"

I don't know what to say to that. I hang ineffectual posters. I'm not exactly a shining example of next steps.

The window slides up and we both jump in surprise. Max's ruffled head pokes through and he grins from ear to ear. "Hey!" he says, climbing into the room.

I stand. "Sure, come on in. Join the party."

Max moves the whiteboard to the floor and sits in my desk chair. "What's up? Your dad said you needed a ride to school tomorrow. Cops finally took the Trooper?"

"And…you decided to break into my house to make sure?"

He laughs. "I tried to call, but your phone is on silent or something."

"So naturally your next step was to come in through the window?" Autumn asks. "Have you heard of the front door?"

"Pot, meet kettle," I mumble.

She glares at me. "Whatever."

"You came in through the window too?" Max asks.

"Well, I don't make a habit of it."

"Really? I used to do it all the time. So what's up? Are we going to find Lola, or what?"

I hold up both my hands to stop them. This conversation is making my head spin. "Wait. What?"

Max stretches his long legs and crosses his ankles as he folds his hands behind his neck. "I heard you from the tree. You said you were the only one looking for Lola, right? Let's fix that. I'm in."

"You're in…what?"

"This, dummy," Autumn says, picking my Lola board from the floor, and propping it against the headboard. "We're in this. Let's find her."

I rake my fingers through my hair. "Five seconds ago you thought I was an evil piece of shit and now you want to join forces? You wrote 'Murderer' on my damn locker today."

She winces. "Sorry about that. Five minutes ago you were a probable creep. Now you're her piece of shit ex-boyfriend who's trying to make amends."

The "ex" in that sentence makes me flinch. But fuck, that's what I am.

I push that supremely uncomfortable thought from my head. "Okay…but how are we going to find her? Hang more fliers?"

Max snorts. "Yeah, because that's been so helpful."

"It's not like I had another option. Besides, the fliers would have been helpful if anyone called in real information," I say, trying not to grumble.

"What about the official tip-line recordings? The number is all over the news every time they show her face," Max says, using his fist as an imaginary microphone. "*If you see this girl, or have any information regarding her current whereabouts, please call five-oh-three blah blah blah.*"

"Yeah right, and how are we going to get ahold of those? They go straight to my dad's office," Autumn says, stuffing her hands into the pockets of her sparkly sweatshirt. "What could they even tell us? She's been gone too long. All the information is old now, and my dad already talked to everyone who saw her that night."

"New information could still help," I say. "The official tip line would have more reach because of the media coverage, and I'm sure Roane isn't keeping up with new tips if his focus has shifted entirely to me."

"What if we ask my dad to review the recent ones?" Autumn asks. "I can tell him I was wrong about the voicemail."

I roll my eyes. "Yeah, okay. I'm sure his teenage daughter's sudden change of heart will be *just* enough to make a seasoned police official completely change the direction of his investigation. Maybe you can also tell him I'm a Libra, and my sign is known for diplomacy, not murder."

She scowls at me. "You're stupid."

"Not as stupid as that plan."

"I have a better one," Max says, leaning back in the chair. The front legs lift off the floor, and he almost wipes out before he catches himself.

He carries on like it never happened. "We should bypass Roane and listen to them ourselves."

"And how are we going to do that?" Autumn asks.

Max grins, and I already know I'm not going to like this. "Duh. We break into the police station."

TWELVE
DREW

This is it. This is how I get arrested for real.

I stare at myself in the bathroom mirror and sigh. I look like shit. Bags under my eyes. Skin a color that would make a zombie wince. Angry red lines crossing the whites of my eyes.

The two stooges didn't climb out of my room until almost eleven. It's a minor miracle my dads didn't hear them clambering down the side of the house. I barely slept after. I couldn't stop running through Autumn's plan.

It sounded a lot more substantial last night with the sweet twenty-four-hour buffer before we had to carry it out. The plan hinges on her dad being on night shift, which he is tonight. But now, I'm rethinking our collective sanity.

Tonight, I'm either taking one massive step closer to Lola or a prison sentence.

I pull my phone from my pocket to check the time. Almost ten. I swear under my breath. Max is supposed to pick me up down the street in about five minutes. I splash my face with cold water, and someone knocks on the bathroom door.

"You okay in there, hijito?" Papá calls.

Shit. I dry my face with a towel, hoping to draw some color into my skin before he worries. "Yup, getting ready for bed."

I open the door and he's waiting patiently in the hallway. He smiles at me, and I try to match it. "Did you need the bathroom?"

He shakes his head and fluffs his dark hair. "No, no. I wanted to check on you. Haven't seen much of you these last couple days. The last few weeks, really…"

"I know, Dad mentioned that too. I just need time."

"You take all the time you need. I'll be around if you need me, okay?" His gaze is sad, angry, and animated, all at once. Like he wants to say so much more and it's a physical effort to hold back the words. To support me without asking me a thousand questions, to give me space when he wants to make sure I don't vanish too.

I wrap my arms around him. He hugs me so tight that it hurts my ribs, but I don't say anything. I let him hang on for as long as he wants, and only step back when he does.

"Don't worry, Papá. I'm okay. I promise."

His shoulders relax a bit. "Do you want to talk?"

"Not yet. But I will."

Once I'm done doing things you'd disapprove of.

"Okay. Just…remember, you're made of hopes and dreams, hijito. We wished for you for so long. I'm here. Whatever you need."

A vice tightens around my throat and all I can do is nod.

He pats me on the shoulder and goes back down the stairs as I slip into my room.

"Goodnight, my boy," he calls. I hear Dad shout goodnight from downstairs too.

"Goodnight," I yell back, shoving down the guilt about everything I'm keeping from them. I can't deal with that now. There's no time.

I close my door, flip my hood up, and make sure the mound of pillows under the blankets looks like a curled-up sleeping me. I always thought that was cliché, the whole fake-person-under-the-blankets thing. But if they look in, there has to be something in my bed or I'll be fucked. I guess it's a classic for a reason.

I turn off the light and climb out the window. The cold makes my lungs ache, and my breath comes out in a cloud. I slide the window shut behind me, balancing on the eave over the kitchen window. My shoes slip against the frost-covered shingles, but I manage to slide down and bounce into the backyard without much noise.

Max is idling at the corner in the Liberty when I come around the side of the house, and I wonder if he'll let me drive. But when I get closer, I see the driver's seat is empty. He's sitting on the passenger side with his feet propped up on the dash.

I climb in and raise an eyebrow at him.

He shrugs. "I knew you'd want to drive, so I moved before you could hassle me about it."

"You knew I'd want to drive?"

"Yeah, you've got control issues on a normal day, never mind when we're about to do something stupid."

He may have a point. "It's like you know me or something."

He laughs. "Or something."

Only Max could drag a smile out of me on a night like this.

When I turn down Autumn's street, the amusement curdles.

Fuck. I can't believe we're about to do this.

Autumn's house is a hunter-green single-level ranch with wide windows and a dead lawn. Her old, dented Volkswagen sits in the pebbled driveway. I pull up behind it and spot her anxiously pacing the front porch in her sparkly sweatshirt.

She climbs in without a word and buckles herself into the middle seat. I drive off before anyone can back out of our plan—including myself.

I try not to look at Lola's house as we come to the stop sign, but I can't help it. Tonight all the lights are off except for her bedroom.

"They'll never turn that off," Autumn says from the backseat. "The bulb will burn out, and they'll replace it again and again until they're a hundred years old."

I look at her through the rearview mirror and catch her wiping a tear from her cheek.

The atmosphere in the car changes.

Max sits up straighter. I tighten my grip on the steering wheel. Autumn puts her hood down and her face turns to steel.

"They'll turn it off when we find her," Max says.

"Right," I say. "Let's go over the plan one more time. We can't mess this up."

"Okay, first step. Go."

"You guys drop me off at the park," Max says. "I wait until ten thirty, then call 911 from the ancient pay phone. I tell them there's a creepy guy chasing a woman in the park, then scream like a frail old lady and hang up."

I try not to smile. The "scream like a frail old lady" part is new.

Autumn rolls her eyes. "It's the night shift, so the call will get the two deputies out of the station. That should make it easier to get around the office without so many eyes. They'll drive around the park for a bit, so Max, you gotta get out of there."

He nods. "I'll get back to the car and hunker down."

"I'll park around the block from the station," I say

"Then I go inside and distract my dad," Autumn says. "He never answers his personal cell at work, and I already called it six times tonight telling him I can't remember the Wi-Fi password, the laptop charger is gone, and Netflix froze up on me. I'll get him out of his office and complain until he goes blue in the face, giving Drew a chance to get past him."

I nod. "I'll go in, download the recordings off his computer, slip back out, and we'll all meet back in the Liberty."

Autumn leans forward, sticking her pointy little nose into the space between the front seats. "Last time I was in his office, he had folders with open cases across the top of his home screen. The 'Scott.L' folder was in the middle, the tip-line recordings should be in there, but they also get emailed to him, so they might be in his downloads folder instead. His computer password is my mom's birthday. Twelve, twenty-eight, nineteen seventy-six. With periods between the numbers and no spaces. I already texted it to you so you won't forget."

I gape at her in the rearview mirror again. "Damn, Autumn, you're not messing around."

She shrugs. "I'm a Virgo. I always come prepared."

I don't know if she's piling onto my Libra joke or if she's being serious.

We stop at a red light. The park is up ahead on the left. The police station is another quarter mile away.

Max looks around the outside and unbuckles his seatbelt. "I'll get out here. We're the only car on the road anyway. Good luck. I'll see you after."

He snatches a few quarters from the junk in his cup holders, and then he darts across the street and down the road. Watching Max run off alone suddenly makes this feel like a bad idea again.

"The light is green, Drew."

I hit the gas. We can't stop now.

10:25. He makes the call in five minutes.

My hands shake as I pull into one of a dozen empty street spots around the corner from the station and throw the Liberty into park.

Autumn opens her door. "Wait until you see the cars leave and then come to the door. I'll cross my arms when the path to the office is clear."

Then she's gone too.

I pull at the collar of my sweatshirt. It's all happening so fast. If I fuck this up both Max and Autumn could get caught up in my mess, and it would be one hundred percent my fault.

I close my eyes.

Get a grip, Drew.

I relax my hands and sit back. I can do this. I'm not going to get caught. Neither is Max or Autumn. We're stealthy, sneaky teenagers. If anyone can get away with this, we can.

Blue and red lights illuminate the intersection ahead of me. A police car jolts out of the station's parking lot and disappears down the road. I jump out, lock the car, and look at the time on my phone.

10:32.

Cops are gone. Max is on his way back. Autumn is already inside. Time to go.

My fingers find the USB drive in my pocket and close around it. Hard plastic edges bite into my hand. Without this, I'm toast.

There are a few scattered cars in the lot, Roane's sheriff cruiser, and the white SUV I saw the pretty receptionist climb out of the last time they brought me in.

Shit. The receptionist. Why is she at the office this late?

I peek through the glass double doors and scan the entryway.

The front desk is a big half circle about fifteen feet from the door. To the left sits the bathrooms and a coffee station in a three-walled alcove. The space behind reception is mostly desks, and special offices line the walls at the back and to the right. Sheriff Roane's office is the first, almost directly beside the front desk.

Autumn stands near the coffee machines with her father. Roane's back is to me, his shoulders tense. It's clear from his posture the last thing he wants is to deal with Autumn's drama, and oh man, do I understand how he feels. Not that he doesn't deserve whatever she's leveling at him. Her arms hang by her sides, and whatever she's saying is low and angry. I can't hear it through the glass, but her face is full fury.

I have to wait.

The receptionist sits behind the desk, but she hasn't seen me yet. She's from Alabama or something. I can't remember her name. Maybe I never knew it. I think someone told me she married a guy in college who was from here.

She tucks a piece of her long dark hair behind her ear and squints at the screen in front of her. Something about how she holds herself makes me think she'd tackle me if I caused any trouble. Frilly lace blouse be damned.

She stands and I jump back.

"Sheriff Roane," she calls, "can I get you another cup of coffee?"

He turns and shakes his head. "No thank you, Savannah. I'm fine. But the boys might want some when they get back from that call."

"It's cold out there, for sure. I'll make a fresh pot," she says, but rather than heading toward Autumn and the sheriff, she walks toward one of the doors in the back. There's a separate break room.

More importantly, she's left her desk.

Roane turns back to Autumn and puts his hands on his hips. She folds her arms. There's my cue. I slip in the door and their conversation finally reaches my ears.

"What do you mean the internet is broken?" Roane says. "How can it be broken?"

"How the heck am I supposed to know? It...stopped. Which you'd know if you answered any of my calls."

"Autumn. I told you. I can't answer a bunch of personal calls. I'm at work."

"And I'm stuck at home with no internet. I'm *dying*."

I creep through the lobby as fast as I can. Thankfully the flat old carpet muffles my steps.

"I don't have time for this," Roane says. "I have a million things to do, and each one of them is more important than standing here, arguing with you about the internet."

"So what I'm hearing is that work is more important than your daughter? Wow. It's finally out in the open."

"Good lord," he mumbles.

Good lord indeed. I can't tell if she's making this up as she goes, or if this is genuine bottled-up angst she's unleashing tonight for our benefit. But either way, it works, and I slip into Roane's office.

This room is sixty percent stained red wood and forty percent black leather. Even the walls are paneled. He may be shooting for *sophisticated and judicial*, but it looks more like *grandpa's living room*. Also? It smells like old Chinese food in here.

I pass the black armchairs across from his opposing man-in-charge desk and push his office chair aside. Pictures of Autumn, her mom, and a long-dead family pet face the chair next to his nameplate, and a thousand mismatched pens. I shake the mouse and the screen lights up, flashing the password box at me.

I pull out my phone and find Autumn's text.

Evil Spawn: 11.28.1976.

Evil Spawn: No spaces. Only periods. Good luck!

I should probably change her name in my contacts.

I type in the password and the desktop appears. I fumble taking the USB out of my pocket. It slips between my fingers and clatters across the desk, hitting three pens and a big red file before I snatch it back up.

I freeze, and my already racing heart flies into my throat. I'm half expecting Roane or Savannah to come barreling in at the noise, handcuffs ready. But the front desk is still empty. Half a second later Autumn wails, "I'm on my fucking period, what do you want from me?" and bursts into tears.

I'm good for a few minutes.

Hell, she could keep him occupied until the end of his shift if she really wanted to. If fashion design doesn't work out for her, she should take up acting. She'd conquer Hollywood, one dramedy at a time.

I find the Lola file in the middle of the desktop, right where Autumn said it would be, and click it open. The screen floods with information. Files with statements, pictures of where they found her phone, pictures of my Trooper. All the evidence they have from the second Lola was reported missing. Even the original report, filled out by her dad the morning after.

My eyes race to read everything, and I have to remind myself that this isn't why I'm here. I scroll through it all, but there're no recordings, and most of it is about me anyway. The big bad boyfriend. None of the information even ventures outside of Washington City.

I open his downloads next. About two hundred things have been downloaded in the last ten days, and I'm looking for five weeks of recordings. That could be upwards of a thousand downloads to sift through.

My blood pressure is going to pop a vein in my neck, I swear.

I hit the search and type "Lola," but he hasn't named the recordings that way. I try again with the name of her folder, and that doesn't help either.

"New pot of coffee is on," Savannah sings from the main room. "Do you want anything, Autumn?"

Fuck, I'm running out of time.

"Do you have any hot chocolate?" Autumn calls back.

I hear Savannah's footsteps retreat.

Fucking saved again. If we get out of this, I need to buy that girl a car. Hell, she can have mine as soon as they give it back.

I refocus on the files downloaded in the past few days—if I find one, maybe I can search by that saved name. The mouse drifts over the results, and I look for anything that's an MP4, or playable in any capacity. I don't know what format I'm looking for.

Boom.

S.L.09.29E

Scott, Lola, and the date she went missing. I do a search for "S.L." and find five total. S.L.09.29A, S.L.09.29B, S.L.09.29C, S.L.09.29D, and S.L.09.29E. Five files for five weeks. I drag and drop all of them into the icon on the desktop for the USB and wait with absolutely no patience for them to download.

The icon jumps when it's done. I eject it and log out, pocketing the drive again. Practically buzzing with anticipation. Something on here might tell me where she is.

The screen goes dark, and I fix the desk chair as Roane throws up his hands in the lobby. "No, Autumn. You have to go home. I'll take a look at the router in the morning, and I'll send a pizza to the house, but I can't do this right now. I have too much on my mind."

Footsteps stomp toward the office and I dive behind the far end of the desk to hide.

Fuck. Fuck, fuck, fuck.

"What kind of pizza?" The crack in Autumn's voice is the first sign that she's not in control anymore. This is her last-ditch effort. I have to get out of here.

I peek around the back of the desk, weighing my options. Roane's back is to me, but he's between me and the exit.

How the hell am I—

Something moves outside the window, and I about pee my damn pants. Max's panic-stricken face presses against the pane.

I unlock the window and try to yank it open, but it sticks a few inches up. I crouch down. "What are you doing here?" I whisper.

"Checking on you! What do you think? Plus, you locked my car, and it's cold as fuck out here. Hurry up, let's go."

But I can't. Roane's arguing with Autumn about pizza toppings. I can't go out the way I came in without being seen. And unless I want to make a whole lot of noise, the window isn't a viable escape option either.

For me anyway.

I take the USB out of my pocket and slip it to him along with his keys. The least I can do is make sure I'm not caught with the evidence. "Go wait in the car. If I'm not out in ten minutes, leave without me."

"Wha—"

I close the window on his protest and point toward the Liberty. He stands on the other side of the glass for two more seconds, mouths something that looks like "I fucking hate you," and then stomps away.

I throw the latch back into place, jump away from the glass, and slip into one of the leather chairs facing his desk, slouching like I've been waiting here for hours. My pulse pounds in my neck and I tuck my chin to hide it.

"Fine, Autumn, fine. Whatever you want. Vegan pepperoni it is, but I'm not eating the leftovers, so you're getting a small," Roane grumbles as he walks back into his office. He spots me and halts in the doorway.

I smile up at him. "I hope I'm not interrupting anything, sheriff."

THIRTEEN

MARY

DAY 3

The double dose of medicine wipes me out even faster this time. I wake up with my forehead pressed against the passenger window and a cloud of steam from my mouth stretching across the glass. The van bumps along a dirt road, and I blink at the trees surrounding us.

We're back up the mountain already.

I rub the nap from my eyes, scratching at my neck again. The cloud disappears from the window, and I absently wipe at the remaining condensation with the beanie that fell off my head while I was asleep. I tuck it into my jacket pocket.

"How are you feeling?" Wayne asks, watching the road carefully.

"Tired. Itchy. A little better, I think."

He nods. "I'm so sorry. I can't say it enough."

I smile at him but don't respond because I still don't understand how this happened. How did he forget what I'm allergic to? How did he look at the strawberries and the eggs, side by side on my breakfast plate, and not immediately know which one was making me sick?

How does a father not remember what could kill his own daughter? And more than that, if he did mix them up—with the stress of everything that's happened the last few days, I guess that wouldn't be a reach—why didn't any alarm bells ring in his mind when I ordered a strawberry smoothie this afternoon?

None of it makes sense, and it's a confusing end to an otherwise good day. I finally felt like I had a handle on *me*, and now everything is all fuzzy again.

He looks over; he must be waiting for me to say something.

"These things happen, right?" I think I'm talking more to myself than to him.

His features droop. "I suppose they do."

The road straightens out ahead of the van, and I spot the cabin, blinking in and out of sight through the trees.

Wayne sighs. "Home sweet home."

He slows to turn into the driveway as someone rounds the corner up ahead. An old man in a buffalo-plaid baseball cap and puffy blue vest walks in our direction. His smile lights up the road. He waves both hands over his head, and Wayne grumbles under his breath, glancing again at the V-neck beneath my jacket.

The tires lurch to a stop half a foot short of the cabin stairs. "Why don't you head inside," he says, stabbing the latch of my seatbelt with his finger. "I'll see what he wants."

I turn in my seat. The man's reached the end of the driveway and waits there with his hands in the pockets of his vest. "Who is that?"

"I don't know. A neighbor, maybe? Seems friendly."

Then why do I have to go inside? To keep him from seeing my collarbone? Oh, the horror. Also, the old guy *may* be a neighbor? If we come up here all the time, wouldn't Wayne know who lives nearby and who doesn't?

I climb out of the van.

The old man catches my gaze as I ease to the ground, and he pulls a hand from his pocket to give me a little salute. "Afternoon."

Wayne shuts his door and reappears around the back of the van a few steps later, shrugging into his jacket. His heavy footfalls echo in the quiet. "Afternoon. Can I help you?"

The old guy smiles again. Tufts of gray hair peak out beneath his hat, and reading glasses hang from his vest pocket. Wrinkles the size of canyons line his face. The good kind. Like he's spent decades smiling.

"No help needed," the man says, reaching out a hand. I wanted to introduce myself. "I'm Ben Hooper, and I live about a quarter mile up the road."

He points in the direction we came from.

Wayne clears his throat and shakes Ben's hand. "Nice to meet you, Ben. I'm Wayne."

Ben shifts his gaze to me. "And who might you be, darlin'?"

I don't have to look at Wayne to know his gaze slides to me. His stare weighs more than that scratchy afghan on the couch. "This is my daughter, Mary."

"It's a pleasure to meet you," Ben says, with as much lightness and enthusiasm as I've ever heard a person use. He's effortlessly casual and happy in a way that makes me sad.

I don't know how to be…that. Have I ever been able to smile that easily?

I want to.

"You too," I mumble.

He smiles, tips his head to the side, and squints at my face. "You know, something about you looks so familiar. I can't put my finger on it."

I match his squint. "Really?"

"She gets that a lot," Wayne says with a grin. "She has one of those faces."

I do?

"Huh. Okay," Ben says with a shrug, and turns his smile back to Wayne. "Well, anyway, just wanted to say that if you guys need anything and don't feel like stomping back down the mountain, you let me know. Okay?"

"Thank you," Wayne says. "That's very nice of you. We really appreciate it."

"Nah, it's nothing. What are neighbors for, right? We've lost that sense of community these days, and I'm doing my damnedest to get it back."

Aw. That's kinda sweet. I think I like Old Man Ben.

"We should be helping each other," he goes on, "not isolating ourselves with screens and the internet. Take away the iPhones. Get back to family values."

Ah, nope. He lost me.

"I couldn't agree more," Wayne says. He looks back at me and frowns. He meaningfully flickers his gaze toward the cabin.

I shrug and jerk a thumb at the door. "Locked."

Realization dawns on his face and he drops a hand into his pocket. "My bad. Here."

He tosses the keys in a high arch, and I reach up with my free hand and snatch them from the air without even thinking about it. I turn my palm over to stare at them in surprise. Huh. I'm coordinated. Add that to my list too.

Mary Ellen Boone. Seventeen. Good student. Senior. Lizzo. Strawberry allergy. Floral jackets. Dead mom. Bit of a homebody. Cinnamon rolls. Purple. Homeschooled. Good catch.

"I'll be inside in a minute. I want to grab some more firewood first," Wayne says. "Go get warm, Mary."

Ben takes the hint. "I'll let you both get back to your day. It's wonderful to finally cross paths." He squints at me again before I turn to unlock the door.

Pretty ironic that he should think I look familiar, considering I wouldn't be able to pick out my own face from a hall of mirrors.

"It was great to meet you too," Wayne says behind me, "And you know what? We're here if you need anything. Firewood, first aid, whatever. We're prepared—"

The door creaking open blocks out whatever else he says, and the blast of warm air from the woodstove feels so good on my itchy, irritated skin that I immediately close the door and let them finish their neighborly conversation in peace. I gravitate to the sofa and sit close to the fire. I didn't realize how cold I was until now. I sit with my hands stretched toward the heat until my fingers pink up and get their warmth back. And with it comes exhaustion in another wave.

I hear a thump against the side of the house. I pause to listen and hear it again a few seconds later. Maybe firewood tumbling against the siding? Honestly, I'm too tired to care. All I can think about is taking a nap.

I haul myself off the couch, throw my jacket on the peg by the door, and hang Wayne's keys on the little hook beside the light switch. They swing for a second, and I freeze.

A flash of another doorway invades my mind. A narrow white door with a key holder beside it. This one isn't a screw hook in a log, it's a plaque with four silver hooks and "Family Forever" in white cursive across the top. I blink and a woman appears between me and the door. Her back is to me, reaching out to hang her keys on the hook. She's in scrubs, I think. They're teal and shapeless. Her dark hair hangs down her back and she throws it up in a bun and drops her purse on the red couch beside the door.

I blink and I'm staring at the cabin wall again.

Holy shit. Was that a memory of my mom?

The door opens and Wayne steps inside, startling me. He doesn't notice. He shivers, running his palms over his bare arms, and holds out the bright pink bag I forgot in the van. "Nosy people. We came out here to get away from neighbors," he says, irritated, before he looks at my face. "What?"

I take the bag on autopilot, my mind still on the woman with the dark hair, and I blurt, "Was my mom a nurse? Or a doctor?"

He takes a step back. "No. She stayed at home, with you. Why?"

Disappointment prickles at my insides. I guess that wasn't my mom after all. "Just curious what she did for a living. Do we know any nurses or doctors? Anyone who wears scrubs?"

He gives me a furrowed look. "No. Why?"

I shrug. "Thought I remembered something, but I guess not."

His face softens. "Today was a lot for you."

"Yeah, the Benadryl kind of killed the fun."

"No, I meant the whole day: The people, the shopping, being out in the world."

I blink at him, surprised he thinks leaving the house is the problem, not the allergy attack. If that smoothie didn't take me down, I'd have asked to stop at the beach somewhere, stretching our trip out as long as possible. "Oh yeah, that too."

The woman's image comes to mind again. I see the outline of her so clearly. It *has* to be a memory. She has to be a friend's mom or something? I wish I could have seen her face—maybe that would have helped me place her. But she's gone, and so is the remainder of my energy.

Wayne reaches out and brushes some hair from my face. His fingertips are ice cold. "Are you feeling okay? Do you need to go lie down?"

"I guess, yeah." I start to turn away, but my gaze lands on his bare forearm and I frown. "Where did your jacket go?"

He looks down at his T-shirt. "Oh. Must have left it in the car. I'll get it later."

I could have sworn he was wearing it when he got out of the van. This stupid Benadryl is wrecking my brain. "Wake me up when dinner's ready?"

"You got it, kiddo," he says, firing more wood into the stove.

I close my door to block out the noise and kick off my new shoes beside the bed. The heavy blankets lure me in, and when I fold them over me and sink into the mattress, it's the closest to content I think I'll manage for the rest of the day. My eyes close, but my brain won't stop.

"*Did you eat the eggs?*" Wayne asks, before he tells me I'm allergic to the wrong thing.

"*Large, please,*" he says, as he orders me more of something that'll cover me in hives before the last batch has fully faded.

I want to sleep, but the confusion weighs on me.

I couldn't prevent what happened today, but he could have. I mean, what else might I be allergic to? How can I keep track of food allergies when I can't remember what they are? And how can I trust him to do that when he keeps proving he's not up to the task? I get the feeling I'm used to advocating for myself with him, which I can't do until I remember what I'm supposed to be advocating for.

How many hits am I going to take in the meantime? How many

days am I going to lose to a drug-induced haze of exhaustion while I figure out what isn't safe for me to eat and drink?

I stare up at my irritatingly happy beach poster and find myself wishing he were better at this whole dad thing. But the guilt is immediate.

He's done so much for me the last few days. So he got one allergy mixed up. It sucks, but it's not the end of the world. He probably hasn't been sleeping much since my car crash. It doesn't mean he's incapable of taking care of me. We're both adjusting to this new normal.

I take a deep breath and try to relax. My gaze drifts to Officer Bowman's wrinkled business card. Still propped against my lamp.

"I'm okay," I whisper, closing my eyes. "Everything is fine."

I hear the front door open and close again as the Benadryl yanks me under.

FOURTEEN

MARY

DAY 4

My breath comes out in annoyed puffs as November tries to sink its claws into me. I grip my dinner bowl tight and kick off the ground to move the river swing again. It'll be full winter soon—well, as *winter* as Oregon ever gets anyway, which is mostly freezing rain and a constant chill from the moisture in the air. Soon I'll have even more reason to be cooped up in that cabin.

The thought makes me so anxious I could claw all my skin off and throw it into the river.

It's been *four* days since I woke up in that ditch, but it feels like months. I don't know if it's the endless uncertainty, the Benadryl fog, or Wayne watching me every single second, but it's exhausting.

Yesterday's nap quickly morphed into a nineteen-hour sleep marathon. I woke up late this morning with ghost hives still dancing across my skin and a deep-seated hesitation to eat.

I knew bread was safe, so I ate toast for lunch, but nothing about this taco salad tempts me to roll the dice. I focus on the calming sway of the swing, and not the fact that I've been analyzing every single ingredient in this bowl for an hour, wondering if I'm also allergic to the tomatoes or the cheese or the romaine…

The last thing I need is three allergy attacks in four days, and there appears to be nothing Wayne or I can do to prevent it. Both of us seem to have the same amount of information about my allergies. Which is decidedly nothing.

I scowl at the tomato on the end of my fork, setting the bowl on the seat beside me. That *normal* teenager feeling I had in Waybrooke feels laughably out of reach, and I want it back more than anything. Now everything feels suffocating and wrong.

The sound of Wayne chopping wood echoes in the yard behind me, but I don't look back at him. I know he's keeping an eye on me. God forbid I sit within six feet of a slow-moving body of water. I might drown from the proximity alone. I roll my eyes and push myself a little higher.

"Mary, be careful on that swing. It's not as stable as it looks," he calls from the other side of the woodpile.

Mary. My name rings in my ears, like my brain won't allow it in.

I throw a hand above my head and wave in acknowledgment.

I probably only have a couple more minutes to myself. It'll be dark soon, and then it'll be back to the cabin. Back to TV, and this quiet, homebound life. I'm itching for something to do. To move. To go. To live. To have a purpose beyond sitting on the couch wrapped in a scratchy blanket like a sickly Regency heiress.

I'm getting so tired of this fucking cabin.

I want to go for a run, or explore the coast, or hike a mountain. Anything to get the energy out, but I can't because all I'm allowed to do is watch Netflix. Even convincing him to let me come out here while he chopped wood was an endeavor.

"It might rain later..."

"What about your dinner?"

"There are coyotes in this neck of the woods, you know."

"You hate being outside, what's gotten into you?"

He's really shoving this homebody trait down my throat.

I'm supposed to be a shut-in, I get it. *Mary* never leaves the house, but if that's true, why do I feel like I'd rather burn this cabin to the ground than sit on that couch and watch another season of *Schitt's Creek*? Nothing against the Roses, I'd die for Moira, but I'd also kill to get the hell out of here.

I pick at a tiny periwinkle flower printed on the sleeve of my ugly jacket and sigh. This cabin might be cute and peaceful, but it's also drafty, isolating, and empty of the things I want. Even if I don't remember what they are.

I focus on the water and take a deep breath, letting the cold settle into my lungs again.

I'm okay. Everything is fine.

The holes in my memory are unsettling, that's all. Maybe it will get better once we move back to the old house. According to Wayne, McMinnville isn't huge but it's bigger than this tiny nowhere town. I need to give myself more time.

I eye the abandoned dinner bowl. If I don't starve to death before then.

Maybe I can get an allergy test or Wayne can call my doctor? I'd like to eat in peace. My stomach growls, and I wrap my arms around my body.

There's movement in my peripheral vision, and I jump. Wayne stands at the end of the swing, axe over his shoulder, and tips his head to the side. "Did I scare you?"

My Lizzo heart spasms inside of my chest, but I shake my head. "Nope."

He smiles. "You look cold. Want to go inside and get some hot chocolate? I have a few packets of the instant stuff, and you can use the last of the milk if you're interested?"

Goodbye, fresh air. Hello, Netflix. "Yeah, sure. That's fine."

But even as I agree, I wonder if I'm allergic to milk. Or marshmallows.

Is anyone allergic to marshmallows?

He stops the swing with the back of his arm and picks up my bowl. "You didn't eat much."

I pull my jacket closer, but the cold tightens my muscles until I shiver. "I wasn't very hungry."

Wayne looks at me like we both know I'm lying, but he doesn't say anything. I reluctantly slide from the swing and walk across the yard.

Mary Boone wouldn't care about being in the cabin all the time. Netflix is her best friend.

I don't understand her at all.

A bubble of anxiety threatens to burst as I get closer to the front door, but I step inside the house. There's no reason to have a panic attack about resting for a couple days. I'm not in danger. I'm watching TV for god's sake.

I need to get a grip.

One day I'm going to look back on all this worry and feel like a drama queen. The memories will trickle back any day now, and all the puzzle pieces will fit together. I'll feel like myself again.

I hang up my jacket, plop down on the sofa, and reach for the remote. Again.

"What's on the TV agenda tonight?" Wayne asks a few minutes

later, setting a black ceramic mug on the coffee table. Wisps of chocolate-scented steam remind me of the hot chocolate at the precinct, with a wave of relief. Hot chocolate is safe to drink, and he didn't add marsh-mallows. "Something more interesting than last time, I hope?"

His expression is open and happy, and I tell myself this is because *he* is open and happy. "What do you mean? I thought that one about the lady who wins the bed-and-breakfast in New Zealand was fun. Especially the goat."

He laughs and sits in the rocking chair by his bedroom. "The goat was the *only* good part of that movie."

"Agree to disagree."

I hit the down arrow, skimming movie descriptions, and linger on the classics section. The covers for most of these movies are in black and white, with the occasional rom-com from the eighties or nineties. Vague hints of plot sift through my mind at a couple of them, and I can almost remember what happens at the end of a few, which is fraction-ally comforting.

Ever After pops up and a tingle of emotion rolls through me. Happiness? Nostalgia?

I turn in my seat. "Have I seen this one before?"

Wayne leans forward and squints at the screen. "Is that the Cinderella one? With the butterfly wings and the books?"

"I think so?" I click on the summary and we read it.

He smiles. "That was one of your mother's favorites."

That explains the emotion, I guess. "I think I remember this."

"It won't be long now. You'll remember it all."

"Can't come soon enough." I press play. This movie feels like the kind of comfort I'm desperate for today.

The room darkens around us as the movie plays. The poor girl on the screen shifts from a child to a mistreated adult who has killer aim with an apple, and I'm lost in it. I start mouthing every single word, and by the halfway point, tears sting my eyes because this finally feels like me. I know this. This movie belongs—in some small part—to me.

I don't realize I'm openly crying until I get to the end. The music swells, the girl on the screen is crying too, and suddenly I'm not on *this* couch anymore. I'm in the middle of a big red sofa with about ten fluffy blankets on my lap, a giant bowl of buttery popcorn wedged between me and someone else. The room is dark except for the light cast from a TV on an antique stand. *Ever After* plays on the screen. A woman with long dark hair sits beside me, shaking a familiar fist at the prince as he turns his back on the girl he loves. The woman with the dark hair yells, "I hate this part!"

It doesn't sound like she hates it at all.

I look over at her and say, "You've seen this ten thousand times, how can you still get so mad at this movie?"

"I'll stop being mad when he stops making her cry. Drew Barrymore is a gem."

"Can't argue with that."

She throws popcorn at me. I throw some back and she looks at me with all the outrage of a kitten. "You're a brat, you know? Quit making a mess or you'll have to clean the whole couch."

"You started it!"

"Lies."

And it's done. I'm back on the couch in the cabin. I clutch at the arm of the sofa so hard my fingernails dig into the stuffing. That was definitely a memory. And I *know* know her.

I can see her face *so* clearly now. The warm eyes, freckles across her nose, hair up in a bun for the third day in a row. I can hear her voice in hundreds of conversations about school and boys and friends. Yelling at me for sneaking out of the house. Picking me up at the pool. Hiding the cold brew from me so I don't vibrate right out of U.S. history. Reminding me about dentist appointments and teaching me to drive—squealing that I'm too close to the curb.

Everything, all wrapped up in *her*.

Now the tears are really falling. I sit there, dissecting every sliver of her face for so long, I don't realize the movie's over until Wayne clears his throat.

"You okay?" he asks, turning on the lamp beside the rocking chair. It bathes the room in warm light. He comes to sit next to me. "What happened? Did the movie upset you?"

I put the remote on the arm of the couch so I can wipe the tears from my face, but I can't get the words out. "No…I think…I might remember *Mom*."

His whole body stills. "You do?"

I nod, and heave in a bone-rattling breath. Is it all finally coming back to me?

Wayne rifles in his back pocket and pulls out his faded wallet. He flips it open. There's one of those little photo sleeves in there. The top picture is a baby wrapped in a green blanket—me, I'm guessing. He flips to the one behind it, tugs the picture from the sleeve, and holds it out to me with a smile. "Is this who you remember?"

He has a picture of her? Of the mom I couldn't remember? And he waited until *now* to show it to me? Excitement churns my mostly empty stomach at the idea of having a real, confirmable memory, and I swipe away the last of the tears, composing myself. I pull the photo closer and squint at the two people standing in front of a giant fireplace in a fancy building. The mantle is covered in red and white flowers, and the couple in front of the fireplace wear giant matching smiles on what's clearly their wedding day.

Wayne is easily recognizable, though a lot less gray. He has the same sharp cheekbones, and his arms are wrapped around a pale woman in bright white satin and lace.

A woman with long, honey-blonde hair and huge blue eyes.

I blink at the photo, closing one eye, then the other. I imagine her face with a torrent of thick dark brown hair, freckles, but it's like cramming the wrong piece into a puzzle. No matter how I twist her thin delicate features, I can't make her into the woman on the red sofa.

I must have gotten it wrong.

"Well? Is it her? Do you remember?" Wayne asks, intently.

I smile to hide my tornado of emotion. He looks so hopeful. I can't bring myself to tell him the truth. "Yeah," I say. "Yeah, that's her."

His grin splits his face. "See? What did I tell you? Be patient and it'll all come back in time. Was I right, or was I right?"

I cement my smile in place, but I'm still as stone. "You were right."

He nods to himself and moves back to his chair, humming a song under his breath. I slide my hand over to the remote and click play to fill the silence.

I need a minute—or ninety—to figure out what I'm feeling. Sadness that I got it wrong? Anxiety about consistently "misremembering"? But why do I feel more dread than disappointment?

Details from the last four days tangle in my mind, a mix of comforting, supportive fatherly gestures...and mistakes. Wayne cleaning out the pharmacy of first aid stuff and tampons to make sure I had everything I needed. Wayne buying the wrong-sized clothing. Wayne showing up at the precinct in a full panic, looking for me. Wayne telling me I'm allergic to eggs. Wayne supplying a birth certificate, with a smile on his face. Admonishing me for wearing a V-neck—*You can't remember. You don't know the rules.* Leaving clean, dry clothes outside the bathroom our first night here. *It must have been the strawberries...*

Soon the credits for whatever movie I played fill the screen, and I absently start another one.

Wayne laughs. "*Legally Blonde?* Are you trying to torture me?"

I blink at the screen, surprised to see Elle Woods snort crying as she's dumped over dinner. I glance over my shoulder at the clock on the stove. It's almost midnight.

I don't want to be awake anymore. Or in this room. Or in my head.

I hit the pause button and stand. I feel like I've been hit by a truck. I'm exhausted, the Benadryl drowsiness like a distant, energetic memory. "Um, no, you're off the hook tonight. I'm going to bed."

He nods. "Okay. Sleep well, my Mary."

My name rings in my ears again.

"Goodnight," I mumble, trying to ignore how he watches me cross the room.

He doesn't so much as blink until I close the door. And for the briefest second, I consider locking it.

I *really* need to get a grip.

FIFTEEN
DREW

What the hell are you doing here?" Roane growls. He stalks around the desk and shoves his chair back. "And how long have you been in my office?"

He relaxes when he checks his computer screen and finds it on the password page.

I shrug. "I don't know. A few minutes? I came to talk, but you were busy with Autumn, so I waited here. Should I have listened to your conversation instead?"

He sits at his desk with a huff. "Next time, wait to be asked in."

I give him a mock salute. "Sir, yes, sir."

The regret is instant. He leans forward, bracing his arms on his unnecessarily large desk, and the mood in the room goes still and sour. "Why are you here?" he repeats, in his most calm, controlled, officer tone. "You can't have your car back, if that's what you're after. We won't be done with it for some time."

Of that I have no doubt. I wouldn't be surprised if he "accidentally" blew it up in a training exercise.

I shake my head to banish that mental image. "Ah, no. I actually came to talk about what you said at the boat launch. I do know something else about the night Lola disappeared."

He sits back, clearly surprised, and shuffles for his little silver recorder, because apparently this is 1975 and he doesn't have an app for that. He presses play, and says, "Andrew Carter-Diaz, additional statement" into the mic, and then turns it toward me. "You have more to tell me?"

I hate that he's recording me, but I got myself into this. I can't exactly say I changed my mind and walk out. That'll only make him suspicious, and this place is full of cameras. If he thinks I'm being weird, the first thing he'll do is pull the recordings and catch me messing with his computer. I'll be handcuffed long before I can sort through anything on that USB.

I have to seem genuine, and the only way to do that is to tell him something real.

"Yeah, I do."

"And you're doing this without parental supervision, without your attorney, and of your own free will?"

"I am."

His chair groans as he leans back. "Proceed."

Ugh, I hate him. Does he have to be so many police clichés all at once?

"You asked me at the river why Lola got out of the car."

"I did."

Pain ripples through my chest as I relive it again. The look on her face. The sound of the door slamming. The sight of her walking away from me. I take a breath. "I…ended things. That's why she got out, and that's why I didn't go after her."

Like a fucking asshole.

Roane scratches his chin stubble. "You broke up with Lola? Why?"

I hate this part. "Because I'm an idiot. Because she was talking about getting married, and I panicked. She accused me of cheating, and we got in a fight. She stormed off. I drove home. That's the whole story."

"*Did* you cheat on her?"

I flinch. "Of course not."

"If you only broke up with her, what's with all the secrecy? Why not tell me this the first time we spoke?"

"Because I hate myself for it. Our last conversation turned into an argument, then she vanished into thin air. I didn't want anyone to know I hurt her like that."

"Why tell me now?"

"Because I *did* hurt Lola, just not the way everyone thinks. And while I've been beating myself up about breaking up with her, the whole town's decided I killed her. I…I thought you should know the truth. Because you're right—this *is* all my fault. If I hadn't ended our relationship, she wouldn't have stormed off and none of this would have ever happened."

Saying that last part out loud makes my throat burn.

I move to stand but he holds up a hand. His expression shifts from that serious cop stare to sadness, regret maybe? I sit back down.

"Now, hold on. You two are young, way too young to be thinking about the future, and that kind of conversation would make a lot of people, particularly kids your age, lose their cool. It makes sense that Lola would look to you for support she felt she wasn't getting from her parents, but it wasn't on you to promise your life to her at seventeen. I'd be more concerned if you didn't freak out a bit, honestly."

I shake my head. "We're not talking about a little freak-out. If this was only about me breaking Lola's heart, then sure. But I left her out there on her own. There's no excuse for that."

"This is a safe town. She should have been able to get home from the river."

"But she didn't, did she?"

"No. She didn't." Roane's eyes narrow, and what he really means clicks into place. She should have been able to safely get home *if* she walked away like I'm saying she did. Because Washington City is perfectly idyllic. This is a *safe* town. So *I* must be a liar.

When I don't say anything, he pushes the recorder closer to me. "One more time, Drew. What happened to Lola after you broke up with her?"

I pinch the bridge of my nose, suddenly more exhausted than I've ever felt in my entire life, but I answer his question. "She got out of the car and ran down the road. I went home."

"That's the truth? All of it?"

I let my hand drop. "It's all the truth I have."

He shuts off the recorder with a dismissive jab of his finger. "I'm glad you shared this with me. I'll add it to the report."

I stand. "Thanks. Sorry for coming in unannounced."

"It's late. Head straight home, okay?"

"Sure."

I leave the precinct, and as soon as I'm past the front windows, I sprint around the block. Autumn and Max are standing side by side in front of the Liberty. Their faces go from panic to relief.

"Holy shit, Drew. I thought you were done for," Max says.

Autumn points to her dad's office window. "I about crapped my pants when he walked in there. What happened?"

"I talked my way out of it."

"How?" they ask in unison.

"Doesn't matter. We need to get the hell out of here and see what's on those recordings before someone busts us with that USB."

"Let's go to my place," Autumn says, pulling open the passenger door. "My dad's on shift until four. The house is empty."

I nod and climb back into the driver's seat. Max hands me the keys from the backseat—grumbling about how he should at least get shotgun in his own damn car, but we ignore him.

I park a little ways from Autumn's house in an alley where people stash their trash containers, and we hurry down the sidewalk before any of the neighbors see us.

She ushers us inside and slaps at a light switch. Overhead lights illuminate a wide living room with vaulted ceilings, a sectional, two beanbag chairs, and a TV over a fireplace. I've never been inside Autumn's house before. We always ended up at Lola's. The shadow of a kitchen stretches out to the right, but she leaves those lights off and flops on the couch. "Well, that was stressful."

Max flings himself into one of the beanbags, and half his lanky body's swallowed by the chair. "I can't believe we did it. We're like... secret agents. Man, I'm so hyped. I could stay up all night. I'm not even tired."

"Good, because we're probably going to need all night to listen to these recordings," I say. "Give me the USB."

His mouth drops open. "What? I thought you had it?"

All the blood drains from my face. "You *lost* it?"

He barks out a laugh. "Just kidding."

I imagine the wheeze his lungs would make if I tackled him. "I'm going to kill you for that. Roane will finally have a real reason to arrest me."

Autumn rolls her eyes and gets up. "You two are annoying. I'll get my laptop. Try not to get any blood on the sofa."

I stare him down. "Give me that USB or I'm going to punch you."

"You're killing my secret agent high." He fishes around in his pocket and produces it with two fingers. "There. Happy?"

I snatch it away from him. "I'll be happier when this tells us something."

"Me too," Autumn says, reappearing with a laptop in a purple, blue, and black galaxy cover. She props it on the cushion in the middle of the sectional, and I hand her the USB. The recordings load, and she presses play.

The computer speakers fill the room with a whiny teenage voice. "Hi, hey, hi. Is this the tip line? I have a tip for you. Check the mall. She's super stuck up. I hope she never—"

Autumn hits the skip button.

"Thank you," I mumble.

The next recording plays.

"Hey, there. Ya know, that Lola girl is in Texas. My aunt just saw her here. She joined the rodeo circuit. You can see her on the Rodeo Austin website—"

Skip. Yeah fucking right. Lola in the rodeo. She'd rather die.

Autumn groans and hits the pause button. "So what's the plan here? Do we listen to all of them? It's going to take a while to sort through five weeks of prank calls and it's already after eleven."

I dig my phone from my pocket and hand it to her. "Here. We can download the recordings onto our phones and split them up. If we each take a set, we can get through them three times as fast."

"Cool. Catch." Max whips his phone across the room, and Autumn snatches it from the air before it hits me in the face.

Fifteen minutes later she's back in her spot on the couch, headphones in, listening to the thousands of S.L.09.29A recordings from the first week. Max is lounging in his beanbag, listening to S.L.09.29B and S.L.09.29C, and I'm on the other side of the couch, staring at the dozens of "D" and "E" files now in a playlist. Each of us has a notebook, but I have a feeling tonight is going to be more skips than scribbled notes.

I listen to people insist they saw Lola wandering around town or eating in the Dairy Queen dining room. The same man calls six different times to say he saw her being abducted by aliens. Three separate old ladies call to say they hope we find her, all with vitriol for that "evil boy" who turned on her. Apart from the quick interruption of Autumn's vegan pizza being delivered, we don't move for hours. Some callers give their names, some leave phone numbers, but most of them spew garbage and hang up. It's incredibly frustrating, but tip-line sleuthing is a marathon, not a sprint.

By about three in the morning, my brain is a slurry of annoyance and people's voices. Mr. I'm-So-Pumped-I-Could-Stay-Up-All-Night is straight-up snoring, and Autumn nods off, then changes positions on the couch to wake herself up at least every five minutes. I stand, and my back cracks a thousand times. "Let's call it a night before we all fall asleep here."

Autumn looks up at me and pulls out a headphone. "Hmm?"

"I'm going to be toast if my dads wake up and I'm not in my room. Plus, can you imagine what'll happen if Roane comes home from his shift and finds us all here?"

She shudders, and Max lets off another throat-rattling sound that makes us both flinch.

Autumn gathers her phone and her laptop. "That's a good point. We can pick this up again tomorrow after school. He's back on shift at one."

Her conviction, like it's not an option to quit until something worthwhile comes of it, makes me smile. "You hang onto the USB though. Just in case? This is the last place he'd look for stolen data from the precinct."

"Yeah, of course." She nods toward Max. "Get him home too, please. The last thing I need is my dad thinking I'm sneaking around with Max."

I nod, and kick at his foot until he sits up with a snort.

"Where's the…what?" he mumbles.

I laugh. "Come on, Sergeant Sleep Apnea. Time to get up."

"Huh?"

"Go. To. Your. Car."

It takes him a full five minutes to pull himself to his feet, and another three to get to the front door. The cold wakes him up though, and by the time we get to the Liberty, he's making grabby hands for the keys so he can drop me off.

The sleeping town slides by around us. Hundreds of recordings ring in my ears.

That evil boy…

Nobody in this town sees a teenager when they look at me. Or even a person. They see a threat. A warning. A red flag. Someone they wish disappeared in Lola's place. I think the only way I'm ever going to feel at home again *in* my home is if I find her. I have to fix this.

Max pulls up to the curb a couple houses away from mine, and I reach for the door handle.

"Hey, Drew?"

I look back at him. "Yeah?"

His eyes droop with exhaustion, but he smiles. "You're pretty great for doing all of this, you know."

"Doing what?"

"This," he says, gesturing to my phone in my lap. "The station and the map and the recordings and the posters—everything you're doing for Lola."

"I'm doing what anyone would for someone they care about."

"Maybe. But not everyone cares this much."

I roll his words around in my head as I climb out of the car and watch him drive off.

Shit, I hope he's wrong. I hope he's wrong more than anything because I can't imagine doing less than this.

I creep around the back of my house. All the lights are off, so I'm in the clear. I use the tree in the backyard to climb up, and I slip back through my window. My room is undisturbed. Fake-pillow-Drew is still under the blankets, and there's no sign my dads ever came in. I slide the window shut behind me and lock it to ward off any more surprise visitors.

The heat pumping from the vent under the desk makes my hands prickle as they warm. I kick off my shoes and pants and shove the pillows aside to climb into bed, dropping my phone on the nightstand, with a relieved sigh.

I can't believe we actually did it.

It's so late. I need to sleep and give my brain a break, but when I close my eyes all I can see is Lola. Waiting for me to find her.

I open my eyes again and grab for my headphones. The voice of another caller fills my ears, insisting she saw Lola flying through the air yesterday morning, before they bust up laughing and hang up.

I know I need to sleep. But I can't let go.

SIXTEEN

DREW

I wake up with a jolt and almost smack my head on the nightstand. Fragments of whatever dream I'd been having fade from my mind— rough dirt floors, fingernails scratching against the earth. A shiver raises all the hair on my arms, and I force myself to sit up.

A cord tangles around my arm. When I tug on it, my phone pops out from beneath the blankets. I blink at it, slowly scrubbing at my eyes until I remember the night before. I must've fallen asleep listening to the recordings.

I roll over to grab the end of the fast charger from the floor, hoping my dead battery will juice up enough to get through the day while I get ready. I set the phone on the nightstand and squint past it out the window. Sunlight streams through the glass. A *lot* of sunlight.

The clock on my nightstand says it's almost twelve thirty.

Fuck. Dead phone means no alarm. I'm *super* late for school.

I press the heels of my hands into my eyes and swear. A lot.

I don't know if there's any point now, since my dads have

probably gotten that automated, "Your child...*Andrew Carter-Diaz*...has been marked absent from school today" call from the attendance office. I also feel like total shit. My eyes hurt, my head hurts, my muscles hurt. All I want is to pop in my headphones and not move all fucking day.

But Roane's face flashes in my mind. The *good* sheriff doesn't give a shit about what I want. If he hears I've missed school, he'll be knocking on my door to make sure I didn't skip town.

I throw on a clean pair of jeans, a dark blue T-shirt, and my black "No Sleep Till Brooklyn" Beastie Boys hoodie, a Christmas present from Lola last year. The "no sleep" part seems fitting for today.

I move my phone to the outlet by the bathroom sink. It's already up to fifteen percent. If I can get it to twenty-five before I leave, it might last until the end of the day, but I'll have to charge it again if we're going to listen to the rest of the recordings after school. I type in my passcode and all my missed calls and text messages flood in.

There's a call and voicemail from each of my dads, asking why I'm not at school. I stick my toothbrush in my mouth and send them each a text saying I overslept and I'm getting ready now. I have similar messages from Max and Autumn. Max's first message is from this morning, saying he's outside my house, wondering if I still need a ride. Looks like he waited about fifteen minutes, and climbed up and tapped on my window, before he gave up and went to school.

Shit. I quickly type out an apology, with about a dozen head-smacking emojis, and almost immediately those three little dots appear on the screen.

Max: Dude u were sleeping like the dead
Me: sry. i didn't even hear you

Max: clearly. i feel you tho. i barely got up myself. My mom
        barged in after I hit snooze the second time.

Luckily both my dads are at work long before I have to leave for
school or I'd have suffered the same fate.

Me: sounds about right
Max: I can leave at lunch and come get you, if you want?? Or are
        you ditching????
Me: Can't. Roane would be on my ass
Max: Okay, i'll be there. I have third lunch today.

I send him a thumbs up, grateful for his never-ending willingness
to help, but also because third lunch means I have an extra thirty minutes to listen to recordings and charge my phone. I set it back down
beside the sink and finish brushing.

At least I have a ride. It's over a mile to school, and I barely have
enough energy to wash my face, much less walk there. I put the recording on speaker. Might as well multitask. I press play on the next recording while the water warms up.

"Yeah, is this the tip line?" a woman asks. "My name is Diana, and
I think I saw that girl in Eugene yesterday. She was with a bunch of
college students, but she looked way older and her hair was orange,
and she—"

Skip.

"Anonymous here. That Lola girl ran away. Stop looking, it's
annoying to see her and her sad-sack parents on the news all the damn
time—"

Skip. Though that sounded suspiciously like the preppy golf team captain from my third-period political studies class. If I find out he's calling the tip line to complain about how Lola's disappearance is such an inconvenience for *him*, he might find the tires of his Jetta mysteriously slashed.

"I'm tellin' ya. She was abducted by alie—"

I roll my eyes and splash warm water on my face. Skip.

"Um, hi. My name is Meredith Hoyt. I already called 911, and they said they'd pass on the information, but I googled this number too, just in case. I think I saw that missing girl, Lola? She came out of a diner in Waybrooke with a man, and I'm not positive it was her, but—"

I reach over to skip when I hear, "—she was wearing the same jean jacket from the picture on the news. The one with the floral arms."

I freeze, water dripping from my chin and down my forearms.

Did I just…hallucinate? Am I still asleep? I blink at my reflection. There's no way. I must have heard that wrong.

I dry my face and rewind the recording.

Meredith Hoyt's shaky voice fills my tiny bathroom again. "…the same jean jacket from the picture on the news. The one with the floral arms."

I press pause because I think my heart stops beating.

A thousand memories of that jacket fly through my mind. At school. At the beach. At my kitchen table. At the pool. Faded jean fabric, with rose gold buttons that Lola picked out herself from the fabric store. Custom floral sleeves that Autumn meticulously hand stitched with rose gold thread as part of her final project for fashion design last year.

She made it for Lola. Even sewed her initials into the tag.

Lola wore it everywhere, including the night she disappeared.

I hit play again, needing to hear the rest.

"She had dark hair, short to her chin, and she was wearing a pair of jeans, a black T-shirt under the jacket, and a white hat thing," the woman continued, taking a second to cough. "She left with the man. Older. Forties? Maybe her dad? He was pretty tall, sharp face, and he drove a big gray van with peeling paint. I didn't get the license plate. This was at about noon. A couple minutes ago, actually. I swear it looked just like her."

Holy *fucking* shit. I check the date and time on the recording. The call came in just shy of twenty-four hours ago.

Lola was alive yesterday. She was standing outside a diner with some stranger, and I have the proof right here. Meredith Hoyt leaves her contact information, and the recording stops. I scramble to pause before it skips to the next one because whatever it is, it's not important. Not as important as this call.

I brace my hands on the vanity and try to process. She's been gone for weeks, and she's casually hanging out with a guy in a creepy van? Nothing good ever comes from a nondescript van with peeling paint. And the man she's with is definitely not her father, so who the fuck is he?

And why hasn't she come home?

My stomach hollows. Maybe she can't. Maybe he won't let her come home.

Is he with her right now? What happened in the last five weeks while we all sat around wondering where she was?

The mirror catches the wild look in my eyes. I think I might be sick again.

I rip the charger from the wall and run to my computer to search for Waybrooke. The map pops up down the coast, near Florence. It's a few hours from here. At least she's still in Oregon. Or was yesterday. If she's this close after all this time, he probably has no immediate plans to leave the area, or the state. Maybe there's still a chance…

But what am I supposed to do now? I have a lead, but what the fuck am I going to do with it? I call Autumn but she doesn't answer. I don't bother calling Max because he never puts his phone on silent, and he'll get it taken away for the rest of the day if it rings in class.

I stare down at my phone screen, paused on Meredith's call. A minute and seven seconds just changed everything. I don't have a choice. I need Roane. He'll know I broke into his computer, but he'll recognize the description of her jacket, and he'll know what to do. He has the authority to talk to the people at the diner or get the cops down there to do it. Maybe someone else saw the van and got the license plate, or it's on a security camera. He can follow the bread crumbs straight to Lola.

She can come home.

This can all be over.

Hope makes my pulse pound in my throat. I need to make him listen.

I open my missing-flier file and retype the information at the bottom. Underline it. Bold it. Make the font bigger.

Name: Lola Elizabeth Scott

Age: 17

Hair color: Dark brown

Eye color: Green

Last seen: 12:17pm on September 29th

Waybrooke, Oregon diner, with a man in his 40s. Tall, sharp face.

Driving a utility van with gray, peeling paint.

I delete the picture on the flier and replace it with my desktop photo. The one of us at the beach. I crop it so it's only her. The jean jacket clear as fucking day. I hit print, stuff my feet in shoes, and the phone charger in my bag. I snatch the flier from the print tray and sprint from my house.

I don't even stop to lock the door. I just run.

All the way through my neighborhood. Into downtown.

I gasp for air, dodging pedestrians on the sidewalk. People shout at me to slow down, but I don't stop running until I burst through the doors of the precinct, clutching the straps of my backpack and the new flier like a wild-eyed animal.

Poor Savannah jolts out of her seat and throws a hand to her heart. "What in the—" she yells, but I'm already at her desk.

"Is the sheriff in yet? It's an emergency," I say, gasping for air.

Roane appears in his office doorway, still wearing his jacket. He must have just walked in. "Drew? What are you doing here? Why aren't you at school?"

"Overslept." I round Savannah's desk. "I need to show you something."

He gives me the look. The *you're acting like a damn fool* look. But he steps to the side and lets me into his office, kicking the door shut behind us. "Have a seat."

I sit in the same chair as last night, letting my backpack slide to the floor. Sunlight streams through the windows and hits me right in the face. I lean forward so it's out of my eyes and rest my elbows on my knees.

Roane shrugs out of his jacket and knocks the mess atop his desk into a pile. "What can I do for you, Drew? Have more to add to your statement?"

THAT'S NOT MY NAME | 163

My chest is still heaving. "No. I have a lead on Lola."

Roane's eyebrows shoot up, and he sits down. "I'm listening."

"Good. Keep doing that." I pull my phone from my pocket and start Meredith Hoyt's message. Her voice fills the space between us, and I watch him as he listens to her story. I slide the new flier across his desk, pointing at the time and the details about the man as she describes them. When it's over, I play it again for emphasis. When she mentions the jacket, I pause it.

"That's her. The description matches perfectly," I say, jabbing my finger at the jacket in the photo. "It's right here. It's her."

He stares at the photo on the flier for a very long, very silent minute, and then looks up at me. "I remember it. Took Autumn a month to finish that thing." He jots some notes on a pad by his elbow, and it looks like he's copying what I typed onto the flier almost verbatim. "But what are the chances it's the same one? A lot of people have jean jackets. We live in the Pacific Northwest."

"A lot of people have handmade custom jackets with pastel floral sleeves and Lola's initials sewn into the tag? Hell, you probably have scraps of the fabric at your house."

He huffs out a laugh, writing something else down. "I probably do."

"It should at least warrant a trip out there, right? The jacket might not be enough on its own, but maybe the diner has footage of her wearing it? Or of the vehicle? Or the man with her?"

He nods to himself, looking over his notes, then looks up at me with a frown. "How on Earth did you get ahold of the woman from the diner? Did she find one of these?" he asks, gesturing to the flier on his desk with the back of his pen.

Yeah, I sent them by carrier pigeon to the goddamned coast. "No, she called the tip—"

The rest of my sentence dies on my lips and the weight of my mistake drags me back in my chair, into the blinding sunlight. *Fuck, fuck, fuck.*

Roane slowly lifts his eyes to me, his face growing redder by the second. "The what?"

Fuck. "I ah…"

"You can't possibly mean the tip-line recordings, right Drew? *Our* official, police-monitored tip-line information? Because that would mean you stole evidence, and there's no fucking way you're that stupid, right?" he bellows, standing so fast his office chair flies back and hits the paneled wall behind him.

I put my face in my hands. *Fuck.*

"How the hell did you get onto my computer?"

I have to salvage this. He was listening before I opened my stupid mouth. "Roane, I know you're hulking out, but I need you to pay attention, okay? How I got the information doesn't matter. What matters is what I found—"

He glares at me. "What did you do, come in through the window? I knew something was up last night. You've been avoiding me and this investigation for weeks, hiding behind your dads and your lawyer, and then you suddenly come in willing to share your feelings? Bullshit. You got caught in the act and lied your way out of it, like you do everything else."

"No. I told you the truth about Lola, but *none* of this matters, Roane. Lola's the only one who matters. Listen to the recording again. It's her jac—"

"Fucking teenagers," he mutters to himself. "I'm going to check the security tapes and when I catch you on camera stealing from my office, you're done for."

He crumples the flier and throws it at me. I catch it against my chest and gape at him. I literally hand him a lead, and he throws it aside? Sure, be mad about last night. Whatever. Arrest me. I don't even care. But don't throw out viable information because you don't like who it came from.

"Roane, please. You need to talk with this woman. I'm begging you."

He reaches forward, and for a second I think he's going to press play on my phone, listen to Meredith tell her story again, but I'm wrong. Instead, he throws it across the room. It hits the door and falls, clattering to the carpet with a hollow sound. "I'm the sheriff. I don't take orders from the prime suspect in a missing person case."

My shoulders deflate. "You're really not going to do anything about this?"

He folds his arms. "I'm not buying this smoke-screen bullshit. You were the last person to see her, and now you conveniently have all this evidence that points to her being on the coast with a strange man in a creepy van? Come the fuck on, kid. The most obvious answer is usually the right one. So you tell me, which sounds more plausible: That she got in a fight with her boyfriend and things went too far, or that she and her very specific jacket were abducted by a stranger who's treating her to lunch at a coastal diner?"

"Roane, I—"

"My team will sort through the tip line calls eventually, so if this turns out to be a genuine lead? We'll handle it. But I think this is a load of BS. Hell, the call from Waybrooke could have been your doing for all I know. You're trying to play it off like you're the concerned boyfriend, but *you* put her in harm's way in the first place."

All the fight leaves me. My head drops back until I'm staring at the ceiling. I don't know why I came here. Why did I think this would make him deviate from what he's already decided happened that night?

If Roane's in charge, Lola's as good as dead.

I grab my backpack and snatch my phone off the floor. I turn it over in my palm, this thing that holds the first hope I've had in weeks. "Someone has her, Roane, and if you don't look into this and she turns up dead, nobody will ever forgive you."

"Enough with the dramatics, Drew. We're not looking for some Ted Bundy wannabe. There's no bogeyman serial killer hanging out by the river. Things like that don't happen around here."

"Would you bet Lola's life on it?"

He falters, just for a second. I turn and march out of his office, but of course, he can't let me have the last word.

"Tell your parents to take a lot of family photos over the next few days, kid," he calls after me, as the stares of half a dozen police officers and Miss Savannah follow me out the door. "Might be the last time they see you outside a jail cell for a long, long time."

SEVENTEEN

MARY

DAY 5

I shuffle to bed and sit down beside my pillow. Annoyed with the colossal weight of the everything I don't know. I don't know why the woman with the red couch is taking up so much space in my head. I don't know why I have no memories of the blonde in Wayne's wallet photo. I don't know why I keep remembering the wrong details, or how to make it stop.

I need something to be clear, and overtly mine.

I run through my list again. Mary Ellen Boone. Seventeen. Good student. Senior. Lizzo. Strawberry allergy. Floral jackets. Dead mom, who's not a nurse and not a brunette. Bit of a homebody. Cinnamon rolls. Purple. Homeschooled. Good catch.

This is who I am. Right?

I dig my legs under the blankets and curl into a ball. The brown-haired woman floats through my mind like a mirage. I tug at her image, trying to make her appear in a movie I've seen, or arm in arm with the blonde woman, or in a neighborly conversation about a shared fence.

Anything that'll place her in my life, but nothing fits and her face leaves an ache in my chest.

A tear slips down the side of my face.

Sleep washes over me like a river, so fast I don't even remember closing my eyes.

I'm at the edge of a softball field, fidgeting in my uniform, anxious to take my turn. I flick my wrist and twirl the bat in my hand. I'm going to knock the crap out of a ball today, and I'm so excited for it. I stare at Kelly's back, still at the plate as she tips the third pitch and sends it skittering toward third base. She makes it to first with a breath to spare, and now it's time. I smile. I live for this shit. The pressure. The eyes on me. All three teammates tense on their bases, ready to run. They know what's coming.

I walk toward home plate, Coach clapping me on the shoulder as I pass, and look up into the bleachers. She's right there, in the front row, like she always is. Still in her work uniform, she tugs her hair up off her neck and winks at me. She knows what's about to happen too, and the pride is already there on her face.

I step up to home plate and the field fizzles away.

I'm in the car with Wayne on our way back from our trip to Waybrooke, fogging up the window in my Benadryl haze. The trees loom over the car, getting closer and closer every time I breathe, until they brush the top of the van. I sit up in alarm as the branches scrape the paint off the vehicle, clawing at the windows.

"What's going on?" I ask Wayne.

He smiles at me, and all his teeth are fangs. "Everything is okay."

The branches break through the glass. I disappear.

I'm sitting with a girl I know in an assembly. She props her feet beside mine on the bench in front of us. We're wearing identical sequin Converse, though hers are silver and mine are black. The gym bursts with sound, a thousand voices all screaming at the top of their lungs. A teacher brandishes a microphone in the middle of the gym, surrounded by students amped up on school spirit. Behind him, at the top of a huge set of bleachers is a long paper sign with Freshman painted in red. The juniors have a maroon one with white letters to the left, and the sophomores have a black and gold one on the right.

"I can't hear you, seniors!" he yells, looking up at our section.

My side of the gym erupts in screams.

The girl with the matching shoes laughs and says, "School spirit is dumb, but holy shit is it infectious."

I couldn't agree more.

The gym dissolves, replaced with a dimly lit kitchen.

I'm sitting at an island with metal stools. The woman with the brown hair beams at me and pushes a gold plastic plate across the counter. The lump on the plate looks vaguely like a cake, covered in fudge frosting. A set of black glitter "17" candles blaze on the top, but the whole thing tilts to one side like it's melting, and I laugh. She's never been a baker—or a cook of any kind, really—but she tries every birthday. No matter what's going on, or how much attitude I've thrown at her.

She starts singing happy birthday with a soft, breathy voice, but she changes some of the words. Like always. "Happy birthday to you, happy birthday to you, you're gorgeous and perfect, annnnnnnd I love you lots too!"

I blow out the candles and swipe a glob of frosting off the top. "You do know the actual song, right?"

She pretends to be offended, clutching her hand to her chest. "I've been singing it wrong since the day you were born, sweet thing. I'm not about to change it up now. I'm too old. Set in my ways."

I shove a chunk of chocolate cake into my mouth. "You're thirty-nine. You're not old. Now are you going to help me eat this monstrosity or not?"

"I thought you'd never ask." She brandishes a fork, unlike my rude ass, and scoops up a bite. "Happy birthday, baby girl."

The happy feeling in my chest spreads through my entire body, and I smile. "Love you, Mom."

As I say the words, the kitchen gets darker. Clouded. Plunged into grayscale.

The cake curls in on itself, molding, sprouting little black mushrooms and decay that spreads across the counter. It touches her hands, turning her skin to mold. She smiles, and her eyes sink back into her head.

"Where are you, baby girl?"

I scream and her head splits open, peeling away like a costume to reveal Wayne.

Staring.

Always staring.

I sit straight up in bed, gasping for air. My fists tangle in my comforter, and I almost rip the fabric, exposing the feathers. No matter how tightly I shut my eyes, she's still there. The woman from my dream.

I see her mixed into countless memories. Yelling at me for breaking curfew. Cheering at my softball games. Doing my hair for homecoming. Fighting with me about driving, or the two phones I lost in the same month. Trashing the kitchen and filling the house with the smell of burning butter and chicken before ordering Thai that we eat on the living room floor. I see my whole life with her, blurry at the edges as it connects with other people and places I can't quite reach yet, but *she* is clear as day. And the sight of her, so perfectly clear in my mind, brings tears to my eyes. Fat, hot tears that feel like they're coming from the deepest reaches of me.

Painful, persistent tears that are half grief, half fear. Because I now know two exceedingly significant things.

My mother is not dead.

And Wayne lied to me.

Why would he tell me she's dead if she's not? Who is the blonde from Wayne's photo? Why would he tell me she's my mother when he knows she isn't? I think of the joy on his face when I pretended to remember her. I told him I remembered a *lie*, and he reacted with *joy*. Why? Why does he want me to misremember my life?

And maybe the most concerning question of all: If he's lying about my mom, what else is he lying about?

I picture the assembly from my dream. Am I really homeschooled? Was that a freshman memory, and I simply imagined myself on the wrong side of the gym? Or am I actually an in-person high school senior, and Wayne doesn't want me to know?

Again, why would it matter if I went to public school or not?

A lightning bolt of an idea makes me stare wide-eyed at the Don't Worry poster. What if this is a custody situation? No other parent, homeschooled, renovations that require us to stay in the middle of nowhere—all of these details keep me away from other people. Did Wayne lose a court battle and…take me? Did he take me away from my mom?

And how the fuck does any of this relate to me waking up in a ditch? To losing my memory?

All the bad feelings from the last four-and-a-half days are like living breathing monsters, looming over me, whispering, "I told you so" and "you should have listened." A throbbing pain pulses through my temples. I don't know if it's from the tears or the panic or the adrenaline, but it hurts.

I sit up, swiping tears from my face, and force air in and out of my lungs. I fight against the panic, so I can sort this out. I need to focus on the facts. I start with the easiest one.

Fact: Wayne lied about my mom.

There's no sugarcoating it, no way around it. He straight-up lied. She's a nurse. He said she was a stay-at-home mom. Wrong career to go with the wrong face. He told me she was dead, and I can feel it in my bones that this isn't true. So why did he lie? So I wouldn't ask to see her?

Fact: He forgot about my strawberry allergy.

Simple mistake, except when I add in that he's also forgotten what his own wife looks like, which throws everything he's said into question. Is he a distant dad? Has he been out of the picture for a while? Did he snatch me to punish her and didn't know I'd developed an allergy in the interim?

Fact: He said I was a homeschooled homebody who hates leaving the house.

I think I'm an athlete. Not only that, I think I'm a damn competitive athlete who thrives on attention. I'm a lover of pep rallies and school spirit. The gaps in my memory are filling with school, friends, laughter, and fun. Not Netflix on the couch and classes at the kitchen table. Is homeschooling a cover for why I can't go back to a real school? So my mom can't find me?

Fact: He has documented proof of who I am.

He had my birth certificate. My Social Security card. My old ID. Photos from when I was little all the way to now. Losing custody might explain why all the photos of him and I together seem to be older, while the newer ones are just of me. But the rest holds up.

I drop my head to my hands. I'm guessing, and none of it is getting me closer to any real answers. Other images come to mind too. Wayne's panicked expression in the police station. The clean clothes on the back of the bathroom door that first night. The massive bag of first aid supplies he bought to make sure I had everything I needed to recover.

The patient way he let me shop, and the smile on his face as he ordered me that cinnamon roll. The teasing about my movie choices. Bringing me blankets. Running full speed to the pharmacy when he saw I was having another reaction. The love in his eyes every time he assured me that I'd get my memory back.

He hasn't raised his voice to me. Not once. In fact, he's been downright gentle, and he's given me every single thing I've asked for and then some. He's gone out of his way to make sure I'm comfortable. Worried too much at times, but worried nonetheless. Like a parent who cares.

I can't make the attentive father of the last few days fit with the kind of man who would kidnap me and pump my head full of lies. Good people don't kidnap teenagers—not even their own kids. So *what* is going on?

I squeeze my eyes shut, pressing the heels of my palms against them until my bruises protest. I'm being ridiculous. Honestly, what's more likely? That I'm a confused teenager with a concussion who's putting way too much stock into dreams…or that I've been kidnapped and I'm being spoon-fed fake memories by a sociopath? Everything he's said has added up, *except* for dreamed memories that contradict it all. Dreams that were half nightmares anyway. So who's to say any of it is real?

Besides, the paramedics were the ones who diagnosed my concussion. They were also the ones who suggested I might have been in a car accident. That didn't come from Wayne; he only corroborated it at the police station.

After everything Wayne's done for me, it feels incredibly unfair to let a few flashes of recognition derail everything this life of ours is made of. Am I really ready to accuse Wayne of horrible, unthinkable things simply because I'm confused?

I don't have an answer for that. I don't have an answer for any of it. I force myself to take a deep breath. The dreams are probably bullshit. I've been so eager to remember something that I'd probably label anything a memory. The fact that four days ago I was knocked so senseless I couldn't even remember my own name makes it harder to put faith in anything my brain supplies. I might wake up tomorrow and know exactly who that blonde woman is, and all of this might make a lot more sense.

The reality is that I'm struggling through a really hard week, and this memory-puzzle is proving to be more challenging than I thought. It doesn't mean the world is ending. And if it is…

I look up at the end table. Officer Bowman's business card shines in the moonlight.

I'm not alone.

Everything is okay. Everything is—

Heavy footfalls in the living room pull my attention to my door. It's almost four in the morning. Why is Wayne still awake?

The footsteps stop outside my room, and I slide under the blankets and cover my face with my comforter. The last thing I want is to hash all this out with the man at the center of the mess. If he is lying, talking won't help. And if he's not lying, this will hurt him more than anything. Which is the last thing I want.

I slow my breathing and close my eyes.

My door creaks open. The metal hinges whine until the doorknob taps on the wall. I try to ignore the anxiety these tiny sounds send down my spine. The room goes silent.

Another few heartbeats, and I hear soft *thump thumps* of heavy boots taking gentle steps.

The foot of the bed creaks beneath his weight as he sits down.

My veins are about to burst through the skin on my neck. What the hell is he doing?

He doesn't speak. He doesn't move. He just sits there in silence.

Is he watching me sleep? Does he know I'm awake? Why is he sitting on my bed in the middle of the night?

My pulse is too loud. I'm sure he can hear it. I don't breathe. I don't move. Panic grips me. He has the upper hand, and I don't know which Wayne is in this cabin with me—the attentive father or the kidnapper.

After an impossibly long moment, the bed creaks again. He stands with a sigh and leaves the room. My bedroom door clicks shut again, and after several long beats of silence, I peek around my comforter to make absolutely sure he's gone.

The room is empty.

I release all the air from my lungs and melt into the mattress.

What the actual fuck was that?

EIGHTEEN
MARY

DAY 5

I have no idea when I fall asleep again. One second I'm staring at the wall listening to the silence of the house and the occasional coyote call in the distance, and the next I'm flopped on my back, blinking at the weak bits of sunlight making their way through my window.

It's almost ten in the morning.

I sit up with a start and look outside. Thick clouds pepper the sky. There must be a storm coming in.

My gaze falls on the foot of the bed. Anxiety rockets through me, and I wrap my arms around myself. Last night was freaking strange. Creepy even. It felt…invasive? He didn't knock. He didn't give any indication that he knew I was awake, which means he…what? Came into my room to watch me sleep?

Has he been doing that every night we've been here?

Is he being strange because the accident freaked him out?

Either way, I don't like it.

Voices catch my attention from outside. I think they're coming from the driveway.

I grab for the thrift store bag, yanking the tags off the first outfit I get my hands on: A pair of black leggings and the long maroon plaid button-up. I throw that on over the black non-V-neck T-shirt I fell asleep in and listen at my door. The living room is silent on the other side, so I peek out. Wayne's not in here.

I shuffle toward the front door, stopping in my tracks when I spot Wayne and Officer Bowman through the window.

Bowman stands by his open cruiser door, smiling. Wayne's right beside him, holding a piece of paper. The front door is still open a crack, letting their voices through.

"I appreciate it, Mr. Boone. I really do. If you hear anything, or you happen to see him, please call the number on that flier immediately. His wife is understandably upset, and we're really hoping for a happy ending on this one."

Wayne tips the flier toward him with a nod. "Of course. I'm sorry I couldn't be more help. We haven't had a chance to unpack, much less meet any of the neighbors."

"I appreciate you taking the time to talk to me. Tell Mary I said hello, would you? I'll come by soon to check on her again. We probably need to have another talk about her car anyway. We haven't found any trace of it or the crash site. I'm hoping she's remembered more and can point us in a direction."

Wayne's hesitation is so short that I almost miss it. But it's there. Then he smiles and shakes the man's hand. "Sounds good to me. Have a great day."

"You too. We'll be in touch." Bowman gets back into his cruiser and pulls away.

I start to reach for the doorknob, to ask Wayne what's going on, but his face changes. His easy smile vanishes, and he glowers at the paper in his hands. He smashes it into a ball between his palms, and stomps toward the house, fury rolling off him.

I freeze. I don't know why, but I do. I don't think I've ever seen him so angry before. Not like this. And all because of a piece of paper?

I whirl around and race back to my room. My door clicks shut half a second before I hear the screen door open. Wayne clomps into the kitchen.

I don't realize how scared I am that he'll catch me snooping until I hear pans clatter and the *click click click* of the gas stove. A minute later, something lands in the pan and sizzles. The smell of fennel sausage makes its way under my door, and the familiarity of this makes my shoulders relax.

Everything is *fine*.

To prove it, I open the door and walk into the kitchen like nothing is wrong. Like he didn't watch me sleep last night. Like I don't care if he did.

Wayne smiles at me. A bright, open, happy smile, with absolutely no trace of the anger from outside. "Well, good morning, sunshine. I thought I'd have to hold breakfast under your nose to get you out of bed."

I blink at him for a second, shaken by the about-face of his emotions, but I sit at the island and force myself to smile back. "Yeah, sorry about that. I had a hard time falling asleep. I didn't mean to sleep so late."

He waves the spatula at me. "Don't worry about it. It's been a long few days. A little extra sleep isn't the worst thing in the world. We won't make a habit of being lazy once you're recovered. To be idle is a short road to death, after all."

Whoa, *what*? I stare at him and he winks at me over his shoulder. Oh. Was that a joke? Everything about my life seems to be idle, so he can hardly judge me for sleeping in when there's nothing else to do in this godforsaken cabin.

"I'm making more of those sausages you love," he says, when I don't respond.

I try to smile again. "I know. I smelled them from my room."

He turns back to the stove, and my eyes drift to the door. Or, more specifically, the empty driveway beyond it. My foot bounces on the little rung of the stool. "Um…did I hear someone in the driveway a little bit ago?" I ask. Slowly, carefully.

I know I'm testing him, but it feels weirdly important that he not know what I saw. If he says it was Bowman, shows me the flier, and tells me what's up, I have nothing at all to worry about. I can stop overreacting and—

"Oh, that?" he says, flipping a sausage patty. "It was some minivan mom trying to sell cookie dough for a school fundraiser. I told her we didn't need any, since we'll be getting out of here soon."

The lie hits like a sledgehammer. He turns and smiles at me as he lies to my face. I work to keep the smile on mine while every molecule in my body is sounding an alarm.

Why is he lying? Why doesn't he want me to know about Bowman's visit?

I wish I walked outside. I wish Officer Bowman saw me and we got to talking. I wish I hadn't listened at the door and let him drive away.

I must've spaced out because he sets a full plate of sausage and scrambled eggs and a fork in front of me. I blink at the eggs for a second, hearing his panicked voice drift back to me from three days ago. *"I made breakfast on autopilot. The eggs were for me—it never even crossed my mind that you wouldn't remember you can't eat them..."*

I stab at a sausage, all the thoughts in my mind spinning together like a tornado of worry until my fork scrapes the plate. I've inhaled everything.

Wayne stands on the other side of the island and raises an eyebrow. "Hungry?"

"Yeah. I guess I was."

He takes my plate without finishing his own breakfast and sets it in the sink along with the sausage pan. He doesn't touch his food when he comes back to the island. "So I have some pretty fantastic news."

You're going to tell me the truth for once? "Yeah?"

"I got a call from the contractor this morning. He says they'll be done with the floors by this afternoon. They're just cleaning up, but it'll look like they were never there by about lunchtime."

I stare at him.

He must read the confusion on my face because he leans forward. "We can go home."

A wave of fear nearly knocks me off my stool. The floors brought us to the cabin in the first place. And now the floors are done. Which means he wants to leave...

The moment I've been waiting for has arrived. I get to leave this isolated hellhole and be around people. My real house. Places that might do more for my memory than this cabin. I should be happy, but all I feel is a crushing panic.

What if we're headed to another kind of isolation? I'm homeschooled, so I might not see another soul for a long time. At least here, Officer Bowman knows where to find me. Nobody I remember will know where I am once he takes me home.

Unless Wayne allows it.

The tips of my fingers go cold. I'm acutely aware of his eyes on my face, so I grin. Like the happy, complacent daughter he expects me to be. Mary would be excited to go home. "That's amazing news."

He smiles too. "I knew you'd be excited. We can pack up and head out in a little bit. Might beat some of the afternoon traffic if we can hit the road by eleven."

That's in less than an hour.

I hold onto my smile, but inside I'm hearing Officer Bowman promise to come back and check on me. Wayne smiling and agreeing. Like we'd be here. He didn't take a call between the driveway and the house, so it's not like the contractors called him on the porch and gave him the news. He had to know that we were leaving soon, but he didn't say anything to Officer Bowman.

Also, how did they replace a whole house full of floors and kitchen cabinets in five days?

Something's happening here. I don't know what it is, but I don't like it one bit.

"Mary? What do you say? Want to head out?"

No.

"Sure, yeah. That sounds good to me." I claw my way out of my own head, so I can pretend I'm not drowning in bad vibes.

Everything is fine.

Everything is fine.

We're heading home. It's fine.

He clears the rest of his dishes from the counter, polishing off his coffee before setting the mug in the sink. "Why don't you get your things from your room ready to go, and we'll hit the road? I'll grab you a box as soon as I'm done with the dishes."

I nod and as I get up from the island, my gaze falls on the basket beside the fireplace, where all the burnable materials from the last few days have accumulated. Frozen sausage boxes. Paper towel rolls. An egg carton. Various other cardboard food boxes.

And on top—a crumpled piece of white paper.

I spin back around. "Actually, with all the packing and prep to go home, you've got enough on your plate today. Let me do the dishes."

He tips his head to the side. "That's very thoughtful of you, Mary. Thank you."

I take his place at the sink, and he heads straight for the front door. "I'll get a box for you. Shouldn't take too long to load up. We packed light thanks to your little detour."

He winks. I try not to flinch.

The second I hear the crunching of gravel under his boots, I race over to the burn pile and snatch up the piece of paper. I need to know what made him so livid, because it sure as hell has nothing to do with minivans or fundraisers. I tuck it into my bra and run back to the sink, washing everything as fast as I can. Wayne reappears as I'm rinsing off the sausage pan and holds a microwave-sized box out to me. "This should be perfect. You don't have much."

I dry my hands and take it straight to my room with a mumbled thank you, but my mind is on the scratchy paper pressing against my chest. The mystery of Officer Bowman's visit literally itching at me. I drop the box on the bed, dump all my Nana's purchases into it, and then I listen. I hear him sliding something around in his room. Hangers in the closet, maybe? I kick my door halfway closed, hiding the paper behind the box as I smooth it flat on my blanket.

Ben Hooper's kind, neighborly face stares back at me, under big red letters.

MISSING.

It's a "Have you seen me?" type flier for the old man next door. Name. Date of birth. Height, weight, eye color. And the last time he was seen. On an afternoon walk. Two days ago.

My breath comes too fast. Hissing in and out of my lungs.

I see Bowman in the driveway, asking Wayne to call if he happens to see *him.*

He was talking about our neighbor.

Breath. Breath. Breath. Breath.

I hear Wayne apologizing for not being any help. Because we haven't had a chance to unpack, much less meet any of the neighbors.

Breath. Breath. Breath. Breath.

I see Ben's face, smiling in the driveway as he stares at me. *You know, something about you looks so familiar. I can't put my finger on it.*

Breath. Breath. Breath. Breath. Breath. Breath.

Wayne saying, *She has one of those faces.*

And then I can't breathe at all.

A sweet old man meets us by the side of the road, looks at me like he's trying to place me, and then vanishes before he ever makes it home? The flier said he went missing on his afternoon walk, not later that night. During. Which means he disappeared between talking with us and returning to his house next door.

Once again, Wayne lied. And immediately made plans to leave…

I really shouldn't have let Bowman leave. I automatically turn to my nightstand, looking for his business card. It's gone.

Maybe everything *isn't* okay.

Maybe it never was.

NINETEEN

DREW

The doors to the precinct shut behind me with the finality of a gavel. I look over my shoulder and Sheriff Roane is glowering at me through the glass. I give him the finger and stomp off.

How could he do this to Lola? How could he put her in danger like this? Who the fuck cares what I stole if the evidence proves she is alive? Not to mention, if she was in Waybrooke twenty-four hours ago and I was here, wouldn't that clear my name? Roane said I'm his last suspect, but wouldn't this recording prove that's not true?

Hell, the call from Waybrooke could have been your doing for all I know.

I run my hand down my face. That's how he can ignore it so easily. Roane never wanted to investigate a serious crime; he wanted to find a runaway, and when that didn't work out, he went straight to "lock up the boyfriend." This recording doesn't fit his narrative.

Which means by the time anyone follows up, it'll be too late. I can't let this happen.

I stop at the corner to smooth out my flier and check my phone. It's almost one. Max will be leaving school soon to pick me up, but I can't think of a next step with the weight of failure pressing down on me.

I can't believe how stupid I am. I *had* him before I slipped up about the recording. Maybe I should have anonymously dropped the USB into the station mailbox. Maybe then they would've sprang into action. Or maybe I should have given it to Autumn. Maybe he would have believed it if the information came from her. I turn and kick the stop sign.

Screw him, if Roane won't follow up, someone else should. Maybe three someones.

I set off down the sidewalk with newfound determination. I jog the last five blocks until the school pops into view. I spot Max coming out of the building as I reach the parking lot. The fluorescent yellow of his T-shirt is impossible to miss. His head is down, phone in hand. I slow to a walk so I can grab my phone from my pocket and sure enough, a text comes through.

Max: Hey man. I'm on my way.
Me: Look up.

Max squints at his screen for half a second before he spots me. He throws up his hands. "How'd you get here?" he yells over the cars between us.

I ignore his question and meet him by the hood of the Liberty, my breathing heavy. "Where's Autumn? I found something."

Max doesn't ask any questions, just wheels back around and speed walks toward the school doors. "Maybe still in the cafeteria," he says over his shoulder.

So that's where we go. The halls are packed with kids. I feel their eyes on me. Glares. Double takes. People I've partnered with on lab projects, former teammates, members of our old friend groups, all stop to stare at me as I walk by. Today, it's easier to ignore. Today, I'm going to find Lola, and everything will go back to normal.

We pass long stretches of blue lockers and open classroom doors as we make our way to the other side of the school. We reach the double doors of the cafeteria. Two huge windows sit beside each door. Max stops in front of the first and presses his nose to the checkered safety glass.

"I think I see her in the back," he says.

Sure enough, Autumn's fluff of red hair catches my eye. She's wearing an oversized white sweater and doesn't look like she got much sleep.

She gathers her trash and chucks it into the garbage behind her before wading into the mass of kids leaving for their next class. When she's about twenty feet from the door, she spots us and her eyebrows shoot up. She tugs a wireless headphone from her ear, and I wonder if she was listening to more recordings.

When she's through the doors, I press a finger to my lips and jerk my head toward the hallway behind us. This isn't the place to talk about anything we want to keep to ourselves. We duck into the first empty classroom we can find, and it happens to be the History 12 room. Mr. Moore must be on lunch this hour.

My eyes go straight for Lola's empty desk again.

"What's going on?" Autumn asks, half talking, half whispering.

I smooth the crumpled flier across one of the student desks in the front row and place my phone on top of it. "I found a witness."

They blink at me and Max's mouth falls open. I press play on Meredith Hoyt's recording. They both step closer, almost in sync, when she mentions the jacket.

When it ends, I tap my flier. "A girl matching Lola's description exactly—short brown hair, green eyes, floral jacket—was seen at a diner yesterday."

Max scrubs his face with his hands. "Holy shit, Drew. I mean... It's been a long time and I started to think..."

She was dead. I meet his gaze and he looks away, like he's ashamed to have thought it at all. "I think everyone did," I say, letting him off the hook.

Autumn hasn't taken her eyes off Lola's picture. She looks terrified. "What does this mean? Like...she's with some old man? Why? Is she in danger?"

My stomach churns, thinking someone is holding her against her will. "Lola wouldn't just take off without her phone, without telling anyone."

"So what now? We take this to my dad, right?" she says, pulling her thick hair into a ponytail with the elastic on her wrist.

An angry twitch runs through my jaw. "No, I already went to the station. He didn't want to hear anything about it. He threw me out the second he realized I stole the recordings. He thinks I'm making it all up, trying to cover my ass."

"The fuck?" Max yells, then looks behind him at the now-empty hallway and lowers his voice. "Why would you do that? Handing him information you stole from his office only brings you more trouble."

I shrug. "He doesn't want this to be a bigger crime. He actually said, '*We're not looking for Ted Bundy*' or some shit."

"Someone at the station is bound to listen to the tapes soon though, right?" Max asks. "They have their own copy. They'll hear this and go after her, right?"

I look at Autumn. The bleak look in her eyes matches the feeling in my chest. We both look away.

"It might be too late by then," I say. "We have no idea who this guy is, what he's doing with her, or how long he'll stay in the area. I mean, it's a miracle she's still in Oregon after all this time, but that doesn't mean they'll stay put. Especially if he thinks someone spotted her. And if the sheriff arrests me, nobody's going to listen to those recordings."

"Shit," Max says. "So what do we do? Call your lawyer? Call the media? Go above the sheriff's head? I mean, what choice do we have now? And what the fuck is wrong with Roane?"

"He doesn't want a mess. A tragic turn to a teen romance is easier to handle than an abduction."

"Except that's what happened," Max says, fuming. He scowls at nothing and everything at the same time. "It's bullshit. It's leaving Lola vulnerable all because he's…what? Too lazy to do his job? Fuck that guy."

Autumn flinches and takes a step back from the desk.

I reach out for her. "I'm sorry. I know he's your dad and—"

She holds up a hand. "Don't. You shouldn't apologize. I can't believe he's not doing everything he can to find Lola. He's known her since she was a baby. Hell, he went to this school with Mrs. Scott. Hearing that his friend's daughter, *my* best friend, is off with some stranger should have him driving to Waybrooke himself. There's a potential eyewitness on this tape, and that's more substantial than anything he has on you. Even if he thinks it's fake, he should still make sure."

"Which is why we need to go to Waybrooke," I say.

"*What?*" they say at the same time.

I turn to Autumn. "If your dad isn't going to drive to Waybrooke, we need to. We know Lola's with an older guy in a gray van. We know she went to this diner. Let's go and see if anyone else saw them leave together. If we gather information, eventually we'll have so much evidence the police can't brush us aside anymore."

"Now we're talking," Max says, clapping me on the shoulder. "Force his hand."

"We could leave now. Be there in a few hours," I say.

"I'll drive."

Autumn wrings her hands in front of her, looking at the photo of Lola again. She doesn't say a word.

"What?"

"How are we supposed to do anything like that ourselves? Why would anyone talk to us? And what about school? We can't leave in the middle of the day. We'll get in trouble. I'm already late for class. And who's to say that was even her? A lot of people have jean jackets…"

She must see the disbelief on my face because she trails off. I don't know if she's trying to talk her way out of going, or if the idea of Lola being kidnapped by some stranger has her so freaked she wants to go home and hide with her vegan pepperoni, but we don't have time for this.

"I might have a lead on your best friend's disappearance and you're worried about your attendance record? How many of these floral, rose gold jackets have you made for people, Autumn?" I ask, jabbing my finger at the flier. "If you don't want to come, then don't. You're not obligated to. I'll do it with or without you. But don't sit here and tell me this isn't a lead because you're too scared to follow it."

For a brief second she looks ready to fight me. I don't know if it's because I basically called her a coward or if she hates being in the wrong, but either way I'm out of the classroom and headed for the parking lot before she gets her thoughts together enough to respond.

Max's long legs catch up to me before I reach the end of the hallway. "For the record, there's no fear on my end. I'll punch Ted Bundy in the face if I have to."

I push at my headache again. "Don't start, Max. We're not hunting down a serial killer, we're gathering information until we can force the cops to take over for us. That's it. There'll be no punching."

"Ugh, fine. What about Roane? He's going to be pissed when you leave town, right?"

"Probably, but with any luck we'll get to Waybrooke and back before anyone figures out we left," I say.

I check my watch as we push our way through the doors and into the parking lot. It's almost 1:30. It feels like days since I've slept.

Max unlocks the Liberty and jumps into the driver's seat, starting the car. Remnants of a Post Malone song blast from the speakers, and he fumbles with the radio to turn it down as I climb in. "My bad," he says.

"Hold on, you sanctimonious asshole!"

Autumn sprints toward us, flushed and angry. I fold my arms and lean back in my seat.

She stops a few feet away. "I'm coming too."

I narrow my eyes at her. "What about school? You'll ruin your picture-perfect attendance if you take off in the middle of the day. The horror."

"Oh shut up. I was clearly freaking out. You don't have to be a dick about it."

Yeah. Probably didn't.

I shrug. "Fine. But you can't bail after we leave. You have to be one hundred percent in, or stay here. If we have any chance of figuring out where Lola is, we don't have time to freak out or backtrack. Deal?"

I hold out my hand.

Autumn grips my hand, hard, and shakes it. "Deal. Let's go find Lola."

Max leans over from the driver's seat. "Get in, losers, we're going sleuthing."

I roll my eyes.

"No, for real," he says, gesturing toward the school. "Get in. The security guard's coming."

We whip around and sure enough, the school's security guard is walking toward the parking lot, shaking his head.

I shut my door, Autumn piles into the back, buckling herself into the middle seat again, and Max backs out of his parking spot. I look out the back window and see the guard disappear back into the school. Maybe he doesn't care enough to report our ditching to the office staff, but considering my track record lately…that's unlikely.

"Our phones are going to start blowing up if he tells the front office we left campus," I mumble, turning mine to silent so I can more easily ignore it.

Autumn props her foot up on the center console to tie her shoelace. "Who cares. We have more important things to worry about. Like what the heck we're supposed to do now."

Max turns onto Main Street, and we all eye the police station as we pass it on our way to the highway. "What do you mean?"

She drops her foot and leans into the space between the two front seats. "What do we do once we get to Waybrooke? Do we go to the diner and ask around? What if nobody remembers Lola? What then?"

I don't have an answer to any of these questions, and Max's focus on the road tells me he doesn't have a clue either.

"What's the plan, specifically?" she continues. "Because if we march into town and we don't have a clue what we're doing—"

Frustration curls my hand into a fist. "I don't know! Okay? I've been formulating this scheme for a half hour. I just want to get to where she was last seen. I don't know what to do beyond that. Maybe the person who waited on them will be working today and we can go from there."

Autumn snorts from the backseat. "That's not a plan."

"I don't see you coming up with anything better."

Her hand flashes open between the two seats. "Fine, give me your phone."

I side-eye her. "Why?"

"You want a better plan? Give me your damn phone."

I roll my eyes, but hand it over.

Autumn balances it on one knee and presses play on the tip-line recording as she rummages through the mess in Max's backseat. She sits up with a scrap piece of paper and a marker, and smooths it out on her other knee. Looks like a discarded Spanish test. Autumn scribbles down Meredith Hoyt's contact information from the end of the recording, and she hands my phone back.

"What are you doing back there?" Max asks, peeking at her in the rearview mirror.

"Shhh," she says, holding up a finger. She grabs her phone, blocks her number with star six-seven, and then dials the woman. "Calls from the police department always come through as No Caller ID."

Holy shit. She's calling Tip Line Meredith? Pretending to be a cop? This is a very bad idea.

"Can she do that?" Max whispers.

"We're going to get arrested for impersonating a police officer," I mumble, covering my face.

In the silence of the car, I hear it the second the woman answers the phone.

"Hello?"

Autumn clears her throat, and says, "Hello, Mrs. Hoyt? This is Savannah Bateman from the Washington City police department," in a flawless impersonation of the sheriff's secretary.

Max gapes at me.

"Washington City?" the woman says.

"Yes, ma'am. I'm reaching out concerning the tip you phoned in about the disappearance of Lola Scott. Our officers went through yesterday's recordings, and we believe your tip may be of great importance. We have an officer headed out to Waybrooke this evening. Would you be willing to sit with them and give an official statement?"

Silence.

Autumn shifts in her seat. "Mrs. Hoyt? Are you there?"

"I...yes. Was that really her? At the diner?"

"We believe so. Would you be willing to give a statement?"

More silence. I suppose I could do that. "When will your officer be in town?"

Autumn snaps her fingers at me. I grab my phone and quickly type Waybrooke into the GPS again. I show her the screen with a 4:30 arrival.

"Probably around five o'clock, give or take with traffic," she says. "They're on the road as we speak."

"That works," Meredith says. "Where am I meeting them?"

"How about the diner, so you can walk us through what you saw?"

"I'll be there."

The line goes dead and Autumn beams at me. "Done."

I shake my head, incredulous. "I can't believe that worked. Where in the *hell* did that southern accent come from?"

"You pick it up when you hear someone talk enough. Do you know how many afternoons I've spent in that office doing homework?"

Max barks out a laugh. "You're amazing."

The heat from Autumn's blush fills the car as she looks away. Max too, looks away, hyperfocused on the completely empty highway ahead.

I clear my throat, super uncomfortable in the midst of whatever the hell that was, and steer the conversation back to the mission at hand. "So what happens when Meredith gets to the diner and meets a bunch of teenagers, not a uniformed officer?"

Autumn says, "Hell if I know. But getting the witness to come to us seemed like a much better idea than wandering around asking if anyone saw a girl with her fake dad."

Yeah, fine. I guess the worst Meredith can do is refuse to talk to us. "Step on it, Max."

He gives me a mock salute and presses on the gas. "Aye, aye, captain."

We rocket down the highway toward the coast, each mile feeling like it's finally bringing me closer to Lola.

TWENTY
DREW

I spin a red plastic saltshaker on the table in front of me. This place smells like cinnamon rolls, with a side of red, black, and white nostalgia. I want to break it all with my bare hands. I look up at the clock on the wall again and scowl. 5:42.

Meredith Hoyt is almost forty-five minutes late.

Max sits beside me, practically lying on the wide window at the end of the booth, and Autumn taps a thumb against the fake marble table in front of us at a frantic tempo. A stack of plastic menus sits untouched by her hand, and I see the waitress giving us the evil eye again from the hostess station. She's come by at least a dozen times asking if we want anything, and I keep shooing her away, saying we're waiting for someone. I'm pretty sure she thinks we're lying or about to rob the place. She bats her gigantic eyelashes at us and wipes the nearly empty front counter. We're one of only three occupied tables.

The saltshaker tips over, spilling the little crystals all over the menus, and I swipe it on the floor before the waitress sees the mess and sets me on fire with her eyes.

I shove the shaker back toward the center of the table and grip my hands on my lap. Where is she?

The front door dings, and we all turn. Again. Like we have every other time someone's come into this diner.

A woman stands on the threshold. She's short and thin, dirty-blonde hair filled with streaky highlights. She's about Lola's mom's age. Nobody's with her. She scans the booths with a nervous energy.

Bingo.

I tell the others to wait and slide out of the booth. When she sees me walking her way, she barely glances at me.

"Meredith Hoyt?" I ask.

She freezes and narrows a set of dark eyes at me. "Yes?"

I'm suddenly filled with gratitude that she was so late, otherwise I might not have had a clue what to say. The words come easily now that I'm sure of them.

"I know we're not who you were expecting. My name is Drew, and me and my friends called you about Lola. We think you might be the key to finding her. If you'll give us a minute of your time, I'll explain everything." I gesture to the table where Autumn and Max are waiting.

She looks over at them and then folds her arms.

"I'm really sorry for tricking you into coming here," I add. "We didn't think you'd agree to meet with us if we told you the truth, and this could be a life or death situation."

I let that linger, hoping that she'll be curious enough to ask me about it.

"Life or death?" she asks with an arched eyebrow. Like she's annoyed at her own curiosity. And us. Mostly us.

"We're collecting information about Lola's disappearance for the police," I explain. "Sort of like a...neighborhood watch. We've been hanging missing person's fliers, making calls, and trying to track down any leads to help the police find her."

"Do you know the missing girl?" She shifts on her feet. She hasn't bolted yet, so that has to be a good sign. "Is she your friend or something?"

"Yeah, we know her," I say, carefully sidestepping having to admit that Lola's just my friend, if she's even that anymore. "We all grew up with Lola. Autumn's dad is the Washington City sheriff, and she and Lola have been best friends for—"

Meredith's gaze narrows again. "Wait. She's the *sheriff's* daughter? Why is she here instead of her father?"

Great fucking question. Would it be appropriate to call the sheriff a prick in front of a total stranger? Probably not if I want to sound even remotely credible.

"It's a really long story, and we'll absolutely tell you everything, if you could sit down with us for a minute. Please? You can leave at any time. We won't hold it against you. A lot has been going on in the search for Lola, and we're trying to piece it all together to help the investigation. Your story is part of that."

She unfolds her arms and glances at the door. But I can practically see the curiosity burning on her face.

Finally, she says, "Five minutes. But I'm not happy about this."

"I wouldn't be either," I tell her, truthfully, and lead the way to the table.

She settles herself on the edge of the bench seat beside Autumn, and I slide back in next to Max. Almost as soon as we're seated, the waitress walks back to our table. She gives a genuine smile to Meredith, but side-eyes the rest of us. "Hello, Meredith. You're the one these three have been waiting on? So happy you've come in."

Meredith smiles at her. "Hi, Sandra. How are you?"

"No complaints." She looks around the table, eyeing me specifically, though I have no idea what I've done to annoy her more than the others. "Can I take your drink orders *now*?"

I order a coffee for myself and offer to pay for Meredith's too. She smiles a thank you. Autumn waves her off, happy with water, and Max studies his menu like he's making a huge life decision. "Can I get a few of those giant cinnamon rolls?"

Sandra frowns. "We only have those in the morning."

"Why is it on the all-day part of the menu then?" he asks, jabbing a finger at a photo that takes up almost half the page. She glares at him, and I wrestle the menu from his hands. "Fine, fine," he says. "I'll have the platter of fries."

Sandra writes it down, takes the menus from me, and leaves the table in a wave of annoyance.

One that I understand completely. "A *platter* of fries?"

He shrugs. "What? I'll share. We skipped lunch, remember? I'm starving."

Autumn rolls her eyes. Sandra is back in record time with our coffees, then she takes off again for the kitchen. Meredith wraps her hands around the red mug in front of her and stares at the coffee like it'll explain why she decided to sit down with us.

"I don't have all day," she says, looking around at us, apparently ignoring the fact that we'd have three quarters of an hour longer if she'd shown up on time. Her gaze lingers on Autumn, and her expression turns sad and thoughtful. "Was that missing girl really your best friend?"

My entire train of thought catches on the *was*. She *was* her best friend. This little piece of past tense shoots a pain through my chest.

Autumn seems surprised, like she didn't expect me to have covered that already, but she smiles at Meredith. "Yeah. I've known Lola since we were little."

Meredith turns her coffee mug on the fake marble tabletop. "What about you? How did you know the girl?" she asks me.

I mentally correct her past tense again—how *do* I know the girl—and then wonder why she insists on calling her "the girl" instead of using her name. "She's my girlfriend," I finally say.

Autumn clears her throat, and for a second, I think she's going to contradict me, but she doesn't.

Meredith's eyes soften with pity, and I hate it. But this is important. "We're trying to build a timeline," I say. "We know she was in this diner, but anything else you can share about what you saw will help us figure out where to go next."

"I'm sorry. I still don't understand why *you're* doing this." She turns to Autumn. "What kind of neighborhood watch looks into a missing girl? Why isn't your father sitting here? Why didn't he follow up on the tip?"

I want to answer for her, but Meredith's attention is fully on Autumn. Telling her *I'm* the prime suspect will end this. Meredith and the lead she holds will go up in smoke if she hears the truth.

Autumn smiles sadly. "My dad is, unfortunately, on the wrong track. He thinks someone from back home is involved in Lola's disappearance, and he won't consider any other theories. He's too stubborn, and we didn't want Lola to pay the price for it. We thought if we came here and got the information ourselves, it might make him pay attention."

"Who does he think is involved?"

"Someone convenient. It's an easy story for him to spin, so he wants it to be true. We need to know what really happened. And you can help, right? You're sure you saw her?"

By the end of her sentence, Autumn's voice is so full of hope that it's dragging her forward. She leans toward Meredith like she holds the key to the universe.

Meredith's eyes shine. "I think I did, yes."

The waitress leaves a massive platter of fries on our table, and Max slides them over to himself. "Can you tell us about it?" he asks, then shoves about nine in his mouth at once.

Meredith looks at him like she forgot he was sitting there, but to be fair, he's basically scrunched himself into the corner. She nods. "I'd like to help, but I don't know if I have much more to share. Besides, what I already called in, I mean."

I cross my arms on the table. "Can you start at the beginning and go through the whole experience? You might know more than you think you do."

"Okay. Well, I had the afternoon off, so I came to eat lunch with a friend of mine. I was running a bit late and hurrying toward the door, and I saw her in the parking lot."

Autumn points out the window. "Where were they? What spot?"

"Um, that one. The one by the entrance," she says, with a wave. She gestures to an unoccupied spot beside Max's car.

The thought pins me to my seat. Lola was right there, yesterday.

"She was standing outside the passenger door of the van," Meredith says, holding her coffee with both hands again. "I wouldn't have noticed her except that she was *really* scratching at her neck. She looked dazed, and I thought she was on drugs for a second, but then I realized she was covered in hives. Her dad ran—"

"That's not her dad," Autumn, Max, and I all say at the same time.

She looks between us. "Okay…*the man* she was with came running from the drug store and gave her some Benadryl, I think. He seemed really upset that she wasn't feeling well and helped her into the van. When he saw me watching, he got in and drove off pretty quickly."

"And you just let them leave? Why didn't you call the cops right away if you knew who she was?" I ask. Desperation seeps into my voice and makes me sound angrier than I intend to. She bristles and I put up my hands in apology. "I'm sorry. I'm not upset with you. I'm trying to understand."

Meredith narrows her eyes at me and takes a sip of coffee. "I would have called the cops sooner, but I didn't know it was her. Not for sure. I saw a girl in distress and watched to make sure she was okay. There was something familiar about her face, but I couldn't place where I knew her from. I didn't put it together until she smiled at me as the van pulled away. She's smiling in all the photos on TV. That's when I knew it was her."

"What happened next?" I ask, too loud. Too intense. Again. I force myself to sit back and I shove my hands beneath my legs. "Where did they go?"

She takes another long drink of her coffee, finishing it off, and points up the road. "They headed in that direction. Through town, then they turned north, up the coast."

"Are you positive?" Autumn asks.

"Absolutely. They went north. That's all I know."

Silence fills the booth. Autumn stares out the window in the direction Meredith described. Max eats another handful of fries.

This isn't enough. We can't take the highway north, blindly looking for a van. There're hundreds of little towns and roads that branch off that highway. She could be anywhere north of here, and since we're about halfway down the state, that's a lot of road to cover before we even hit Washington. Or they might have headed north long enough to get to a gas station, then doubled back to Mexico.

"North" isn't a lead.

"Is there anything else you can tell us about the van?" I ask. "Any stickers, or a parking pass? Did it have Oregon plates? Was there anything inside? Anything that might help identify it?"

Meredith pauses, staring into her now-empty cup. Her eyebrows pinch together while she thinks. "I don't remember any stickers. I think it had Oregon plates, but I honestly can't remember. I only remember the girl. I can't stop seeing her face."

"Is there *anything* else?" Autumn presses, and the desperate look on her face tells me she's feeling the weight of this potential dead end as much as I am. "Anything at all?"

Her face lights up. "Oh, actually, yes. They'd been to Nana's."

"Huh?" we all say at once.

"Nana's. Nana's Favorites. It's a thrift store up the road. Real gem of a place. You can always tell when someone's been to Nana's because she has these bright pink shopping bags with her logo on the side. There was a Nana's bag in the van with Lola. They must have gone there before they came to the diner. Maybe you could add that to your timeline?"

Autumn and I exchange a glance, and she grins. "Yeah, that'll work," she says.

The waitress comes by and asks Meredith if she wants a refill on her coffee, but she holds her palm over the cup and shakes her head. "No thank you. I should get going."

The waitress leaves for another table, and Meredith gives us a sad smile. "I'm sorry. I wish I had more answers for you. I wish I'd thought to follow them or something... I thought it was her, but honestly, until you all showed up here, I wasn't sure."

"You helped a lot. Thank you," I tell her with a smile. "This is the best lead we've had since Lola went missing."

She slides out of the booth but hesitates at the end of the table. "You're all clearly invested in finding your friend if you drove all the way out here. I don't want to hear about the three of you going missing next, so don't be foolish, okay? Take this information to the professionals, then let them deal with it."

We mutter a blanket, "Yes, ma'am." She gives us each a poignant look before clutching her purse to her chest and walking out of the diner.

Max flicks a French fry across the table. "Bummer, huh? That didn't help at all."

Autumn throws the French fry back at him, and it bounces off his chest. "Hey, dummy, were you even listening? She just told us someone else in this town could have seen Lola. How is that not helpful?"

Max throws the same fry back at her, and it gets stuck in her hair. "Do you always have to be so smart about everything?"

I slap the fry out of Autumn's hand before she can throw it again. "Hey, this waitress already hates us. Let's not get kicked out of here. We're in enough trouble already."

They both fold their arms and frown at me, but they stop.

204 | MEGAN LALLY

"We absolutely have to go to that store, but we need something here first."

"More fries?" Max asks with a grin. There's nothing left on the platter.

"More proof. We have to collect every nugget of information so that we can bring it all to Roane and drown him in evidence. We can't do that if all we have is an anecdote from a lady at a diner. We need tangible evidence or we're crafting a story, not a timeline."

Autumn nods, looking down at her phone screen. "You're right. We need to *prove* Lola was here before we leave, but the thrift store closes at six thirty."

Shit. That's soon.

I look around the diner. "Do they have cameras in here?"

"Up there," Autumn says, pointing over my left shoulder. I turn in my seat and spot a tiny black camera mounted above the hallway to the bathroom. "How are you going to get to the footage?"

"Charm?"

Max laughs in my face. "Yeah okay. Good luck with that. I gotta pee."

He jumps straight over my lap and lands on the linoleum like a goddamned gymnast. Grumpy Sandra watches him from the hostess station and gives him a glare that would have withered anyone who gave a fuck. Max disappears down the hallway, and she strides over to me and Autumn, ripping a piece of paper off her little order pad. She slaps it on the table.

"You ready for your check?" she asks.

Like we have a choice.

I pull out my wallet. I don't have that much money on me after that last batch of fliers, but I have enough to cover the bill and a good tip. I put my cash on the table, hoping to soften her mood. Autumn throws a five on top too, catching my eye like she had the same idea. Sandra takes it all to the register without saying a word.

When she returns with the change, I give her my best smile. "The rest is for you."

She looks down at what's left in her hand and frowns like this makes her happy, but she's not thrilled about it. "Thank you."

"No, thank you," I say, standing. "I wondered if you might help us with something?"

She crosses her arms. "What?"

"Did you see a girl in here yesterday? Around lunchtime? About our age, green eyes, freckles, short dark brown hair." I hold my hand to the bottom of my chin for length reference. She might have been here with an older man. "Left in a hurry?"

"What's it to you?" Sandra asks.

Something about the way she holds herself feels protective. Like she knows who I'm talking about and doesn't want to speak about her to strangers, which is both exciting and frustrating. Of course Lola would charm the waitress.

"She's missing, and we're trying to find her," Autumn says. "We were wondering if you had any footage of her on the security system?"

Sandra glances at the camera, then glares at us. "I don't know what you kids are up to, but I've had bad vibes from you since you walked in. I'm not telling you anything about her, or her dad—"

"That's not her dad!" we both say again, exasperated.

"I'm not getting involved. If she's really missing, then the police can get a warrant for the footage, but I'm not handing anything over to a bunch of random kids. You need to go."

"Please," Autumn says, in her softest, most Disney-princess voice. "She may be—"

Sandra shakes her head and stops Autumn mid-word. "Nope, I'm not doing this with you. Get out. I'm not messing around."

Fuck.

I wish her a good day, and Autumn thanks her, but I don't know what for. Sandra hasn't been helpful or pleasant. Bad vibes? If she was going to get bad vibes about anyone, maybe it should have been the kidnapper she served lunch to yesterday.

We push out of the diner and walk to the Liberty. I don't remember that Max isn't with us until I pull on the passenger door. It's locked. He has the keys.

"We still have the store," Autumn says. "We know where we're going next."

I want to agree, but if we can't collect any physical evidence, Roane won't budge. We're going to have to erase any room for doubt if we're going to force his hand. Which means we're probably shit out of luck.

We wait in the cold parking lot until Max finally strolls out the front door ten minutes later, whistling to himself. He flips his phone around in his hand as he walks. He looks...*cheerful.* And it annoys the shit out of me.

"How much do you love me?" he asks.

All I can see is that smile on his face. "Took you long enough. We're kind of in a hurry here, remember? The thrift store closes in ten minutes."

He clears his throat. "I *said,* how much do you love me?"

I glare at him.

He mumbles something about not being appreciated and hits a

button on his phone. Mine vibrates in my pocket. "Are you calling me?" I ask, but when I look at the screen, it's not ringing. He's sending picture messages. Lots of picture messages. I open the first and step back in surprise.

Lola.

I swipe through a dozen grainy black-and-white photos. Dark hair, cut to the chin, floral-sleeved jacket, white hat, and the strange man sitting across from her in a booth. The same fucking booth we sat in tonight.

She's smiling in a few of them—but the man's face is turned away from the camera at all times. Even if he weren't, the image quality is terrible. I doubt anyone would be able to place him from this. It looks like someone held a grayscale photo under a greasy magnifying glass covered in scratches. I can barely make out a sharp nose when he turns his head the right way.

"How…how the fuck did you get this? Did Sandra show you the tapes?" I ask.

He laughs and opens his door to get into the Liberty, forcing me and Autumn to climb in to hear his response. He pulls a banana from his back pocket before he sits and takes a bite of it as he slams the door. "You're joking, right? There's no way she'd ever help us. I knew that from the start."

"Then how?"

"While you guys were asking like sweet baby angels, I found the security system in the closet across from the bathroom and rewound it until I found the lunch footage from yesterday. I snapped a few photos, grabbed a snack from the kitchen, and I got outta there. I told you—sleuthing."

I clap him on the back. "I love you so much."

He beams at me, and for a moment, he looks so much like my Papá. A stab of guilt fissures through me and I have to look away to shake it off.

Autumn's head pops up between the front seats, her whole body vibrating with excitement. "I want to see."

I hand over my phone and she beams from the backseat. "We're really doing this. We're going to find her."

I smile back. "First, we find Nana."

TWENTY-ONE

MARY

DAY FIVE

I'm somewhat aware of Wayne coming into my room to help me pack up the rest of my stuff. He rolls up the "Don't Worry, Be Happy" poster and tucks it into the side of the box. Kicks my shoes toward me. He throws the yellow afghan from the sofa on top of my box, tosses me my jacket, and then I'm outside, stumbling down the steps toward the van. Everything feels far away, like the whole world took a step back, and I can't reach anything that makes sense anymore.

My body numbs. I don't even feel the cold bite of November through my shirt.

Wayne puts my box in the back of the van. Ben's flier is tucked safely into a sock at the bottom. I don't know what's happening. Wayne lied to a police officer. He lied to me. He stole my business card. He might have stolen *me*. And I don't know what to do.

I don't have any options, apart from getting into the van and letting Wayne drive us to wherever we're going next. I don't have anywhere else to go.

Except there's a voice in my head screaming at me not to leave with him.

Never let them take you to a secondary location.

The thought makes me freeze. When I stop, Wayne backs into me. He whirls and catches me by my shoulders in surprise, but his fingers dig a little too hard into my arms. "Mary, watch where you're going, please."

I mumble a sorry and step to the side to let him pass. As I watch him go up the stairs, I feel the ghost of his hands forming fingerprint-shaped bruises. He reemerges a few seconds later with another box, this one full of pots and pans and a duffel bag I've never seen before. He dumps them into the back of the van and heads back to the living room where another couple boxes are waiting. The duffel bag shifts and starts to slide. I reach out to catch it, stepping into the van's open back doors, and a blast of ice-cold memory hits me straight in the face.

I'm inside the empty van, deep in the back.

Bumping down a dirt road.

Going around a corner and rolling into the side wall.

Face pressed against carpet and pine needles.

Dark windows.

And panic.

I gasp, and the images are all sucked away. Pre-storm morning takes its place, filling the van with weak sunlight, as Wayne steps up beside me and pushes the box of personal documents from our first night here into the van beside the duffel bag. "Everything okay?"

I nod. Too fast. Too much. I force a smile. "Yeah, the bag surprised me. It almost fell out."

He looks down at it. "That's fine. It's only blankets and knick-knacks." He points to the passenger side. "Go wait in the van. Buckle up. I have to pull around the side of the house to load up a few things from the basement and we're out of here. It'll only take a few minutes."

A tightness wraps itself around my chest and squeezes until I can barely breathe. Dear god, I need some air, and the thought of sitting in that van beside him has all the hairs rising on my neck.

I try to form words to beg for an alternative, even a temporary one. "C-can I wait by the river instead?"

He smiles at me. "Want to say goodbye to your favorite swing?"

I nod.

"You sure love that thing." He looks at his watch. "Fine, but only for a minute. And only if you put your jacket on. You'll catch your death out here."

I nod again, because it's the only communication I can manage at this point, and he disappears back into the house before I can even slip the sleeves of the jacket over my arms. I knot my fingers in the hem and try to count out even breaths as I walk, but it doesn't help.

Nothing helps.

Because Ben Hooper is missing. And Wayne lied to me about my mom. And about Bowman being here. He's rushing us out of here for no reason, and his fingers are digging into my arms, and I can't shake the feeling that I'm not safe with him.

But I have nowhere else to go. I have nobody else to go *to*. I may remember my mom as the woman with the red sofa, but I don't know how to find her. I don't even know her fucking name. The nice old neighbor is missing. Bowman is gone. And I'm about to be gone too, with a man who barely even lets me outside.

I sit on the edge of the river swing, and it creaks beneath me. The last five days replay in my mind. Wayne looking urgently at me in the entrance to the police station. The relief on his face when he saw I was safe—but also couldn't remember him. The way he pleaded his case to get me back up this mountain. His hesitancy to bring me back into town. His insistence we drive two hours to buy leggings when the ones he bought me were the wrong size.

Cutting up strawberries, then blaming me for eating eggs I'm not allergic to.

Ordering me a strawberry smoothie.

Rushing out of the diner as soon we started to attract attention.

The refurbished floors back home that became floors and cabinets, which somehow all got completed in five days.

The photo of the complete stranger he tried to pass off as my mother.

If it weren't for that birth certificate and all those photos of us, I'd almost think—

Fear explodes in my veins. Now I really can't breathe.

Can't breathe.

Can't move.

Because the thought completes itself: I'd almost think that Wayne's gotten everything wrong because he has the wrong daughter.

The blood drains from my face. The tip of my nose turns to ice, and I feel like I'm about to pitch forward into the river the way my head spins.

Oh my god. What if...

What if he's *not* my dad? What if I'm *not* Mary?

What if that's not my name?

I launch up off the swing and pace along the waterline because my whole body is itching to move. Mud cakes to my new white shoes, squishing up the sides. The sky churns above the water, turning the river gray and hostile.

What if I'm not Mary?

What if I'm not Mary?

What if I'm not Mary?

The question burrows in my mind. I clutch my temples. Who am I if I'm not Mary Boone?

I look up at the house for Wayne, but he's nowhere in sight. The van is parked by the basement door, but I don't see *him*.

A branch snaps to my right, between the woodpile and the tree line. I whirl toward it, half expecting to see him standing there, staring at me. But there's nothing but the tarp-covered woodpile and the forest.

The breeze shifts, twisting upstream. It brings cool wet air from the woods, and with it, the most disgusting smell. Like bad meat, or old eggs, only way worse. It smells like the forest is rotting, and I instinctively recoil from it, stepping into the water. The splash disrupts the silence, and something moves straight ahead. My gaze slides over the swing, toward the trees beyond it, and I lock eyes with an animal.

A coyote.

It stands about twelve feet away, absolutely still. So still it blended right in with the branches behind it. The hairs around its mouth are pink with blood and there's something in its mouth.

My heart stops beating. I stare at it, and it stares at me, and I wonder if my Wayne panic was pointless, because I'm about to be mauled to death on a mountain that smells like rotten meat.

Without taking my eyes off the thing, I crouch until the tips of my fingers dip into the frigid water around my feet, and I dance them across the bottom until they catch on a rock about the size of a mason jar, but with a long sharp point on one end.

I stand slowly, water dripping off my fingers, rock ready at my side.

I don't know what the hell I'd do with it if the coyote actually ran at me, but the second I'm upright again, it takes off through the trees.

Dropping whatever it had been chewing on in the process.

My poor heart restarts as soon as it disappears, but my gaze zeroes in on what it dropped. The other side of the woodpile is all muck, but it looks like the coyote dug a big hole in the ground. I pull my feet from the water and take a step toward the swing, knowing I don't want to find out what's back there even as I move closer.

I stare at the thing on the ground, stepping around the outside of the swing. It's probably a dead squirrel or something gross like that.

My legs itch to run. To take my rock and get the hell out of here, but I can't stop moving toward the hole. The smell, and the blood… all the fear in my body is trying to figure out what's back there so I can react to it.

I stop a few feet away. The hole tugs at me, begging me to look inside, and…

I see him all at once, in graphic detail. One solid second of images, forever seared into my brain like a gruesome tattoo. Bite marks from animal teeth on the side of a partially dirt-covered face. Blood. Ripped skin. Open milky eyes. Giant gaping wounds on a mutilated neck. A half-exposed buffalo-print hat. One arm sticking out of the hole. Hand missing.

Discarded six feet away by the coyote.

Acid burns up my throat, catches behind my teeth, and goes back down, as I stare at his familiar face.

The coyote dug up Ben Hooper's corpse.

TWENTY-TWO

DREW

I don't know what I'm expecting from a place called Nana's Favorites, but this is not it. We pull up in front of a smallish building with that beachy wood siding and dirty white shutters that look a mess even in the fading light. A bird flies out from behind one of them and takes off toward the ocean, scaring the shit out of Max as he unfolds his gangly self from the driver's seat.

"Shit," he says, ducking long after it's gone.

Max doesn't like birds.

Autumn laughs and tries to turn it into a cough, as the lights inside the store turn off and an older woman with completely white hair and hot-pink glasses steps outside with keys in her hand. She freezes in the doorway when she sees us all standing there and breaks out into a smile. "Well, hello there! I'm afraid you kids are going to have to come back tomorrow. The store's closed until the morning."

She turns to lock the door.

I grab my phone and my missing flier from the seat, then walk toward her. "Actually, we're not here to shop. We're hoping you could help us find someone?"

She looks at me over her shoulder, key still in the door. "Excuse me?"

I tell her our names, and hand her the paper. She lets her keys dangle in the lock while she adjusts her giant purse on her other shoulder and reaches out for the piece of paper. Her purse is the same color as her glasses. And her yoga pants. Pink on pink on pink with this one.

The woman squints at the photo, and her fingers come up to cover her mouth. "She's missing?"

I nod. "For a few weeks now. We spoke to a woman at the diner down the road who said she saw her with an older man and a bag from your store."

Autumn steps up beside me. "Was she here?"

The woman looks between us, and then back at Max, still fidgety from that damn bird, and she nods at the photo. "Yes, they came in yesterday to buy some clothes. Left with quite a few things. Some shoes. They both seemed nice."

Well, one of them is.

I pull up the pictures Max snagged from the diner footage and hold the screen out so she can see them. "Are these the people that came here?"

The woman stares at my phone through her crazy thick glasses, and nods vigorously. "Yes. Same hair, and I remember the jacket—it had the prettiest buttons, but this isn't the best photo. Where did you get this?"

"From the diner," Autumn says, and quickly changes the subject. "Do you remember anything about the man with her? Or the vehicle they were driving?"

"Why would you need to know any of that?"

"We're trying to gather information to help the search effort," I say. "The more you can tell us, the more we can bring to the police and hopefully find her faster. Please, her family is so worried about her, and we think the man she's with may be dangerous."

The old woman takes a step back and runs into the closed door. "You think that man...the one who was in my store, is a danger to that sweet girl?"

She looks so genuinely horrified that I feel a wave of guilt at what I have to say next. "We think he might have kidnapped her. Which is why we're here. We need any information you have."

"But they were so nice," she insists. "They smiled at each other, and they laughed, and the girl put on her new clothes before she left, and everything seemed *fine*." Each word sounds a little more high pitched and hysterical than the last. "If I'd known she was in danger, there's no way I'd let her out of this store. Oh my god. What if they don't find—"

Autumn reaches out and puts her hand on the woman's shoulder. "Hold on a second, okay. Nobody is blaming you, and there's no way you could know that she was in trouble, especially if she wasn't acting strange. You're not to blame."

"But she was in my store..."

"What's your name?" Autumn asks.

"Eloise. I'm Eloise."

"Okay, Eloise, would you blame anyone at the diner for not helping her? Because they all saw her with the same man, and they didn't think anything was up either. You didn't take her, you didn't look the other way, you didn't do any harm here. He did. So we really need you to think and tell us if you saw or heard anything we can pass along to the police."

Eloise nods like it's a reflex, like she's not really listening to us, but a second later she says, "I didn't see their car. Just the people. The girl was young, your age. He was…quiet. Serious. He had bags under his eyes, but then so did she. They shopped and he helped her with her bags, and then they were gone. I honestly didn't think anything of it."

I take the flier from her so she doesn't look at it again and freak out. "Would you be willing to call this into the official tip line? The police set up a hotline for sightings of Lola, and it'll help a lot if they get the information from us and it's backed up by your call."

Her eyes widen. "Oh of course. I'll call right now. I'll do whatever I can."

"Do you have a pen?" Autumn asks. "I'll write down the number for you."

Eloise fishes around in her gigantic purse and produces a pen and a pad of pink sticky notes. Autumn scribbles down two numbers and hands them back.

"The first is the hotline, and the second is the sheriff's cellphone number. He's been a little slow on checking the tip-line calls, so if you wouldn't mind calling him directly, that would be a great help."

Eloise frowns at the second number. "The sheriff's personal number?"

"He's her dad," I say. "And kind of an ass."

I mean to keep that second part to myself, but it slips out. Eloise lets out a surprised laugh. "It would be my honor to hassle your father if it means getting this sweet girl home."

We thank her profusely, and she unlocks the door of the shop to start making calls. I'm filled with a very specific sort of longing. The kind that would place more people like her in charge. To put Eloise in Roane's shoes and see how quickly Lola comes home. Having her so immediately invested in our mission feels like our little capsizing lifeboat might stay afloat.

We turn to leave and Eloise shrieks in the doorway, scaring another bird from the nest behind the shutters. This time Max dives into the car and stays there.

I whip around and the old woman's eyes are gigantic. "They did say something! Before they left, the girl…Lola said she wanted to change into her new clothes before the long drive back to Alton."

There's a strange buzzing in my ear and I realize I stopped breathing. "Wait, she specifically said Alton? Are you sure?"

"Yes! I'm absolutely positive. I remember because my brother used to live up there, and when I heard that's where they were from, the long drive made a lot of sense. Alton is in the middle of nowhere, super isolated. My brother hated how far it was from everything, so he moved to Florence a couple years ago. Alton is a good two-and-a-half hours from here."

I wave my hands to stop her, reeling her back to Lola. "But she specifically said they were driving back there?"

She nods. "Yes."

Autumn grabs my arm in a vice grip of excitement. "And you'd be willing to pass this information along to my dad and the tip line too?"

Eloise puts one hand on her hip and grins. "Honey, I'll call him until he drives down here himself and takes my statement," she says, and slips inside.

I walk back to Max's car in a daze.

Lola is in Alton.

Holy shit.

Max keeps clenching and unclenching his fists on the steering wheel. We all sit in the silence of the car, watching Eloise rip Roane a new one through the glass door.

Finally, Autumn cracks a huge smile. "Holy shit, you guys. We know where he took her."

"Alton," Max says.

Fucking Alton.

"Okay, so what now?" Autumn asks. "Do we go home? Are we done?"

I look at Max. Max looks at me. Autumn impatiently taps her foot on the floorboards in the back. I don't have an answer for her. We should go home. We got what we came for and then some. We even got a bonus witness and a location out of it. If we head home now, we'll be back a little after nine. But—

"It doesn't feel right," Max says. "Being so close to finding her and then going home?"

Exactly.

"So what do you want to do?" Autumn asks.

I scrub my hands over my face and pull out the camera stills of the diner video again. I flip through them, seeing Lola and this man. I wish his face was in focus. I wish they both were. I wish this was the inarguable proof that we need to make it rain on this town and this whole investigation, but I thought I had proof before this, with Meredith Hoyt's tip-line call. "It's just…what if this isn't enough for your dad?" I ask her. "What if he takes one look at this and disregards it because I'm the one who drove down here to make this happen? What if he accuses me of coercing a witness or something?"

Autumn shifts uneasily in the back. "I really don't think he'd take it that far, do you?"

"I brought him Meredith's call, and he accused me of faking it to get myself off the hook. Why would he think this is any different? Any lead he can pass off as tainted by the main suspect, he will. He's proven that."

"Point, Drew," Max mumbles.

"I'm sorry, Autumn. I know he's your dad, but I don't want to go home and assume he's going to do the right thing…and then be fucked when he doesn't. If we go back, our parents aren't going to let us out of their sight for a long time. What happens if he doesn't follow through?"

She stares at her lap, long tendrils of red hair falling in her face, and for one horrifying second, I think she's crying. She looks up with anger in her eyes instead. "No, you're right. Lola deserves more than leaving this up to my dad. But we can't just drive around looking for her ourselves. Meredith was right about that—we can't investigate this on our own. It's too dangerous."

"I said it once, I'll say it again: I'll punch Ted right in the face. I'm not scared." Max throws a punch at the air above the steering wheel and the sigh that comes out of my chest weighs at least a hundred pounds.

"I'm not about to get us all killed trying to track down a kidnapper," I say. "No means no, Max. You're not punching anyone today."

"Aww, fine."

"I think we need to modify the original plan. We came out to find evidence that Lola was here, so we could force Roane to investigate, but what if we bypass him entirely? If we know she's in Alton, why not bring the fight to them? I'm beginning to think the only way we're going to get Roane on the team is if we take away any choice in the matter. So let's give the evidence to another precinct. Someone impartial, who can look at what we have and run with it. Then Roane would have no choice but to work with them and listen to what they have to say, or look grossly incompetent."

"Well, that or he'll convince the Alton precinct that you're guilty and then you'll have two police stations after your ass," Max says.

I glare at him. "Helpful. Thanks."

"So…you want to bait my dad with his pride and reputation by siccing the Alton Police Department on him?" Autumn asks.

I turn to gauge her reaction, but I can't read her expression. "Too far?"

She grins. "No. It's absolutely perfect. I'm only angry I didn't think of it first."

A surprised laugh escapes me.

"Now we're talking," Max says. "The sleuthing continues. Destination: Alton."

Autumn holds up a finger as Max starts the car. "One teeny tiny problem," she says. "Eloise said Alton is a two-and-a-half-hour drive. Meaning we won't get up there until nine, and most small-town stations close after five or six. They'll probably have a couple people on call to handle bar fights and crap like that, but nobody who has the authority to take on the kind of information we have. We should wait until the morning. That way we don't get laughed out of there by some random officer who's annoyed at pulling the night shift short stick."

That…makes sense. But I don't want to admit it.

I look up the Alton police station on my phone and sure enough, it closed an hour ago. "Fuck. We have to stop somewhere for the night."

Max shrugs. "We're already going to be in trouble for skipping school and leaving town without asking. Might as well see this out before we go back to face the music, right?"

"We need to find an actual *place* to stay though," Autumn says. "Because I'm sure as hell not sleeping in this piece-of-crap car."

"Hey!" Max protests.

"Let's find a place in Alton," I say. "That way we'll be close, and we can spend the rest of tonight gathering all our information and figuring out how to make them listen. We'll take it to their precinct first thing in the morning."

"Fingers crossed they're better at being cops than Roane," Max mutters under his breath. "Also, there's nothing wrong with my car, you jerk."

I'm positive Autumn heard him because she presses her mouth into a thin line. "I'm not sharing a bed with you losers. That crosses a line."

Oh sure. Ditch school, impersonate a police station secretary, ambush a witness, get kicked out of a diner, steal security footage, cause an old lady emotional distress, and stay out all night—*that's* all on the up-and-up, but sleeping in the same bed as a boy is where she finds an uncrossable line.

Max backs out of his parking space, and barely has a chance to turn out onto the main road before Autumn's phone lets out a shrill ring from the backseat, making us all jump. She sucks in a breath.

"What?" I ask.

Her face is lit up by the screen. Illuminating every freckle on her nose and the worried wrinkle between her eyebrows. "It's my dad."

"What?" Max makes a sound like a mouse being squeezed.

Autumn looks at me and grits her teeth. She taps the answer button and puts it on speakerphone. "Hello?"

"Where. Are. You?" Roane shouts.

Damn if I don't flinch.

"Busy."

"Autumn! Don't you dare start with me. I know you left school with Max and Drew." Was it my imagination or did he spit my name out like a moldy piece of bread? "The security guard told the principal he saw the three of you leave, and now I'm getting call after call from some woman in Waybrooke who wants me to drive out and take her statement about seeing Lola Scott in her store? Says my *daughter* gave her the number. What the hell are you up to?"

She glares at the screen. "I'm *busy* doing your job. Maybe if you actually looked for Lola, I wouldn't have to."

And…she hangs up. "We should turn off our phones, so he can't track them."

I gape at her.

"What?" she says. "I told you, I'm all in. He'll get over it eventually."

"Oh shit," Max mumbles. "Oh shit, oh shit, oh shit."

I catch his eye. Oh shit indeed.

When this is all over, I'll have to watch my ass for years to keep Roane from turning a speeding ticket into an overnight in a jail cell, but I'm struggling to care about that as much as I should. Nothing is worse than losing Lola and having to wake up every single day not knowing if she's dead or alive. Reliving every word we screamed at each other in that car. Scrambling for my phone every time it rings, for it to never be her.

Compared to that, Roane is a kitten with a butter knife.

Max turns north up the highway. "I think I can hear Roane calling my mom from here. She's going to kill me."

"We'll die together then."

He gives me a grateful look and shuts off his phone, dropping it into the cup holder like the useless brick it is now. I start to do the same, but what he said sinks in. My dads won't kill me, but not knowing where I am right now is certainly killing them. I should have been home from school three hours ago. I imagine Dad sitting on the stairs again, watching a door that won't open again tonight.

At least Roane knows Autumn is safe. Relatively. I mean, we are chasing a kidnapper.

I open the family group chat and skim all my dads' questions and demands to know where I am while I sort out my response. Their last texts beg me to call them, and it hurts to read the pain in their messages. I don't dare listen to the voicemails or I won't have the resolve to finish this.

I don't want them to worry. They deserve to know what's going on.

> Me: i'm sorry. i know ur worried and i wouldn't have done this if i had any other choice. i'll be home soon but not tonight. i'm safe, Max is safe, Autumn is safe.
> Me: we found something important.

I send the grainy photo of Lola in the diner with that pointy-nosed asshole.

> Me: the scotts needs to see this. she's alive, and she was in waybrooke yesterday
> Me: two witnesses saw her, and one spoke to her. Roane won't look into it so we're searching for someone who will. we're so close, i can feel it. tell mr. scott that Roane is messing up. tell him to go to the precinct and ask for an update. tell him we're looking
> Me: I'm sorry but i have to do this. i have to find her or it'll kill me.
> Me: i'm being safe, i promise. i love u both so much
> Me: i'll see u tomorrow.

I shut off my phone, knowing with absolute certainty this is the worst thing I've ever done to them. The guilt of that chases me up the highway.

TWENTY-THREE

MARY

DAY FIVE

Rain starts falling from the slate-gray clouds as I retch onto the dirt. Like the storm is trying to wash away what happened here, but it can't.

Nothing can undo this.

Wayne killed Ben Hooper.

He sent me inside the house, and he killed him.

Wayne is a murderer.

All I can see is Ben Hooper's smiling face. His poor family hanging the same fliers that Bowman gave to the man *responsible* for his death an hour ago.

Oh my god.

Is this why he didn't have his jacket when he came into the house yesterday? Did he get it bloody, hacking this poor man to death? Stash it in the woods, so he could pop in to play devoted dad like nothing happened? What then? Did he wait for me to take my nap to sneak back outside to dig this grave?

I'm over here trying to convince myself that Wayne couldn't have taken me from my mom because he's never raised his voice to me; meanwhile, he's stashing *bodies* in the yard. I'm such a fucking idiot.

I glance at the hole in the debris. Ben Hooper's eyes stare up at the storm like he can't believe what happened to him any more than I can. If Wayne can do this, and then come inside and smile like none of it ever happened, what else is he capable of?

And what is he planning to do to me?

Rage washes over me. White-hot fucking rage. No. No way. He doesn't get to make me disappear too.

The storm picks up, slamming into the ground, and another branch snaps behind me. I whip around and this time I'm right. Wayne's standing behind me.

He glances at the hole in the ground, and then at me, as we're both slowly soaked by the storm. He looks positively bored and tsk-tsks at me. "Oh, Mary. You always ruin everything."

I stare at his blank fucking face and smash my rock into his temple, driving his whole head to the side. He drops to his right knee, his eyes unfocused, as a river of blood runs down his cheek.

And I *run.*

His roar of pain weaves through the trees behind me. I tear through the forest, moving as fast as my legs will take me. Branches rip at my face. Rocks press into the too-thin soles of these shoes. Thorns grab at my jacket, tugging, pulling, scratching.

I have *no* idea where he is. If he's stunned, or bleeding, or dying… or charging through the forest behind me. I don't dare look, and I can't hear anything above the roaring pulse in my ears. I run like my life depends on it, because it most certainly does.

At first, I don't know where I'm headed, considering I just found my neighbor's dead body. But Ben mentioned a wife. If there's any justice left in this goddamned world, she'll be home, because if Wayne's *not* dead, I doubt I'll make it farther than the house next door.

Rain pours through the trees, drenching my clothes and hair until it feels like I've climbed from the river. I burst from the trees, and for a second, I think I've made it to the neighbor's yard, but it's a clearing of weeping knee-high grass and huge rocks the size of picnic tables. The angry gray sky stretches out ahead of me, and a rumble of thunder shakes the trees.

I launch myself through the clearing, heading for the closest patch of trees so I'll be under cover faster. With a jolt, I realize there's smoke rising from beyond those trees. Chimney smoke.

She *is* home.

My legs move faster. My lungs catch fire. I can do this. I can make it.

Something crashes through the trees behind me, and I glance back over my shoulder, stomach filling with dread as Wayne bursts through the branches and into the little field. He looks wildly from side to side before he spots me. Blood coats his neck and the top of his shirt. He pins me with an icy stare, and I dive back into the trees.

I won't look back again.

"*I'll find you. . .*" he calls.

Except he doesn't say that. Not *this* time.

All at once, I remember what happened.

I remember him coming up from behind me as I checked the mail at home. Dragging me away—into this life, into this place. I remember waking up in the van as it rumbled up the mountain in the dark. I remember lying on my side, scared shitless as I pieced together what was happening. I remember using a trick I saw on YouTube to break the zip tie around my wrists. I remember pretending to be asleep when the van came to a stop at the cabin, and then lurching to my feet before he could open the back door. I remember throwing myself against the door when he cracked it open, knocking him flat on his ass in the driveway as I ran for the road in the middle of the night, screaming for my mom.

I remember the trees, branches like fingers.

I remember the cold night air on my bare arms.

I remember his voice behind me, like he wanted me to *know* he was there. That he was close. That I wouldn't get away.

"Get back here right now, young lady."

He doesn't call out this time. He just hunts.

Memories mix with my vision of the trees, flashing between the storm currently raging around me and what happened five nights ago. There was no car accident, no trip from McMinnville, no house renovations. Just Wayne chasing me through the woods until I somehow ended up on that road.

I can't breathe.

I see a house through the trees. I'm almost there. I get glimpses of blue paint and whiffs of wood-burning smoke from the brick chimney. The outline of a bay window with a light inside.

My salvation.

I'm so close she could probably hear me scream if I could only muster enough breath. I'm gasping. I'm on fire. I can't feel my legs, my hands, my face.

Ten feet until I'm free of the trees. I see the lawn, brown and dormant. Five.

The screen door opens. Did I scream? Did someone hear me?

I lunge between the last trees, bursting onto that dead lawn, and an old woman backs out onto the small porch. I suck a lungful of air to scream—

And a hand wraps around my throat from behind. Another clamps down over my mouth, catching the sound with a wrenching squeeze. The trees swallow me again as he drags me back under the cover of the branches. I scratch at his hands, but they only tighten until I feel like my throat is being pinched in half. Black dots dance in my vision, and he breathes in quiet little bursts against my cheek. He doesn't relax the hold on my throat.

"Oh, Mary," Wayne whispers in my ear, his stubble scraping my skin as I scramble to stay conscious. "You'll pay for this."

Black dots pepper my vision until they wipe me out completely.

TWENTY-FOUR
DREW

I pull back the curtain in our motel room and look out at the road for what has to be the five-hundredth time. The streets of Alton have been quiet since we rolled into town. The darkened businesses on the main street sit in silence. The flickering streetlight in the empty motel parking lot was the only movement, until it shut off when the sun came up.

This looks like a place where dreams go to die.

I can't imagine Lola being here.

Max snores behind me, and I let the curtain slip between my fingers, shutting out the morning light. He's in one of the double beds, splayed out with his head hanging off the side of the mattress, mouth open. He looks like one of those thin-armed starfish. Another baritone snore rattles from his throat and practically shakes the abstract motel art from the walls.

Autumn sleeps on one side of the other bed, its ancient comforter tossed to the floor because according to *her majesty*, "They never wash those." She lies beneath the sheets in a tight ball and hasn't moved all night.

I turn back to the window. Ten minutes to eight—when the precinct officially opens. I force myself to be patient, even as I look back out the window.

I should be tired because I barely slept last night, but I'm not. There's something about this town, and knowing Lola was headed here only two days ago. Her shadow lingers here. I can't explain it, but I feel closer to her in this place.

I let the curtain fall again and walk over to the neat pile of documents sitting on the dresser. I spent most of the night getting my presentation ready. Thankfully the motel office had a printer, and the girl behind the counter didn't seem to mind me using it.

I printed copies of each diner photo, a better picture of Lola wearing that jacket from her Instagram, a fresh missing person flier, and a typed timeline of everything we know happened from the night she disappeared to her reappearance in Waybrooke.

It may not be the perfect police report, but it tells the story of a gorgeous, spunky, difficult, annoying perfect girl, and what we think happened to her.

I shuffle the papers for the millionth time, looking for the right order to present this to the Alton PD, but I keep getting stuck on the diner photos. The jacket is the most identifiable thing in this photo—I think that's what worries me the most. Their faces are grainy, indistinct. I hope the jacket is enough. How many girls who look like Lola could be wandering around in a one-of-a-kind jacket?

No. This is enough. It has to be.

Max's rattling snore cuts off as he flips onto his stomach. I've been patient enough. I throw on my sweatshirt and kick his mattress.

He sits up with a jolt. "What the hell?"

"Time to rise and shine," I say, crossing to Autumn's bed. I know better than to kick her mattress if I want my balls to remain intact, so I gently shake her shoulder until she rubs her eyes. "Come on, we have to get to the police station."

She groans, but she flings back the sheets and rolls to her feet.

I leave them to wake up while I snag the key cards and head up to the front office to check out. The windshield of the Liberty glints with frost as I pass it and duck into the office.

The same girl from last night sits behind the counter. She has dyed black hair, a lot of eyeliner, and the kind of bloodshot eyes that suggest she's gotten as much sleep as I have. She drops her chin into her hand and winks at me when I walk in.

"Well, hello. Need the printer again?" she asks.

I shake my head and slap the key cards onto the shiny black counter. "Nope."

She smiles and takes the cards. "I like your don't-give-a-shit vibe."

I ignore her and let my eyes wander around the little lobby. The space isn't any bigger than our tiny room. A small table is set up for "breakfast" when really it's just coffee, a few bananas, and some kid-sized boxes of breakfast cereal. A bulletin board hangs over the table, and two chairs, same as the ones in our room, sit across from it.

"Okay," the girl says, handing me a receipt. "You're all checked out."

Her eyes scan me from head to toe, making it clear she means that in more than one way. I turn away so she won't see me frown. Not because she isn't cute—the eyeliner looks good on her—she just isn't Lola.

I stop and pour some coffee into a disposable paper cup. I stir it with one of those wooden sticks, trying to cool it down, and freeze mid-stir when I see what's on the bulletin board. It's completely covered with missing person posters. All of the same person.

My stomach drops.

The smiling face of an elderly man named Ben Hooper stares back at me in black and white. The poster says he was last seen two days ago while on a walk. The number for the Alton police department is printed at the bottom, but his face takes up the most space. His smile cuts into me as I sip the coffee. It tastes like dirt, but I force it down anyway.

"I don't remember these being here last night," I say to the girl behind the desk.

She rolls her eyes. "They weren't. His wife's been posting fliers on literally every surface in town. She came in super early and took over the whole thing. No wonder he took off. She seems a little out there."

I know exactly how that feels, to be running around posting fliers so you can feel like you're doing *something*. But the flippant way this girl talks about it makes my stomach churn. Like it doesn't matter. Like his frantic wife is strange for looking for him in the first place.

Or maybe that's my baggage weaseling into someone else's life.

I swallow the coffee-flavored bile coming up my throat and look away from the missing man's face. I snag a few bananas for Autumn and Max. "Thanks," I say, heading for the door.

"Sure, but I—"

The door cuts her off as I step outside.

Max and Autumn meet me at the Liberty, and Max tosses me the car keys as I toss him the bananas. Autumn clutches my little pile of "evidence" to her chest as she gets into the car, riding shotgun this time. Max doesn't protest. He gets into the backseat, eating his banana. He offers the other one to her, but she makes a face, so he eats that one too.

The drive to the precinct is short and full of heavy silence. The nerves twist my already unhappy stomach. I have no idea how this is going to go. During our strategy session last night, Autumn thought that connecting the jacket to the diner will be enough to convince the police to talk to Meredith and Eloise. I hope she's right because we don't have a backup plan.

The precinct comes into view two blocks ahead. It's a little one-story building with a small parking lot in front. Only two cruisers and two sedans parked in it. The Alton Police Department sign, painted with a gold badge, sits beside the door, and I'm suddenly back in Washington City, hearing the doors of Roane's precinct slam behind me as everyone inside glares daggers at my back.

My whole body breaks out in a cold sweat.

Fuck. I really don't want to become a suspect in yet another county.

I roll to a stop at a red light.

If this goes south, I'd like to think I'll keep going, find someone else to listen, but what if nobody will see my side? What if there's nothing I can do to bring Lola home, and I'm making everything worse? What if Roane is waiting with handcuffs, and I won't have another chance to follow the clues we've gathered? What if—

"Yo, dude. The light is green," Max says from the backseat.

I blink out of my spiral and force my foot off the brake. I ease the Liberty toward this building that's looking more and more like a black hole by the second. I park in the lot, as far from the door as I can, and Autumn raises an eyebrow at all the empty spots beside us.

"You okay?" she asks.

"Nope."

"Drew," she says, holding up the papers. "It's not just your word anymore. You have us, and we have two other witnesses who saw her.

The police have no reason to ignore this, and they have even less reason to set their sights on you."

"Unless Roane shows up and convinces them you're a sociopath," Max says from the backseat.

Autumn spins around and glares at him. "Shut. Up."

He shrinks back and gets out of the car.

"Don't listen to that nonsense," Autumn says. "We've got this. Remember the speech: we're here with information about a missing girl. We give them the photos, and tell them about Meredith, about Eloise. They'll take it from there."

I take a breath and follow her out of the car, but I drag my feet. It's easy for her to feel confident—she has less to lose. If they don't believe her, she goes home and gets grounded. I could be arrested.

We cross the parking lot, and I hesitate at the door.

Max claps me on the shoulder. "Let's do this thing."

Inside, we're hit with a flurry of activity. Despite the quiet parking lot, this office is bustling. Uniformed officers are everywhere, passing around folders, answering phones, and pinning things to a big bulletin board in the back. A few people in suits with badges on their belts mill between them. Everyone's talking at once, and I see Ben Hooper's missing person flier in the middle of the bulletin board.

"What's going on?" Autumn stage-whispers beside me.

"An old man went missing," I say. "I saw a flier in the motel when I returned the key cards. They must be forming a search party."

"See?" Max says. "Proof that some cops know how to actually investigate."

Yeah, well. We'll see about that. But the clear urgency in the room makes me feel a little better. Maybe this won't be a disaster after all.

One of the uniformed officers spots us standing by the door and comes to the front desk and leans on it. He's tall, with short red hair and a matching mustache. "Can I help you kids with something?"

I freeze completely. He looks at me, maybe because I'm in the middle, and half a step closer than Max or Autumn, but it feels like he's staring down a suspect. Like I've done something wrong just by walking in here. Like he knows who I am. Like he's sure I'm guilty. Did he talk to Roane? Our phones are still off, so how would he know we'd end up here—

"Hello," Autumn says, stepping up to the counter when I don't speak. "We need to talk to someone about a missing person."

"A missing person?" he says. "You mean Ben Hooper?"

She shakes her head and places Lola's flier onto the counter. "No, our friend Lola. We have reason to believe she's here in Alton, and we need to talk to someone about it."

Redhead looks over his shoulder and scrubs his face with his hands. "Okay, well, things are a little hectic at the moment. Normally it's not so busy in here but we have a local who's gone missing as well. Why don't you take a seat, and we'll be with you as soon as we can."

He gestures to the bench to the right of the door. It's a long wooden thing along the wall, big enough for the three of us to sit. The officer goes back to the group forming around the bulletin board and we wait.

Max's knee starts bouncing the second his ass hits the bench. "This is good, right? I mean, they didn't ask us to leave, so we're still on track?"

Theoretically.

Autumn looks at me. "You okay?"

"Yup."

"How long do you think we'll have to wait?" Max asks.

Turns out, over an hour. I lose count of how many times I look up at the clock on the wall, but I watch the minute hand tick around and around, until it's after nine, and my ass is well and truly numb against this unforgiving bench.

Max is slumped against the wall. Asleep. I swear he can pass out anywhere, and at a moment's notice.

At least he's not snoring.

Autumn's abandoned the bench altogether, opting instead to pace across the entryway at a thousand steps per minute. She acts more anxious by the second, which is funny because the wait is having the opposite effect on me. My nerves slowly settle.

Finally, the group around the bulletin board separates, and everyone moves toward the door. Autumn slides against the opposite wall as about a dozen officers leave the building together, and only then do I notice they have different cities listed on their badges.

They called in officers from other towns to help look for Ben Hooper.

Roane never called in anyone outside his precinct to do shit unless someone made him. Preferred to keep everything "close to home." Which as far as I can tell, loosely translates to "within my control."

Officer Redhead is one of the only people left in the precinct.

He sets a stack of fliers that look identical to the ones at the motel on the counter. "Still here?"

I make a face. "Did you expect us not to be? You told us to wait."

"I did. Don't you have school?"

I say no at the same time Autumn says yes.

He looks between us. "Okay, where are you all from? You don't look like local kids."

"Washington City," Autumn says.

He lets out a low whistle. "You kids are a little far from home, don't you think?"

There's that *kid* thing again. It feels dismissive. Like we can't possibly have anything important to say, because we're *just* kids. And kids should not be at a police station at 9:15 in the morning on a random school day, fifty miles from home.

Autumn steps up to the counter and hands him Lola's flier a second time. "Have you seen this girl?"

I stand beside her. Back her up. Neither one of us bother waking Max.

Officer Redhead looks us over, but he takes the flier. Humoring us, I guess. He glances at it and seems to read the information at the bottom before his gaze flickers up to the photo. "She looks like a lot of girls. She's missing from Washington City?"

Autumn nods.

"And you're her friends?"

We nod again, and Autumn introduces the three of us.

He doesn't seem thrilled that we drove all the way out here to show him a flier on a school day. But Autumn has it handled. As always.

"We have information about her disappearance, and we need someone to take our statement. Officially. My dad is a sheriff, so I know how this works. And if you won't I need you to direct me to someone who will, because we're not leaving until *someone* takes a statement."

Redhead sighs. "Come on back."

Even though it's what I was hoping for, I stand there like a moron for two full seconds before my body moves. I scramble after Autumn to one of two desks in the middle of the main room. Officer Redhead eases into the office chair on the computer side, and we pile into the two metal chairs facing the desk.

The officer hits a few keys on the keyboard, grabs a notepad and a pen, and levels us with his attention. "Okay. Tell me what's going on."

This time, I do what I should have done from the start. I tell the truth. The entire truth, even the ugly bits.

I start at the boat launch and run through every single detail exactly as it happened. The fight, the breakup, leaving her there. Realizing she was missing. The weeks since, our search, Roane's botched investigation, stealing the tip-line recordings. The origins of the jacket and what it means to hear about it on the recording. Going to meet Meredith in Waybrooke. What we learned from Eloise.

With every piece of new information, I brace for him to dismiss us. Especially at the "we broke into the police station and stole evidence" part, but besides a deep frown and a circling hand motioning us to keep going, he doesn't react at all, which I find odd as hell. He's a cop. We just told him we stole evidence from another cop. Doesn't that warrant a mid-statement lecture?

All he does is write.

He. Takes. Everything. Down.

In fact, the more we talk, the more he leans forward in his seat. Listens harder, if that's even possible. Asks questions. When he pulls up Lola's case file on his computer and holds our grainy diner photos beside the image from the report, most of the color drains from his face. He demands to know more about the van. About the jacket. About Lola.

At some point I look up and Max is standing behind Autumn's chair. How long has he been standing there? If the grin on his face is any indication, I'd say it's been long enough for him to realize this is going well.

Officer Redhead even calls Eloise himself. She doesn't answer, but he leaves an official-sounding voicemail, asking for a callback, and I'm positive she'll be in touch as soon as she hears it. Then he makes a less fun call.

To Roane.

He's smart enough to make the call in another room. He comes back a few minutes later looking angry, but determined, which I think is a good sign. He sends Autumn off to speak with her father and resumes typing. Then he mentions possibly splitting their search party to look for both Ben and Lola.

And I'm soaring.

I've never been this hopeful in my entire life. In every worried minute of the last twenty-four hours, agonizing over how to get help and how to tell this story, I never dared to think that we'd actually make a difference. But it's happening.

Autumn comes back a minute later, looking flushed but smiling.

"I hung up on him," she says. "He was already on the highway. We've got about forty-five minutes before he rolls in here and starts screaming. Brace yourselves."

I look up at the clock. 10:05.

Roane closing in on us should make my hands sweat, but Officer Redhead—err, Officer McCurry, who does have a name—has a lot more questions. This is what we came here for, so Roane can suck it. I'll deal with whatever he throws at me.

It takes us a long time to answer everything, and we go through the timeline twice more to make sure he has everything written in the report, but he eventually looks down at the *pages* of notes he's taken and leans back in his chair, rubbing his face. "Holy shit. This is a lot."

We nod. Furiously.

He drops his hands and then meets each of our stares. "I'm not going to pretend what you three did to get here is okay or condone how you gathered a single piece of this information. I'm positive there'll be consequences for you back home, and I can't do much about that, but

I can see *why* you did what you did. I need you to let us handle it from here though, okay? No more stealing or sleuthing or running away."

Max grins from ear to ear and I know it's because he called it sleuthing.

Autumn shrugs. "We're only here because nobody else was doing anything. If you take over, we have no reason to keep going."

I say nothing, because I won't stop until Lola is home. Officer McCurry looks right at me, like he knows what I'm thinking, but before he can coax an agreement out of me, the doors to the precinct open again.

Another officer walks in, this one much younger than Redhead. In fact, he looks barely older than us. Maybe it's his giant blue eyes.

His brown hair is a little ruffled, and so is his uniform. It looks like he slept in the office or something. "Hey, McCurry. I'm out of fliers. Do we have another stack ready?"

Officer McCurry jumps to his feet and ushers the other officer over with a wave of his hand. "Bowman, I need you for a second."

The younger cop comes to stand beside the desk. "What's up?"

"This is Drew, Autumn, and Max, and they're looking for their missing friend. They have reason to believe she's in Alton, so I've been taking their statement. It reminds me of your weird night shift. Didn't you pick up a teenage girl a few days ago?"

Autumn looks at me with the biggest eyes I've ever seen, and I imagine mine look exactly the same. They picked up a teenage girl? Is she here? Do they already know where she is?

The young guy takes the photo of Lola and frowns. "Yeah, but she wasn't a missing person. She was in a car accident. Her father came and took her home. I just got back from checking on them, actually."

He tilts his head, still looking at the photo. "I can see the confusion though. They're the same age. Same jacket. But this is not the girl I picked up the other day."

I can't... I can't process this.

Autumn's lightning fast. "But if she had the same jacket," she says, "it might have been her. It's one of a kind. I made it."

"Are you positive, Bowman?" Officer McCurry asks, handing him the diner photos and the rest of his notes too.

Bowman looks again. He flips through all the photos, squints extra hard at the flier, before he shakes his head. "Look, I'm sorry for what you kids have been through," he says, like he's not a minute older than us, "but I think you might have stumbled into a misidentification at the diner, and it led you here, unfortunately. I verified this girl's identity myself, saw all her paperwork, and double-checked everything, down to her birth announcement in the McMinnville paper. I wish I had better news for you, but I'm sorry. It's not her."

A sound comes out of Autumn that's part breath and part sob. Max lays a hand on her shoulder, and she doesn't shrug him off.

But me? I'm losing it. "But... But you said they look the same. What are the chances that two girls who look exactly alike, with the same jacket, end up in this same town, but aren't the same girl?"

I hear my voice jump to a panicked octave, but I can't stop it.

Bowman sets down the papers, looking sad. "I said she looks a *bit* like her. We're talking about two different people. I'm sorry. You have the wrong person."

TWENTY-FIVE

MARY

DAY FIVE

I feel myself moving, but I blink and see nothing at all.

I blink again and see someone's back and the ground beneath hefty work boots.

I blink a third time and go back to nothing.

I'm still moving, and I don't understand.

What's happening? Am I being carried?

The ground below me comes back into view. I focus on those boots, stepping through bracken, onto dead grass, and my brain snaps the details together. I'm on someone's shoulder. Slung over like a duffel bag. My fingers splay out looking for purchase—I need to get away. I see part of the driveway. I lift my head and an elbow smashes me in the face. I know it hurts, but I can't feel it.

I see nothing again.

I can't blink anymore. My eyelids won't work, but I feel something cold against the side of my face. I think some time has passed. Everything is cold now. There's something wet on my nose, dripping down my cheek.

And I remember.

Like a flash flood. A dam exploding. He's knocked all the pieces back into place.

I remember my home. I remember my family. I remember tearing through the trees after escaping the van and running down the mountain, desperate to get back to my mom. To my friends.

To the life he tried to steal from me.

I remember him catching up to me. Grabbing ahold of the back of my hair and slamming my face against a tree. Pain ricocheting around my brain as blood gushed from my nose. I landed a wild, frantic shot to his nuts. He let me go. I remember branches dragging at my face as I blindly sprinted through the trees until the ground dropped out from beneath me and I fell.

Down.

Down.

Down a steep embankment, hitting everything along the way—trees, rocks, branches.

I have no idea how I ended up in the ditch, or how far apart these memories are from each other. Maybe he couldn't find me after he gathered his nuts up off the forest floor. Or was unwilling to jump off the same ledge I fell over. I must have crawled out of the woods, trying to find the road and get help. Trying to get away from Wayne.

A man who's most definitely not my father.

He's the stranger who took me from my family.

Wayne Boone is my kidnapper.

A long creak breaks through the darkness, and I get one eyelid to open enough to spot a lone lightbulb dangling from a fixture. I'm lying on something that yields to my weight, barely, and in the darkness, something cold wraps around my ankle and bites into the skin.

Panic crawls through the darkness and covers me like a blanket made of rocks.

I can't be here.

I have to run.

I have to get away from Wayne. Someone like him doesn't leave witnesses. But I don't know how to make my body move. All my limbs feel too heavy. Too useless. And the cold dampness seeping across my face is most assuredly blood.

I can't make myself function, and all I hear is *him.*

You don't remember me?

Mary?

I'll see you in a minute.

Mary.

Once we get home, we don't have to leave for a long time.

Mary.

Sleep well, my Mary.

Mary. Mary. Mary.

You

always

ruin

everything.

Through the pinkish glow of my eyelids, darkness creeps in, and there's nothing I can do to stop it, no matter how hard I try and claw myself back. I can't do this. I have no fight left.

I think of my family back home, how badly they must want to see me again. I hear them calling my name, looking for me, and one final piece clicks into place.

I know my name.

TWENTY-SIX

DREW

I'm sorry. You have the wrong person.

The words bounce uselessly around my brain. I don't understand. How could a girl who looks like Lola—same age, same hair, same eye color, same one-of-a-kind jacket—somehow *not* be her? Does she have a doppelgänger running around?

What are the chances of even three of these coincidences happening together?

Officer McCurry seems to feel the same, because it's not two full seconds before he's on his feet. "Stay here," he says. "I'll talk to him." He follows Officer Bowman into a copy room in the back.

I watch him through the big interior window. The two men stand beside the copy machine, talking in low voices. The three of us lean forward, equally desperate to hear what they're saying, but all we get is a lot of flailing limbs—Officer McCurry—and resigned looks—from the other guy.

Every time Officer McCurry's lips move, Officer Bowman shakes his head.

"Doesn't look like Redhead is winning this one," Max mumbles.

I stand and look around the precinct, but none of the other officers have come back yet. I have to get closer, or I'll never know what's going on. So I slip over to the back wall, away from the window, and slide over until I'm right outside the copy room door, pressed to the wall.

"This doesn't look right to me," Officer McCurry says. "What are the chances you picked up a girl who looks exactly like this five nights ago? What if the girl you picked up is Lola Scott?"

My whole body goes rigid.

Papers rustle, and Officer Bowman sighs over the noise as he jabs at copier buttons. "The girl I picked up is Mary Boone. She's a seventeen-year-old from McMinnville, and her father provided at least half a dozen forms of identification for her. Without complaint. He's a sometimes-local who owns one of the fishing cabins. I verified it myself."

"How sure are you?" Officer McCurry says. "Sure enough to dismiss what these kids are saying?"

Damn, it's nice to have a person with some kind of authority saying everything you wish you could say.

"Of course not," Bowman says with a sigh. "But do you think I would have let a teenager out of here if I had any question about whose custody I was releasing her into? She got her head scrambled in that accident. You should have seen her. She couldn't even remember her name. Do you think I'm going to let someone that vulnerable into the hands of anyone that walks in here claiming to be her family? Do you think I'd be that careless?"

Officer McCurry is quiet for a moment. "Of course not. That's not what I'm trying to imply…it's just… These kids, you know? They have one hell of a story, and too much of it adds up. There are too many similarities and eyewitnesses. I can't brush it off because you disagree."

"I'm not asking you to. Check it out for yourself. I'll even bring you up there. I promised to check in on Ben Hooper's wife and give her an update before the end of the day, and the Boones live right next door. You can come with me, and we'll stop in and see Mary and her father."

"Yeah...okay. That's reasonable."

"I wish I had better news for you. And for them. Lola Scott and Mary Boone are *not* the same person."

The finality in his voice makes all our evidence feel thinner, less substantial. *Lola Scott and Mary Boone are not the same person.* He says this like it's fact. Like there's no other possibility, and it's a chore having to bring Officer McCurry to the same conclusion.

"In the meantime," Officer Bowman continues, shuffling papers again, "these kids need to go home. I really wish we could do more, but they won't help their friend by getting in the way. Ask for their phone numbers and you can update them once you've checked it all out, but they don't need to be here."

Fuck. I grab my head with both hands, but I can't stop the looping in my brain.

Lola Scott and Mary Boone are not the same person.

She's a seventeen-year-old from McMinnville.

She got her head scrambled.

She couldn't even remember her name.

They have a girl who looks exactly like Lola, with her belongings, who can't remember who she is, and it's still a dead end? How is this possible? After all we've done, it still ends here?

A hand touches my shoulder and I startle. Autumn stands beside me and tears fall down both of her cheeks. She scrubs them off, but more replace them.

"Is it really not her?" she whispers.

Suddenly, I can't be in here anymore. The despair on her face is such a mirror of my own. I can't stand it. I pull away from the wall and head out the front doors. I lean against the cold brick outside.

This is too much. All of it.

I can't come up with a scenario that explains Lola's jacket being worn by an identical stranger, no matter how sure Officer Bowman thinks he is. A stranger so identical, in fact, that she's mistaken for Lola by three people who grew up with her, the witness at the diner, *and* the old woman in the thrift store.

But the officer is adamant. It's not her up the mountain. It's Mary freaking Boone.

What if he's wrong?

I have no way to find out. They're not going to show me a photo of Mary Boone for funsies. She's a kid, right? And so are we. Unless I camp out on the mountain looking for her father's creeper van twenty-four hours a day, I'm out of options.

I have to go home. There's nothing more I can do for Lola here.

And that makes me want to puke on the nearest cop car. Instead, I have a breakdown outside the precinct that was supposed to help us.

I don't know how long I stand there, but it's awhile. Long enough for the cold to seep through the fabric of my sweatshirt and into my bones, and for the tears to turn my eyes raw.

The door opens and Autumn steps out. Her eyes are red and swollen. She stops beside me, leaning her shoulder on the wall. She doesn't ask if I'm okay, which I appreciate. Instead, she pulls a piece of folded paper from her pocket and hands it to me.

It looks like one of Ben Hooper's fliers. I flip it over and find her curly handwriting in sharpie on the back.

93 Ridge Road. Alton, Oregon.

"What is this?"

She shrugs. "I know you. I know you won't be able to let this go without some kind of absolute. You have to see this Mary person for yourself. That's Ben Hooper's address."

I almost drop the paper. "I'm sorry, *what*?"

"He said they were neighbors, right? Mary and Ben? So go see for yourself."

"But how did you…?"

She points her thumb at the door. "When the redhead got up to argue with the other cop, he didn't lock his screen. Ben Hooper's file was still open on the desktop. I copied the address before he came back."

This is Ben Hooper's actual address. *The Boones live right next door.* Mary Boone—maybe Lola—is one house from the address in my hand.

"Go, Drew. For all of us. Go see if it's her."

"You're not coming?" I ask, already taking a step toward the Liberty.

She shakes her head. "My dad will be here in, like, ten minutes. It's up to you. Max knocked over the coffee pot in the back to give you a few minutes to slip out unnoticed."

Of course he fucking did.

I hug her. She laughs. "Hurry up before my dad Tokyo drifts into the parking lot."

"Thank you, Autumn. Thank you."

"Find her."

I run to the Liberty and whip out of the parking lot, plugging the address into the GPS on my phone at the red light. My entire body vibrates with purpose.

I have a plan. And in—I look at the arrival time on the GPS—eleven minutes, I'll be face-to-face with this girl and have my answer.

Doppelgänger or Lola.

But it's her. It has to be. Nothing else makes sense.

At the end of town, I make a right onto a road that climbs into the trees. Just as I pull off, a cop car goes flying by in the opposite direction on the main road. Lights on. Washington City logo on the side.

"Well, that was close," I mumble.

And if Roane made any phone calls before he left, my dads and my aunt are probably right behind him. I got out of there just in time.

The road winds all the way up the mountain, splitting off every few minutes into other narrow roads and private driveways. Eventually the dirt road straightens, bordered by dense evergreens on both sides, and the GPS starts to glitch. But I'm already on Ridge Road and creeping by numbers 85 and 88.

The trees thin on the right side, and I slow to find the next house number. A rusted old mailbox up ahead has a 91 on it. The log cabin behind it sits in silence.

It hits me that I don't know which neighbor I'm looking for. Which side? I slow to a crawl and stare at the cabin for a long second, then press on the gas again. The house looks closed up. I don't think anyone's here.

About a quarter mile down the road, I see the Hooper house. It's a little ranch-style home, with their last name painted in bright yellow letters on a sign by the porch.

The straightaway ends, and I find myself twisting and turning back through the forest, looking for the next nearest neighbor. They end up being about a mile away, on the other side of the road. Two old ladies stand in the yard, raking leaves. Their rainbow-painted mailbox lists them as 128 Ridge Road. The name on the box is Brown, not Boone.

Shit. It has to be the log cabin. I went too far.

I turn around at the end of their driveway, my pulse beating fast in my ears. Then I'm off through the curves again, zeroing in on the cabin.

I don't know how I'm going to do this. Do I pull up in the empty driveway and wait on the front steps for someone to get back? Knock loudly and hope someone's home? What if *she* answers and it's the wrong *she*? What if Officer Bowman is right?

Maybe I shouldn't knock at all. Being here is enough. I could park across the street and pretend to have car trouble. Lift the hood? Stab around at hoses or battery connections like I know anything about engines until I catch a glimpse of her?

The cabin pops up through the trees and I pull over about fifteen feet shy of the driveway and cut the engine. My palms start sweating.

Jesus, what if it's not Lola?

What if it is?

I feel nauseous.

I decide to go the fake-car-trouble route, when I spot it. A van is parked down an incline, way back on the left of the house beside a basement door. Hidden between the house and the trees. *A gray van with peeling paint.*

A branch moves out of the corner of my eye and I freeze.

A man bursts from the trees and strides across the yard, about fifty feet from me, with his back turned. Heading for the basement door.

Carrying something over his shoulder.

My entire body goes cold all at once as I watch the lifeless form dangle facedown across his back. Girl. Short brown hair. Jean jacket with pastel floral sleeves.

Lola.

TWENTY-SEVEN

MARY

DAY FIVE

I think I might be dead.

Again.

The same impenetrable dark wraps around me, and I wait it out. Wait for another wall of pain, or...something else. Something more permanent, maybe. But the limbo drags on. The darkness presses in, holding me down.

A throbbing in my face demands my attention. My hand moves to my nose and comes away wet. I realize a few things at once. One, there's no blood or throbbing noses in limbo. Two, I'm not dead. I'm not even unconscious. I'm lying in an extremely dark place. Three, I think my nose is all the way broken this time.

And four, I'm fucking freezing.

I throw my arms out to try and gather my bearings and smack into something near my cheek. I splay my fingers against it and feel the porous cold of a concrete wall. My breath rasps in and out so quickly it hurts the muscles around my lungs and my head swims. I might pass out again. But I can't do that. I have to get away from—

Wayne.

Terror sends a chill down my back that rivals the cold, and I try to roll over. I'm not on the ground. I reach down and feel something like canvas under me. I follow it away from me and wrap the tips of my fingers around something tubelike. A metal frame. I'm on one of those camping cots. The kind you use to keep yourself off the ground in a tent.

Where the hell am I?

I sit up a little more, and shards of light catch my attention as my eyes adjust to the darkness. Thin bands of daylight make a rectangle.

It's a door. Set into the wall to my right. Rain beats against this side of the house. I turn to the other side of the room and find the outline of a set of stairs that ascend into shadow and now I know exactly where I am.

I'm not *in* the cabin anymore.

I'm under it. He put me in the basement.

My breath comes heavier and heavier. I have to get out of here before he comes back to finish what he started. My hand comes up to my nose, and pain spikes through my face. My neck aches where he tried to squeeze the life out of me until I passed out.

I can't let him get his hands on me again.

I move to swing my legs off the cot, mentally mapping out where the house sits and which direction will get me under the cover of the forest fastest—what direction he'll expect me to go—when something twists into the skin on my ankle. Metal rattles when I move. I lean forward, and in the slivers of light from the door, I see a thick silvery chain coiled on the floor. One end disappears into the shadows, and the other end is attached to a set of handcuffs, one of which is fastened around my ankle.

Panic pools in my stomach. I'm going to throw up. I yank at the chain with desperate hands, but it pulls taut on something farther into the room. No matter how hard I yank, it won't come loose. I'm trapped in here.

Hot tears slide down my face. I let go of the chain and kick the links off the cot. I want to scream. I want to beat down these walls with my bare hands. I want to break this cot over his head.

A light flickers on above me, and I jump, slamming my back into the concrete wall. A lone lightbulb hanging from a loose wire dangles above my head, illuminating the rest of the basement. Cracked concrete walls. Dirt floor. A long workbench, empty except for a few boxes stacked on top, is straight ahead of me. The silver chain shackled to my ankle winds across the uneven floor and wraps around a metal foundation pole by the stairs. My heart sinks. No way can I break that.

The stairs creak and I look over. Wayne's sitting at the bottom. I see the light switch right by his face. I didn't hear anyone come down the stairs. Which means he's been here this whole time.

Watching me.

He sighs and puts his head in his hands. Like he can't believe this is happening either.

"I'm so disappointed in you," he says, after a long minute of silence. "I thought we were making so much progress. I finally got you onto the right path, and you were *listening*. Things were going back to normal, like before when you were little. Then you had to fuck it up again, like always. What's the matter with you?"

I don't say anything because my mind is churning. When I was little? I remember *everything* before this, and I don't remember *him*. Before he snatched me, I'd never met this man.

"I don't know what to do with you," he continues. "How am I supposed to trust you when you're so determined to run back to all your mistakes?"

He glares at me, like he's waiting for a response, so I say the first thing that comes to mind. "What do you mean?"

"I mean your whore friends, their nasty parties, and inappropriate behavior. I'm talking about your disgusting music and your hooker clothes, and the sneaking out. The drinking. The boys. The sinning. Why won't you leave that behind? Why? Why do I have to take such drastic measures to save you?"

Music and drinking and sneaking out?

What the fuck is he talking about?

"Don't ignore me, Mary!"

I flinch. "I'm not Mary."

I don't mean to say it. The words come out on their own.

They're a mistake.

Wayne launches himself off the stairs and screams, "Yes, you are! I'm sick of this fucking game. Every time I find you, it's the same! You need to stop before you take it too far again. You know exactly who you are! You. Are. Mary. Boone."

Every time I find you...

Oh god. What does *that* mean?

"Say it!" he screams. "Say you're Mary!"

My mouth is so dry that it comes out like a ghostly croak, "I'm Mary."

He sits back down on the bottom step and puts his head into his hands again. He lets out a sob that shakes his entire body.

Realization hits like a full body punch.

He really thinks I'm Mary Boone. He *needs* me to be Mary Boone.

His insistence that I'm the quiet girl who stays home and loves her dad, who doesn't watch, read, or listen to anything inappropriate was all him trying to mold me into her.

Which makes all of this exponentially more terrifying. How do I escape a man who's unhinged enough to believe I'm his daughter? When *he's* the one who kidnapped me. He's not only dangerous, he's delusional.

And…what happened to the real Mary Boone?

"I don't know what to do with you, Mary," he mumbles. "Why do you insist on playing this foolish game? Pretending you're not my daughter so I'll let you leave for good? You push and you push until I have no choice but to hurt you. Don't you see? I love you too much to let you ruin yourself."

Again, I say nothing. I'm too filled with rage. Until he has no choice but to hurt me? Like this is my fault?

"Oh the silent treatment, very mature," he mutters.

I swipe tears and blood from my face. "I'm not pretending. I just want to go home."

"You are home!" he roars. "Why do you keep doing this to me?"

I recoil so hard I hit the back of my head against the wall. "*I* didn't do anything!"

He leaps to his feet again. In a blink he's crossed the room in three long strides and backhands me so hard I fall off the cot onto the floor. I flip my hair out of my face and press my hand to my flaming cheekbone.

"Don't you raise your voice at me, you little bitch. I won't be disrespected." He backs up against the workbench. "I thought we were past this. But clearly you're incapable of staying on the right path. Maybe all of my efforts were for nothing. Maybe there's no saving you."

I'm too scared to make a sound. I don't know what else will set him off. But saying nothing will—

"Don't ignore me!" he shouts.

I flinch, and tears fall down my face. "Sorr—" My voice breaks. "I'm so sorry."

His hands tighten on the workbench, and he walks closer to me again. He takes my arm, touching my skin so gently I can barely feel his fingers. He helps me off the floor and back on the cot.

When he looks at me, his face has gone completely cold and hollow, and it scares me shitless. "I know how sorry you are. Maybe the blame is on me. I shouldn't have been so lenient. I should have fixed the problem the first time instead of tracking you down, time and time again, trying to beat the evil out of you. But I'll keep you pure and good if it's the last thing I do, Mary. I swear it. We'll do it together this time."

He stands and stomps up the stairs. I hold my breath until the bottom of his boot disappears, the door shuts, and the basement goes silent.

His words feel lethal. Body-numbing panic grows inside me, but I don't have time. I scramble to my feet and grab at the chain, trying to yank it from the support pole I know damn well won't budge. I yank until the metal links cut into my skin, and my hands bleed, and then I yank some more until I'm out of breath and my arms ache.

I need something to break the handcuffs. I get up and stretch toward the workbench, but my fingers hover a few inches from the boxes. Shit, I can't reach it. I turn back to the cot. Maybe the cot's legs are detachable, or I can break one off. I'll at least have something to defend myself with when he comes back, even if it doesn't help me get free.

I drag it from the wall, and something clinks to the ground. A screw sits in the dirt, the top scratched almost completely flat and it's immediately clear why. I go still as a corpse.

There are names, hand scratched into the concrete.

ALISON
KRISSY
COURTNEY
ARELY
BEKAH
CARLY
SHEENA
ASHLEY

Each in different handwriting. Some names are darker than others, fading away with time, discolored by the moisture coming through the wall. But some are so fresh they look like they could have been carved today.

I look down at the screw. My hand shakes so bad I almost drop it twice before I clench it in my fist. My breath rattles in my lungs.

I'm not the first.

He's taken other girls.

Holy shit.

Holy shit, holy shit, holy shit.

Are they all…dead? Are there other bodies in the backyard? How many fake Marys have been shackled to this cot? Did they all scratch their names in the wall so that someone would know they were here? Before he—

Oh fuck, I think I'm going to hyperventilate.

My eyes find the freshest name. There's still concrete dust in her letters.

The door to the backyard opens behind me and I jump so high I almost fall over the cot. I whirl around, ready to gouge out Wayne's eyes with this little screw, but it's not Wayne.

A boy about my age stands in the doorway.

Chest heaving. Eyes wild.

A boy in a Beastie Boys sweatshirt.

TWENTY-EIGHT

DREW

I stare at her. She stares back. Neither of us blink.

For a solid five seconds.

My mind can't process what I'm seeing in this small, damp basement. Or the girl standing there, staring at me like I'm a threat. Her green eyes are shadowed in bruises. Short brown hair. Floral jacket. Freckles. Bloody nose. Split cheek.

It's not…she's not…

Everything in me crumbles, like I've been holding back an avalanche of emotion, and it's finally too much to withstand. Grief buries me, and I drop to my knees.

"You're not Lola," I whisper.

The complete stranger before me glances down at the wall. I follow her gaze to a set of names scratched into the concrete. The freshest one feels like a punch to the chest.

Lola

The girl shakes her head, the fear in her eyes shifting to sadness.

"No…I'm not."

TWENTY-NINE

MADISON

DAY FIVE

The boy stares at me like he's breaking apart. Tears fill his eyes, and he swipes them away with the back of his hand. Before I can ask who he is, he climbs back to his feet.

"We have to get you out of here," he says. "Quick. Before he gets back."

The strange boy starts digging through the boxes on the workbench. I gape at him, trying to catch up. He must have come looking for Lola, but he found me instead.

One girl too late.

He pulls a pair of long-armed brush trimmers from the box. "This won't cut through the big chain, but it might cut the little one on the handcuffs." His voice is rough.

I want to thank him. I want to tell him I'm sorry I'm not Lola. I want to tell him how absolutely fucking grateful I am that he's risking his own life to save a stranger, but I can't find the words, so I nod instead.

"You're going to be okay," he says, wedging one side of the clippers against the ground and sticking the handcuff chain between them. "I'm going to get you out of here. I tried to call 911 when I saw him carrying you outside, but there's no service up here, so I ran to the neighbor and told her to call the police—she has one of those old-school house phones. Help is on the way."

"Mrs. Hooper?" I whisper.

He looks up at me, eyes wide. "You know her?"

"No. But the guy upstairs killed her husband."

His face goes ashen and he moves faster, slamming the clippers with all his strength. The blades press lines into the metal, but it doesn't snap. He keeps going, the metal giving a little more with every clamp.

"Are there any other girls here?" he asks, but the tone of his voice tells me he already knows the answer.

"No. It's only me."

He nods and clamps down again.

"Maybe Lola got away," I offer, trying to give him some shred of hope back. "She could be—"

"Does that jacket have 'L.E.S.' sewn into the hip tag?" he asks.

I grab at the hem and fold it up. A tag pops out.

L.E.S. is stitched in rose gold thread.

"It's hers," he says. "Lola Elizabeth Scott. If she got away, she would have made it home by now, and if she had, I wouldn't be here. So if she's not here, and she's not at home…she never left this place."

The fabric feels like it's crawling against my skin. Wayne gave me a dead girl's jacket?

I knew the names on the wall were probably other victims, but the reality of Lola makes the others more real. More tragic. More awful. It's proof of what happened here. And the look on this boy's face as he comes to that same conclusion is an image I'll never get out of my head as long as I live.

"You look like her," he says.

"What do you mean?"

"You look like her. Same hair. Same eyes. Same height. Same freckles. Your face is different though." His voice breaks on the last part.

My hands go to my face.

Did we all look the same? Is Wayne hunting the same girl over and over again?

Do I look like Mary Boone too?

"When I saw him carrying you inside with that jacket on…" he says, with another clamp of the trimmers. He looks up at me.

"You thought you found her."

Another tear drips down his cheek and he brushes it on the shoulder of his sweatshirt. He presses the clippers harder. The cuff rips at the skin on my ankle, but I don't say anything.

Boots sound on the floor above our heads, and we go still.

"Go," I tell him, grabbing for the clippers. "Get out of here. I'll finish this."

He looks at me like I'm insane.

"You don't understand. If he finds you here, you're dead. You don't need to die trying to save a stranger. Tell the cops everything. Someone needs to know what's happened," I plead, desperate for him to get out of here before he ends up buried behind the woodpile too. "Tell them my name is Madison Perkins. Tell my mom—" I can't finish the sentence because my throat closes up.

The boy clips at the handcuffs again. The metal is almost halfway cut through. "I'm Drew."

"What?"

"I'm Drew. You're Madison. Now we're not strangers. I leave when you do. He doesn't get to do this to anyone else, ever again. Understand?" He looks up at me with furious blue eyes, and the argument dies in my throat.

"Okay."

The metal groans, and he sets down the clippers. He braces against the concrete wall for leverage, and he yanks back on the handcuff chain. Hard. I have to switch my weight to my other leg to keep from being pulled over, but the metal bends more and more until it looks like it's about to snap.

He's really going to do this.

He's going to get me out of here.

A shadow falls over us. Wayne's silhouette fills the door to the yard. I open my mouth to scream but Wayne's already inside. Drew twists to meet his attack, but he's too late.

Wayne dives at him with a shout, and they crash to the ground in a tangle of fists.

They roll, and twist, and hit at each other. They come to a stop in the stretch of dirt at the bottom of the stairs. Wayne lifts a fist, and clocks Drew right in the temple. His head snaps to the side, but he twists against the ground and knocks Wayne off him. In a flurry of movement, Drew gets the upper hand. He straddles Wayne and lands a solid punch to the wound on his skull. Wayne lets out a screech.

Drew lands another punch to his cheekbone, and Wayne spits blood across the floor. Drew hits *hard*. But even the best punch can't level the playing field against a murderer.

I have to help.

I plant my feet against the concrete wall like Drew did and yank on the handcuffs, trying to finish what he started. From the corner of my eye, I see Wayne throw out an elbow, block the next hit with his forearm, and punch Drew straight in the face. I hear a crack like two rocks slamming together and Drew reels back, hand going to his nose as blood gushes from it. Wayne rocks to his right, throwing Drew off him, and he lands on his back by the workbench.

Wayne leaps on Drew's chest and wraps his fingers around his neck, and I scream so loud it feels like I'll rip the inside of my throat. I can't watch this boy die. Not after he charged into this serial killer's lair to save me.

I jump to my feet, pick up the metal cot, and smash it into Wayne's back.

He grunts. "Cut the shit!"

I bring it down again. And again. He releases one hand from Drew's throat, and catches the edge of the cot frame, yanking it from my grip when the chain keeps me from getting any closer. He tosses it toward the stairs, out of reach.

Drew claws at Wayne's grip as his face turns red. Wayne shifts to put his knee on Drew's chest and presses down until his ribs can't expand.

He's trying to kill him faster.

No, no, no...

Drew's eyes shift to me in panic. I frantically search for anything that will help him, but Wayne was careful in his placement of the cot, the length of the chain. There's nothing in this corner of the room.

Except the clippers.

I spot them on the floor, half under the cot, and grab them. Drew makes a gurgling sound. He tosses his head from side to side, and I slam the clippers against the back of Wayne's neck and he shouts in pain. Drew's not done yet either. His hand curls into a fist and he levels a shot straight into the bottom of Wayne's rib cage.

Wayne's breath comes out in a wheeze. The blows rock him off-balance, and Drew gasps in a breath. He plants his feet on Wayne's chest and kicks out.

Wayne goes down *hard*. He hits his back on the corner of the workbench, knocking one of the cardboard boxes off the edge, and they both land between me and the door. The box scatters its contents all over him, and my legs. He grabs for my ankle, and I scramble back.

"Mary," he groans.

I scream and grab the first heavy thing I can find. I hurl it at him with all my strength and something boxy and black hits him straight in the temple and rolls toward the bench.

Wayne Boone goes very still.

Drew rolls to his side, and tries to sit up, still gasping. He holds out a hand and I grab it. We pull each other to our feet and back away from Wayne until the chain pulls tight. I lunge for the clippers, clamp them down on the metal, and twist, pulling at the handcuffs with all the strength in my leg until...*snap*.

The smaller chain breaks, and my ankle jerks free.

Wayne still doesn't move. I look past him and see what I threw.

"Is that a car battery?" Drew whispers, his voice hoarse and rough from the damage Wayne did to his neck.

"Yup." I push his shoulder, toward the bottom of the stairs. "Go. Upstairs."

He points to the door that leads outside.

"Yeah fucking right. I'm not stepping over him, are you?"

"Good point."

I grab his arm and we clamber over the cot and up the stairs. I'm only halfway up when I feel Drew's arm rip from my hand.

Wayne—face red, bloodstained, and furious—yanks Drew back

by his sweatshirt. I watch him fall in slow motion. His shoulders hit the cot. It collapses under his weight, and the base of his head cracks against the dirt floor.

His eyes go unfocused.

Wayne stomps on him with the heel of his boot.

"No!"

Drew doesn't move.

Wayne looks up at me, like a feral animal. The battery doubled the size of the gash in the side of his face, sending rivers of blood down his chin and across his neck. His chest heaves, and his hands ball at his sides. Fists he'll probably use to beat me to death.

I lock eyes with him—and run.

"You little bitch," he screams, bounding after me.

I have three steps to go when my ankle's snatched out from under me. I drop, and my chin hits the corner of a stair. I feel blood pooling between my teeth, and all I taste is metal. The room spins, and I struggle to right myself.

Wayne flips me over. His fingers close around my throat. But I'm not fucking around.

I well up the blood in my mouth and spit it in his face.

He rears back, and I follow Drew's lead, bringing up my knee to plant my shoe on his chest. I shove as hard as I can, and he throws out his arms to catch himself, but it's all open air.

I don't wait for him to land. The second the weight of his body falls away from me, I roll over and pull myself up. I hear him land with a crunch I can feel in my bones as I launch myself into the kitchen.

My nose fills with the stench of rotten eggs.

All four knobs on the stove are turned to high, but the burners aren't ignited. The stove is pumping the house full of gas.

And the fireplace is lit.

I'll keep you pure and good if it's the last thing I do.

We'll do it together this time.

Holy fucking shit. He's going to blow up the house with all of us inside. *Fuck, fuck, fuck.* I tear around the island, and slap off every single burner, but the air is thick with gas and I can't stop coughing. I have to get the fuck out. I have to get *Drew* out.

I hold my breath and dash for the front door. I fumble with the dead bolt. It flips but the door doesn't budge. Panic claws up my throat. I can't breathe. I start to pound on the door, then realize I forgot to unlock the doorknob.

I flip the latch and the door opens. I gasp a lungful of fresh air as a fist grabs the back of my hair.

"No!"

Wayne's grip tightens, and he drags me back inside. Pain sears through my scalp, and I feel whole chunks of hair ripping away. He pins me to the wall between his room and mine, looming over me.

And ooh is he a sight to see. His face is coated with blood. I got him good.

"Stop fighting me, Mary," he screams, spitting in my face. "This is what you need!"

"Fuck you!" I throw up a knee—aiming for his balls.

He twists to the side, and I miss. He grips the front of my jacket and throws me over the top of the couch. I hit the coffee table, and it breaks beneath me.

Everything hurts.

I roll over, my cheek resting on the hardwood floor, and I gasp in dust bunnies and the stench of sulfur.

"You ungrateful bitch," he says, from behind the couch. "After everything I've done for you, this is how you treat me? I'm doing this for you! For the both of us."

I scrape my arm across the floor, getting it underneath me. "I'm supposed to thank you for trying to kill me?" I croak. "That's funny."

"I'm trying to *save* you!" he screams.

I get my knees under me. One of his boots pulls back for a kick that'll surely break my ribs. I dive forward and twist my back against the wall beside the woodstove. He misses, stumbles, and tries again.

I grab the little metal shovel from the fireplace rack and drive it straight into his leg. He roars in pain, reeling back. Blood pools down the front of his jeans, and the shovel rips from my grasp as he steps back and *takes it with him*, still buried in his leg. The force of his kick must have driven it through bone.

He bends to yank out the shovel, but I already have the fire poker. I grab the edge of the windowsill and pull myself to my feet. A wave of pain rolls down my legs, but I can't pay attention to it. Not now.

I wield the poker like a bat, like I've been trained to do for the last six fucking years, and swing it up over my shoulder. I power it down and catch him in the forearm. The blow makes him drop the shovel and I swing again.

I catch him in the face. The metal reverberates in my hands as it hits bone. I drive him back across the room. He stumbles into the arm of the couch, then around it. I keep coming, pushing him back toward the basement door.

My arms feel like spaghetti, but I can't stop, because if he gets the upper hand, I'm dead. Not later. Not eventually. Right now.

It's him or me.

I step around the couch and swing again. His hand flashes out and catches the end of the poker in his fist. His eyes are wild and unfocused.

272 | MEGAN LALLY

He blinks three or four times, quickly, like he's trying to see straight and can't.

"Mary..." he slurs, spitting blood down his chin.

All the anger and hatred and fear from these last unthinkable days surge through me all at once in a tidal wave of rage.

"That's not my name, you asshole!" I scream, then kick him down the stairs.

I watch him free-fall and land in a heap at the bottom. Right where Drew used to be.

But he's not there.

I stand my ground at the top of the stairs for a second, making sure Wayne doesn't get up. Blood trickles from his ear and down the unnatural angle of his neck. He doesn't move. His chest doesn't rise.

And I smile.

The screen door bangs open, and I whirl in a panic, but it's Drew, gasping for breath. "Is he dead?"

I nod.

He smiles too, but it crumbles as he looks at my face. I'm still not Lola.

My heart breaks for him and for the girls who didn't get away.

Sirens blare in the distance, and he holds out a hand to me. "Come on. Hurry up."

I limp to him and grab his hand. We step outside, and he slouches against me, so I hold tighter, and so does he. Together we work our way down the stairs and away from this cabin of nightmares. We collapse in a pile at the far end of the driveway, and I look back at the house. All those names in the basement are seared into my mind.

Alison.

Krissy.

Courtney.

Arely.

Bekah.

Carly.

Sheena.

Ashley.

Lola.

I look over at Drew as police cars rocket up the road. He's staring at the basement door. I'm shaking. My entire body. He is too. Someone calls my name, only they call me Mary, and I flinch even though I know it's not him. It's not Wayne.

Wayne Boone is dead.

Officer Bowman runs toward me at a full sprint, not even bothering to close the door to his cruiser. Five more officers follow him.

"Are you two okay?" he asks, dropping to my side.

"No. But we're alive."

JANUARY 12TH

THE WILLAMETTE TIMES

It's official. CrimeFlx is set to produce one of the most antici-
pated docuseries of the decade—the tale of Oregon's most infa-
mous new serial killer. Wayne Boone.

CrimeFlx, a new true crime streaming platform, secured
a deal to produce a five-part miniseries with exclusive interviews from family members of Boone's many victims and the
law enforcement officers who finally tracked him down and
ended his reign of terror.

Boone, a "home-taught handy man" from McMinnville
was found dead in his Alton, Oregon fishing cabin last fall by
police after falling down a flight of stairs and breaking his
neck. During the investigation into his death, the remains of
an elderly neighbor and nine teenage girls were discovered on
and around the property. At first, it seemed Boone had a type,
as almost all his victims had short brown hair, green eyes, and
freckles, but a closer look into his past revealed a much darker
connection. An extensive search of Boone's McMinnville house
led to the discovery of additional remains buried under a concrete slab in the backyard: his daughter, Mary Boone, a teen who
had short brown hair, green eyes, and freckles.

Those who knew the family painted a picture of a difficult
household, with a domineering Wayne Boone at the helm. A
friend of the family told investigators that Boone's wife passed
in a car accident when Mary was nine, and after her death,
Boone became increasingly protective and controlling of his
daughter. He withdrew her from public school following an

incident freshman year over the school's sexual education curriculum when Boone verbally assaulted the school's principal regarding the purity of public education.

Boone had new rules. "Clean" television only. No "filthy" books. No "tainted" friends. No drinking. No driving. No staying up late. And soon, no leaving the house at all. These rules left family and friends increasingly concerned. When Wayne and his daughter vanished, they left behind only questions—until his death in Alton reopened the investigation.

The McMinnville coroner's office listed Mary Boone's cause of death as a broken neck. She was fifteen years old. Authorities believe that Wayne Boone killed Mary in a fit of rage after she snuck out to attend a Halloween party—the last time anyone saw her alive. Unable to face what he'd done, Boone set out on a mission to "find" her and bring her home again. The abductions began less than a month after his daughter's death.

Boone used social media in his search. Records on his computer suggest he spent hundreds of hours a week poring over public profiles, looking for his "Mary." He stalked his victims, sometimes for weeks, until an opportunity presented itself to remove her to his cabin—a more remote location than his McMinnville home—where he'd become enraged at his victim's inability to become the daughter he'd lost. He'd take things too far, and the cycle would begin again. Boone even adjusted the age of his targets to fit how old Mary would have been had she lived, and Boone would have continued his abductions undiscovered if not for a critical error in his choice of Mary number nine.

Boone crossed state lines to find his victims, collecting them from five different states, which helped him avoid

276 I MEGAN LALLY

detection. Lola Scott lived a little too close to home. Scott was last seen leaving a convenience store in her hometown of Washington City just before midnight on September 29th. Washington City is a mere hour's drive from the Alton cabin.

Lola's boyfriend was initially suspected of her murder and searched relentlessly for weeks, following every clue until he found himself on Boone's doorstep. While he arrived too late to save Lola, he was able to help free what would have been Boone's next "Mary," Madison Perkins of Bellevue, Washington. Together, the two teens did what none of his victims had—they escaped Wayne Boone, the Daddy Dearest Killer, and ended his reign of terror.

The five-part docuseries follows their harrowing survival story and is expected to smash streaming records when it releases this summer. Viewers can expect never-before-aired footage of the now-infamous cabin and interviews from Mark Roane, former Sheriff of Washington City. The man many consider responsible for cracking the case. Roane worked tirelessly to find Lola Scott, saying, "I knew it was a serious situation from the start. A girl like that doesn't just vanish. I knew right away this was some Ted Bundy stuff."

The Many Faces Of Mary Boone releases this summer on CrimeFlx. Streaming packages start at $11.99.

EPILOGUE
DREW

The sun comes out for Lola's birthday.

It's been raining for basically the last month, so seeing the sun on this February afternoon feels like the universe extending an olive branch. Maybe even Mother Nature knows that today is hard enough without a downpour.

The Trooper idles in the boat launch parking lot—not in our usual spot though. I can't bring myself to park there anymore. Instead, I park in the former home of Lola's shrine. It's long since been cleared away.

I never come here anymore. This place is haunted. Maybe not in the traditional sense, but this is where our nightmare began. The opening credits of a horror movie that hit too close to home. Lola may not have died in this spot, but it was the start of the end for her. The whole parking lot and the river beyond it leave me with an eerie dread.

So, of course, I've been sitting here for hours, hoping the darkness will take me too.

The river rages on the other side of my windshield. Frothy white peaks churn in the dark current. I keep my eyes on the angry water and *not* on the cupcake sitting on the dash.

I grip the steering wheel with both hands until the muscles in my forearms ache.

I've been dreading this day for months. I knew it would be a walking nightmare, but I still found myself dressed and driving into town as soon as the bakery opened. Because this is what I do on Lola's birthday. I go to the bakery. I buy her a red velvet cupcake with cream cheese frosting and gold sprinkles. We stick a pink candle in it, and she makes an outlandish wish.

For world peace.

For every illness to disappear.

For nobody to ever get their heart broken.

For a perfect life.

And then we laugh, and she eats the cupcake, frosting first. Then Autumn comes around—wherever we are—and she too gives Lola a cupcake. And Lola pretends to be surprised that we each got her one, even though we always do.

I couldn't…not go. I couldn't wake up on her birthday and not buy a cupcake. It would feel like I was ignoring her, which is one precarious step from forgetting her entirely.

That I'll never do.

So I sit in my stupid car, looking out at the stupid water, and pretend that I'm not being bested by a lump of sugar. That it's not ripping me to shreds to see it sitting on the dash, lone candle and everything, knowing that she'll never make another wish.

I lose feeling in my fingers.

She'll *never* make another birthday wish.

She'll never turn eighteen.

She'll never open another present.

She'll never get a car of her own, or turn off the light in her bed-room, or go on a road trip, or go to college, or travel, or *live*. She'll never get to really live.

And it's all my fault.

Unshed tears burn behind my eyes, but they won't come out. I let go of the wheel and press my fingers against my lids. The inside of the car feels like it gets smaller and smaller.

This is supposed to be her day.

The memory of that dank, dismal basement creeps into my mind.

"You're not Lola."

"No...I'm not."

My lungs constrict, and suddenly I'm gasping for air. I turn off the car, leave my keys dangling in the ignition, and throw myself into the February chill. I whip my door shut and bound across the parking lot to the boat launch, desperate for space or peace or something I can't seem to get my hands on. I stop short of where the water laps at the concrete and drop my hands to my knees, forcing the cool air into my lungs.

I'm not doing well. Clearly.

Four months later and I still can't keep my head above water.

I'm like a zombie version of myself. The closest I get is a couple days of numb before another memory comes out of nowhere and knocks me on my ass. Today it's been relentless, which is why I came *here* instead of braving the cemetery with everyone else.

I prefer to break down without an audience.

My dads have been begging me to talk to someone for months, but I can't bring myself to do it. I shouldn't get to feel better when I'm the cause of so much pain.

Wayne may have killed her, but I'm the one who left her vulnerable on the night he was prowling for his next Mary. I'm the reason her parents saw that diner surveillance photo and rushed to Alton, only to come face-to-face with Madison the same way I did. That's all on me. I did that to them.

I don't deserve to feel better.

My phone goes off in the pocket of my jacket, and I silence it without looking to see who it is. I lie down on the concrete like a snow angel. My dads won't call today. Max and Autumn would probably show up here if they need something. I don't care to hear from anyone else.

Especially not the reporters.

Ever since the news broke about the docuseries, they've been calling fifty times a day for a comment. I have nothing to say to them, just like I had nothing to say to the documentary people. And neither, would it seem, does Washington City.

When news spread about the show, the town collectively flipped out. It would have made me laugh under other circumstances, because all their anger pointed straight at Roane, the *former* sheriff of Washington City. The teaser clips show him boasting about his investigative ability, how he knew this was the work of a serial killer from day one.

The news vans were driven out of town by screaming locals. And everyone made a point of stopping me all over town to share their outrage.

"Roane is a selfish piece of shit!"

"I think he's the most-hated man in the county."

"Does he have no shame?"

"Can you believe he resigned? Not even because of the case! He signed on to consult for the studio. What an asshole."

And my personal favorite: "The audacity of that man. To pretend like he didn't bungle this investigation from the beginning and try to blame you for everything. I'm so sorry you have to relive this, Drew."

As if I wasn't on the receiving end of their hatred a few short months ago. Like they wouldn't have run me out of town too if my dads hadn't stepped in with a lawyer to make it stop.

I've graduated from "evil son of a bitch who killed Lola" to the "hero who charged into a serial killer's den to save a stranger." I've never seen so many people backtrack so fast. Now I'm a gem. Now they're so sorry for my loss. Now they're protecting me from the media and they have my back. Now they want me to raise my pitchfork against the newest most-hated person in the county like I don't know what it's like to hold that title myself.

Their support is almost worse than the hatred. It's made of nothing but guilt, and I'm not interested in their guilt. I have enough of my own.

My phone goes off again. I silence it a second time.

I take a deep breath and listen to the water. I can't wait for graduation. In a few months I can leave Washington City and never look back. I can't be here when the show drops. All it'll take is one true crime enthusiast asking me for a selfie and I'll end up in jail.

I hope Madison gets away before it premiers. Changes her name. Finds a new city where she doesn't always have to be "the girl who escaped Wayne Boone."

Her face appears in my mind like an old habit. I see her bruised and scared, wearing Lola's jacket, her foot chained to a pole as she tells me what I already know. That she isn't Lola. That Lola is gone. Begging me to leave her to die so Wayne doesn't kill me too.

Nobody should take anything else from her. Ever. She's lost enough.

Hell, we all have. But especially her.

I close my eyes and think of her standing beside me as we watched the authorities cart him from that basement on a stretcher, a sheet draped over his corpse. She gripped my arm with both hands, like she expected him to sit up and drag her back to the basement for round two. Because that's the level of evil that lived in him. The forever kind. The kind that tricks you into thinking he'll always win.

He didn't win in the end.

The man who killed so many helpless girls was bested by a seventeen-year-old nationally ranked softball star in his own house. The corner of my mouth tugs up at the thought. I heard a rumor he was cremated and someone threw his ashes in the trash. I hope to god it's true.

My phone rings a third time and I shimmy it out of my pocket with a huff. Autumn's face shines back at me from the screen. I sit up and hit the answer button. "What?"

"What's with the 'tude, dude?"

Nope. Not Autumn. "Max?"

He laughs. "My phone was dead, so I borrowed hers."

God, I hate couples. "What do you want?"

"Are you still at the boat launch?"

I pause. "How do you know I'm at the boat launch?"

"Ah...I don't? No reason. Don't worry about it."

"Max."

I hear Autumn in the background, "Don't tell him."

"Don't tell me what?" I say.

They both say "Shit" at the same time, then the line goes dead. I stare at the home screen for a few seconds. I don't know what's going on, but I know I don't want to deal with it today.

I climb to my feet. I should leave before they get here. Go

somewhere quiet, where I can punish myself in peace. But I don't want to. As haunted and awful as this place is, it's *our* place. I can't leave her here alone on her birthday.

I start walking back up the ramp to the car when someone appears at the top. I shield my eyes from the sun to see who it is, and the surprise of the face looking back at me hits like a fire poker to the guts.

Madison.

She stands in the middle of the concrete block, in a black hoodie with wide white bands on the arms and ripped skinny jeans. She looks… different now. Her hair is longer and she's dyed the underside of it bright blue. But she still looks so much like Lola. Especially in the eyes.

I blink at her while my brain malfunctions.

"Hi, Drew," she says.

Thank god she doesn't sound like her too. I swallow the lump in my throat and croak out a hello.

"Max and Autumn told me where to find you."

I walk up the ramp, but I can't look her in the eye. We haven't talked in months. She found my Instagram a few weeks after we were discharged from the hospital and sent me a couple messages, checking in, asking how I was holding up. Thanking me. Eventually I stopped responding.

Because I'm a fucking asshole.

I ghosted the girl who saved my life because she looked a little too much like the girl I threw to the wolves.

This is the last place I expected to see her.

"Um…what are you doing here?" I ask.

I sneak a glance at her, but thankfully she's not looking at me. Her eerily familiar green eyes are trained on the river, so I turn to look at it too. "Just saying hi. It's been a minute."

"You look different."

Her cheeks redden, and she runs a hand through her hair. "I had to change something. Every time I looked in the mirror, all I could see was Mary, you know? Her face is all over the news. I needed to get away from his gross list of attributes."

"Chin-length brown hair, green eyes, freckles," I recite under my breath.

"Exactly. I had to look like someone new. Get some distance."

"Your hair looks nice."

She smiles. "Thanks. You look like hell."

Her response makes me laugh. "Thanks for noticing. Now what are you really doing here? I don't think you came all this way to talk about your hair."

She turns back to the water. "I wanted to check on you. One of the articles mentioned her birthday. I asked my mom to drive me over. I . . . didn't know how else to get ahold of you."

That makes me wince. "I'm really sorry. I didn't set out to ghost you, it was just . . ."

"Too much."

"Yeah."

"You don't have to be sorry for taking care of yourself. Besides, if I had anything really important to pass along, I had Autumn tell you."

The slew of investigation updates from Autumn over the last few months take on a whole new meaning. I assumed it was gossip from the Washington City PD, but I guess that doesn't make sense, considering she hasn't spoken to her dad since Christmas. He moved out to consult on the show. Her grandma moved in with her until graduation.

All that must have been Madison.

I can feel the surprise on my face, so I change the subject. "You realize how absurd that is, right? You checking on me? You're the one who got kidnapped. You're the one who lost your memory and had to live with… I simply showed up and—"

"And saved my life."

"I didn't save anyone. I found a pair of clippers and fell down some stairs."

She turns to face me, folding her arms in front of her. "That's bullshit, Drew. And you know it. If you hadn't come looking for Lola, I wouldn't be here right now. I'm only alive because of you and Lola."

Now I know she's full of shit. Wayne never looked for new victims when he still had one in his house. He'd find his "daughter" bring her home, and when she didn't work out, he'd kill her and go searching again. Lola couldn't have had a hand in Madison's survival because she was dead before Wayne ever found Madison's social media. "Empty sentiments aren't going to help me or anyone else."

Madison tucks a strand of hair behind her ear and takes a deep breath. "It's not an empty sentiment. It's the truth. I lived because you loved Lola enough to chase her down. Without Lola, nobody was showing up in that basement. Without you, I'd have died down there. You'll never convince me otherwise."

I turn away from her. Fists clenching at my sides.

"You're angry."

I nod. "But not at you."

"At Lola?"

"No. Everything else. I'm glad you're okay, but I don't want to hear that me loving Lola saved you because it didn't save her. She was the reason I got in the car and did what I did, and it was all for nothing, because she was dead before I even left this town. And maybe if I left to look for her sooner, I might have saved her *and* prevented you from going through this at all."

The stinging in my eyes becomes full tears for the first time in weeks. I wipe my face with the sleeves of my sweatshirt and let out a breath. "I can't function, Madison. I can't go to school. I can't sleep. I barely eat. Everywhere I look is a memory of her, a reminder that I failed her."

Grief splits my rib cage and I don't know what to do with it. I kick a rock and watch it tumble down the ramp and into the water with a *plunk*.

"I'm sorry," she says. "I don't want to upset you or make today harder. If you want to be alone, I can respect that, and I'll even tell Autumn to give you space. I'm not sure how much good it'll do, but I'll tell her anyway."

I roll my eyes.

"And if you want, I'll go back to my mom's car, and you'll never hear from me again—but you absolutely did what you set out to do. You brought her home. You went to find her and you came back with answers. You brought her family closure. That's not a small thing. If you need to grieve, do it however you need to, but taking off for Alton wasn't for nothing. You saved me, you saved countless other girls who look like me and Lola, and you saved nine families from a lifetime of questions."

"I don't want to hear this. I can't hear this. I wanted to save *her*."

Madison grabs my hands and forces me to look at her. "Did you know the police found two computers stashed in a duffel bag in his van? They went through everything on them, and they told my mom that Wayne's search for me began the day after Lola disappeared. The next day, Drew. That means Lola was dead almost before anyone knew she was missing."

I feel like she's slapped me in the face. I rip my hands from her grasp.

"Nobody could have saved her. Nobody. And that's not your fault, it's Wayne's, and now he's dead too and the world is a brighter, better place for it. You didn't fail Lola."

I shake my head because all I can see is her angrily slamming the door to the Trooper and stomping off into the darkness. Into Wayne's waiting hands. "She wouldn't have been taken in the first place if it wasn't for me," I whisper.

"That's bullshit! Wayne followed us for days, for weeks before he took us. That was his pattern, because he was a piece of shit, and he did horrible things. They have him on a few different security cameras watching me for at least two weeks before he grabbed me at my apartment mailbox. If he didn't take her that night, it would have been the next one. Or the next week."

If he didn't take her that night, it would have been the next one.

Suddenly, I can't stop crying. Madison wraps me in a hug and holds tight for a long time. And I let her.

The idea that Lola was doomed no matter what is horrific and awful and somehow weightless in a way I didn't expect. I've been so hyperfocused on how our lives would have been different if I hadn't broken up with her. If I drove her home and made sure she got inside safely that night. Like my actions alone led her to a grave in the woods, but I never thought about Wayne taking her from school the next day, or while she raked leaves in her front yard. Madison's ripped the blame from me and placed it back with Wayne.

"Madison?"

She lets me go, and I look over at the silver sedan parked beside the Trooper. An anxious Ms. Perkins stands outside the driver's side door—not that I blame her. I'm surprised she even let Madison come within fifty miles of this haunted place.

Madison gives her mom a thumbs up. "She's still super overprotective."

Ms. Perkins smiles so bright it feels like a knife sliding into my chest. I hear her in the hospital the day we were rescued, wailing when she was finally reunited with her daughter. Hours later, she doubled back to my exam room, shoved my dads out of the way, and hugged me fiercely, sobbing *thank yous* into my hospital gown.

I have to look away from her before I lose it again. I clear my throat and meet Madison's gaze instead. It's getting easier to look at her. "Good. Do me a favor, and never get the mail again."

A laugh escapes her. "Never. Never again."

Her laugh is different too.

You're not Lola.

No... I'm not.

"Will you do me a favor?" I ask. The words escaping my mouth as the idea forms.

She nods. "Sure. Anything."

I hold up a finger for her to wait, and I walk to the Trooper. I grab the cupcake and a lighter and bring them back to the boat launch. "This has been sitting on my dash for hours, and I can't bring myself to light it. I wanted to do something for her. Make it meaningful. But I don't know how."

Madison's face lights up. "I can help with that."

She goes over to her mom. I can't hear what they're saying, but her mom roots around in the backseat. She hands something to Madison, and my stomach hits the ground when I see what it is.

Madison runs back and pulls me down by the water. She spreads out Lola's jacket on the concrete—keeping it safely out of reach of the waves. She sits on one side, and I sit on the other, carefully placing the cupcake in the middle of the fabric. I reach out and light the candle. The breeze from the river tries to put it out, but I cup my hands around it.

"Happy birthday, Lola," Madison whispers.

My eyes sting again. I watch the flame, knowing exactly what her wish would be if she were here to make another one. It would be a grandiose wish that would cover everyone she loves, forever. So I make the wish for her.

A wish that everyone she loved would be okay.

The breeze blows out the tiny flame and I pretend it was her.

I'm not okay yet, but I'll survive today. I'll survive the days to come. Somehow.

Lola's disappearance left me on the edge of a dark, horrifying cliff. Her death threw me over. But I don't know what to do with this next part. I somehow have to live a life after Lola. I don't have a choice.

I'm still here. She'd want me to make the most of it.

Madison's mom calls for her again, and she sighs. "I'm sorry. We have to drive back. I have tryouts for softball camp in the morning, and we need to stop at the athletic store before it closes, or I'd stay longer—"

I wave her off. "You've done more than enough. More than you know."

She smiles, and I walk her back across the parking lot. She squeezes my arm, like she did outside the cabin, and when I say, "Be careful, okay? I really need you to be okay," I mean it with everything in me.

Madison's smile is emotional. "I need you to be okay too."

"I'll do my best."

She nods and climbs into the car with her mom. I wave as Ms. Perkins backs out.

I'm not the least bit surprised to find Autumn and Max parked a few spaces beyond her car. They look guilty, but I wave them over. The three of us sit side by side at the water, Lola's jacket draped over Autumn's legs, and we trade stories about her until the sun sinks below the trees. We celebrate the girl we'll never stop missing. It's dark when we head back to our cars. Max and Autumn laugh and hold hands on the way to the Liberty. I hang back by the top of the launch and watch them walk away together, imagining what Lola would say right now. Something about them being the cutest. How happy they are. How great our lives are going to be.

I look out at the water one last time. Lola's cupcake sits on the ramp in the moonlight. The weight on my shoulders slips away a bit. Just enough to finally breathe.

"Happy Birthday, Lola," I whisper.

CREDITS

ACKNOWLEDGMENTS

As I write this I'm still a little over eight months from debut, but I still can't believe this is my life. I've been writing for a very long time, almost a decade, and there were many days when I questioned whether this dream would ever happen, and now not only has my dream come true, but you're holding it in your hands. So the first person I'd like to thank, is you. Thank you for reading. Thank you for giving my creepy little book a chance, and thank you for being part of the dream. It means the absolute world to me.

A massive thank you to my agent, Mandy Hubbard. This section of my acknowledgments is a long time coming. You've been in the thick of it with me for a very long time and never gave up, even in the moments when I wanted to. Every panic, every email, every text, every phone call has made me feel like I have a real partner in everything I do, and I couldn't have done any of this without you. When I say you're a superhero, I mean it with all my heart. Thank you, for absolutely everything.

To my editor, Annette Pollert-Morgan, thank you so much for

seeing the potential in this story. From day one you saw straight to the blood spattered soul of this creepy book. You understood all the things that were most important to me and helped morph it into the best version of itself. Working with someone who so completely understands me as a writer has been a literal dream. I couldn't have done it without you, and I'm so excited for what comes next!

Another massive thank you to Dominique Raccah and Todd Stocke. Without your enthusiasm this book never would have made it into the world. Erin Fitzsimmons, Kelly Lawler, Liz Dresner, and Laura Boren, you made my book sparkle in such an incredible way. And to Karen Masnica, Rebecca Atkinson, Michelle Lecumberry, Beth Oleniczak, Jenny Lopez, Thea Voutiritsas, Jessica Thelander, April Willis, and the entirety of the Sourcebooks team, all the work that goes on behind the scenes astounds me. Thank you for everything that you do.

Courtney Gould—you're a life raft in a sea of anxiety. Meeting you in that space between book deal and announcement was a literal godsend. I'm so glad I forced you to be friends with me. You're an absolute gem of a person, a willing partner in crime, a bully when I'm not writing, and an incredible friend. I'm so glad I know you. Here's to many of our books on the shelves together and may your years in the Cult of Megan be pleasant and sparkly.

Rachel Lynn Solomon—your support and advice has been helping me limp along for a long, long time. Haha. Thank you for always being there. For TBT silk sheet fan fiction (that I absolutely still have). For convincing me to query all those years ago. You're such a light, and your willingness to help others through the thick of it is an absolutely beautiful thing. I so appreciate you and everything that you have done and continue to do, sweet friend.

294 | MEGAN LALLY

Sheena Boekweg—I don't know how to thank you, or if there are words enough in this world to tell you how much I love and appreciate you for everything. You've been so steady and constant for so many years, and you're always quick with a reassuring text or a hand to lift up those around you when they stumble. (And being as clumsy as I am, I stumble a lot.) You're one of the kindest, best people, and I'm so lucky to know you and call you a friend.

Jessie Weaver—my thriller-minded love!! You're incredible. Thank you so much for all the support, and the incredible blurb you wrote for TNMN. Publishing is weird sometimes, but it's a bit easier to navigate when you have hilarious people to DM about all the things along the way.

To my TNMN CP's—Kate, I knew when we got lost in the backwoods of Texas and laughed hysterically about axe murderers that you and I would know each other for the rest of our lives. You've read more of my words than anyone else on this planet, and you've believed in every one of them. I've always said that CPs are invaluable, but the real treasure is when they turn into something more. Something a lot more like family. Something like you. Isabel, thank you for treating this book like it was important and worthy, even when it was just a glimpse of an idea sporadically pitched in text message. Your early feedback definitely made this sliver of a book idea build into a reality, and I couldn't have done it without you. Dawn, trading pages with you and having that accountability saw me to the end of a book for the first time in five years. I don't know that I would have seen it through without you. Thank you so so much. Ash, I'll never stop appreciating you or the literal hours' worth of all caps text messages you've sent me about this book. All of your encouragement, and brainstorming, and the hours we've spent commiserating over plot points made all the difference.

D&H forever. (IYKYK.) Hartlee, your constant enthusiasm for this book helped coax the words out of me—even when I didn't really want to. Thank you. I'll never forget it.

To my fellow 2024 debuts—absolute buckets of gratitude. I'd have been lost without your support, and our slack group was a constant source of "I'M NOT ALONE" when I felt very much the opposite at times. Thank you for all the commiseration and celebration; you all are so amazing, and I appreciate you!

An endless amount of love and gratitude to Alison, Bekah, Carly, Arely, Jena, Ashley, Holly, Ryan, Krissy, Karen, Matt, Kelly, Katie B, Katie D, Brittney, Jade, Kate C, Rachael, Kylee, Terri, Mom, and any other person who's listened to me rant about publishing wait times, or talk nonstop about my new book ideas, or dreamily babble about murder over the last decade. Thank you. Thank you. It got me here.

Bekah, I'm convinced you're the only person in the world who can take photos of me that I actually like. Without you, my author photo would probably have been a flower or a brick wall or something. You're an incredible talent and an incredible friend. Thank you so much for every inch of space you occupy in my life. I love your face off.

To my kids, L and P. I've been writing for your entire lives and knowing you've grown up watching me fight for this means everything. I hope you always fight for what you want most. I hope you get as much support as you've given me. You're the most kindhearted little humans, and your joy is my joy. I love you. You're my first and most favorite dream.

To my dad—you always told me I could do all the things, even when I was little and declaring a new life path every other day. You didn't blink an eye when I announced I was going to be a water scientist and stared at mason jars of tap water for two days. Or a week later when

I ditched that in favor of songwriting. Or the week after that when, struck by the magical powers of J.Lo, I decided wedding planning was the dream. You always knew I'd do something big with my life, and it made me more comfortable being different in a town that made me feel like different wasn't allowed. I miss you every single day. I always will.

And lastly, to Brady. You encourage me to spend time on this thing that I love, unapologetically. You support me in every possible way, whether it's a listening ear when I'm ranting, celebrating when I'm excited, or dreaming my dreams right along with me. You help me make space in our busy life for this thing that I love to do, and you're a pro at keeping the house clean when I'm on deadline while simultaneously keeping me sane. I couldn't do this without you. You make my wins feel like your wins too, and I can never thank you enough for that. I love you with my whole heart. Thanks for marrying me twice. XOXO.

ABOUT THE AUTHOR

A long-ago transplant from New Hampshire, Megan Lally now lives in the rainy oasis of Oregon with her family. When she's not writing twisted young adult novels you might find her drinking one too many lavender lattes, stress baking, or arguing about the validity of glitter as a favorite color. (It's absolutely a color, and it's the best one.) *That's Not My Name* is her debut novel.

You can visit her online at MeganLallyWrites.com or on Instagram: @Megan_Lally_